SLUR
by
Diane Mannion

Acknowledgements

I would like to thank the many people who have helped me to bring this book to market. Firstly I will start by thanking the independent author community in general. They are a fantastic group of talented authors who support each other, offering advice on everything from formatting to marketing. Unfortunately there are too many names to mention but the people involved know who they are.

A special thank you goes to my longstanding friend Karen Hopes who was the first person to read a very early draft of the book and give me some honest feedback. Karen has worked both as a librarian and an administration manager with the police so her knowledge was particularly valuable.

I would like to acknowledge the Police History Society for invaluable help with the research for my book. Their website at: http://www.policehistorysociety.co.uk/ contains a wealth of information. I would also like to thank individual members of staff who went to a great deal of trouble to answer all my questions.

Thank you also to my wonderful beta readers who gave valuable feedback which helped me to improve the book. They are the lovely Rose Edmunds, Emma Dellow, Fiona Lang and Rita Ackerman.

Big thanks also go to Chris Howard for designing a stunning book cover. He can be contacted at: blondesign@gmail.com.

I found the following websites useful when carrying out my research: http://www.cps.gov.uk for information on court procedure and http://www.peevish.co.uk/slang/c.htm for helping to compile my glossary of slang. I have to confess, however, that I am already familiar with the slang used, but in many cases I needed to find a polite way to define the words. I also used several websites for research on drugs but this research was carried out several years ago so I no longer have the relevant links.

Lastly I would like to thank my family and friends, particularly my husband Damien and my children, for all the support that they have given me in bringing this book to fruition.

Introduction

Slur is set in 1980s Manchester and the characters live in a deprived area of the city. The language therefore reflects how the characters would have spoken at that time and I have taken the decision to include slang and bad language as I wanted to give an accurate portrayal. Please accept my apologies if anyone is offended by the bad language used but I feel that it gives the novel a more authentic feel.

Although many of the slang words are still in use today throughout the UK and in other English speaking countries, some of them are unique to the North West of the UK. Additionally, some words may only be familiar to the older generation. I have therefore included a Glossary in the back of the book to enhance your reading experience.

Chapter 1

Saturday 21st June 1986

It was Saturday morning and Julie lay in bed dreaming of last night; she could feel the throbbing beat of the disco music. As she came to the throbbing intensified and she realised that this was no longer a dream. It was a loud hammering on the front door. The after effects of too much alcohol meant that the noise multiplied tenfold inside her head.

She staggered out of bed and reached for her dressing gown, but somebody had beaten her to the door. The hammering was followed by the sound of raised voices that Julie didn't recognise, and she dashed to the landing to see what the commotion was about.

As she peered down the stairs her father glanced towards her bearing a puzzled but grave expression. There were two strangers in the hallway; a plain, manly-looking woman of about 30, and a tall middle-aged man with rugged features. Julie's mother stared up the stairs, her face a deathly pallor, her voice shaking, as she uttered, 'They're police. They want you love.'

Julie panicked and began to walk downstairs while asking, 'What are you talking about mam? What would the police want with me?'

She saw the policeman nod in her direction as he addressed her father, 'is this her?'

'Yes,' Bill muttered, and hung his head in shame.

The policeman then focused his full attention on Julie as he spoke the words that would remain etched on her brain for the rest of her life:

'Julie Quinley, I am Detective Inspector Bowden, this is Detective Sergeant Drummond. I am arresting you on suspicion of the murder of Amanda Morris. You do not have to say anything unless you wish to do so, but what you say may be given in evidence.'

Julie stared at the police officer in disbelief and confusion as she tried to take it all in. She wanted to ask – What? Why? When? but the shock of this statement rendered her speechless and she couldn't force the words from her mouth.

Inspector Bowden, heedless of Julie's emotional state, was keen to get down to business straightaway. 'Sergeant Drummond – accompany her to her bedroom while she gets dressed and watch her very closely.'

He then turned to Julie's parents. 'As soon as your daughter is dressed she will be taken to the station for questioning while we conduct a thorough search of the house.'

'What do you mean, search? What are you searching for?' asked Bill.

'Drugs Mr Quinley,' the inspector stated.

On hearing the word 'drugs' Bill was unable to contain himself any longer and Julie watched, helpless, as he metamorphosed into a frenzied maniac.

'Drugs? What the bloody hell are you talking about, drugs? My family's never had anything to do with drugs, never!' he fumed.

He shocked Julie by grabbing her shoulder and shaking her violently as he vented his anger. 'What the bloody hell's been going on Julie? What's all this about drugs and …and …people dying. Just what the hell have you been up to?'

Inspector Bowden took control of the situation. 'Mr Quinley, can you please let go of your daughter and let Sergeant Drummond accompany her while she gets dressed?'

Bill mechanically released Julie and stared at the police officer in horror. This was a side of Bill that Julie, at twenty years of age, had never witnessed. Although he had often complained about her lifestyle, she usually shrugged it off, content in the knowledge that he was a kind and caring father who thought the world of her. Seeing him like this, though, she submitted to tears as she struggled to reply. 'I'm sorry dad, but I really don't know! I've never done drugs in my life!'

Then she began to sob in desperation, 'Drugs? I don't know anything about drugs …Amanda's dead …Oh mam, tell him please?'

Julie's mother, Betty, turned to address her husband, 'Leave her alone Bill. Can't you see she's in a state? You're only making matters worse!'

Inspector Bowden continued, officiously. 'Now, if you will permit me to explain to all concerned - Amanda Morris died of severe intoxication and a possible drugs overdose in the early hours of this morning. As she was in the company of Julie Quinley and one other until approximately twelve thirty this morning, and returned home with them in an extremely drunken state, I have no alternative but to place Julie Quinley under arrest and take her down to the station for questioning. Now, if you will permit me to continue in my duties Mr Quinley, nothing further need be said at this point.'

Julie's father retreated into the living room, mumbling to himself in despair. 'I can't take no more of this, I really can't!'

Led by Sergeant Drummond, Julie mounted the stairs dejectedly. From the corner of her eye she could see her mother standing motionless in the hallway until Inspector Bowden disturbed her. 'Mrs Quinley, could you help me to open the door please?'

When Julie's mother had released the awkward door latch, he stepped forward, shouting, 'in here men, start in that room there, then work your way through to the kitchen.'

Julie's senses were on full alert, the adrenaline coursing around her body, as the police officers charged into the house with her father issuing a barrage of complaints at them. She was aware of her mother's distress emanating from the dismal figure at the foot of the stairs. Apart from that, she could feel her own fear and helplessness, then shame and anger as, turning back, she noticed a group of nosy neighbours shouting and jeering at her mother. When one of them had the audacity to enquire, 'Everything all right Betty love?' her mother shut the front door in response.

Once inside the upstairs bedroom, Julie could sense Detective Sergeant Drummond scrutinising her as she put her clothes on. They didn't speak but Julie tried to dress as covertly as possible while the police officer's eyes roamed up and down her body. She could feel her hands shaking and her heart beating, and could hear people talking downstairs. One of the voices was her father's and he sounded angry.

Julie headed towards the bathroom to wash her face, which still contained traces of make-up from the night before, but she was informed that there was no time to waste and they wanted her down at the station for questioning as soon as possible. 'What about my hair?' Julie asked.

'If you're so concerned about it, you can take a brush and do it in the car.'

Julie grabbed her hairbrush and placed it inside her handbag, which she threw over her shoulder.

'I'll take that if you don't mind!' said the sergeant, indicating Julie's handbag. 'It'll have to be searched.'

Julie, aware of the sergeant's hostile manner, replied, 'That's all right, I've got nothing to hide!'

She passed her handbag to Sergeant Drummond, then cringed with embarrassment as Sergeant Drummond rummaged through it and withdrew a packet of Durex and a small, empty bottle of vodka, which she proceeded to scrutinise. Once Sergeant Drummond had finished her thorough search, she tossed the bag back to Julie.

After several minutes Julie was ready to leave her bedroom without having showered, brushed her hair or even cleaned her teeth.

They began to descend the stairs.

Inspector Bowden materialized in the hallway and instructed Sergeant Drummond to lead Julie out to a waiting police car. He then ordered his men to check the upstairs of the house. As Sergeant Drummond was propelling Julie through the front door, Betty took hold of Julie's arm and wept, 'I hope you'll be all right love.'

The look of anguish on Betty's face brought renewed tears to Julie's eyes, but she was too distressed to utter any words of reassurance to her mother. Her father, who had now calmed down a little, said, 'don't worry love, they can't charge you with anything you haven't done,' and he put his arm around Betty's shoulder in a comforting gesture. Julie knew that this was Bill's way of apologising for his earlier accusations.

When Julie stepped outside the front door she was horrified at the sight that met her. The crowd that had gathered on the opposite side of the street had increased to such an extent that people were spilling over into the road. As Julie stepped onto the pavement with Sergeant Drummond gripping her arm, the excited mutterings of the crowd subsided and there was a series of nudges and whispers.

Julie was now the focus of everybody's attention and she became painfully aware of her unkempt appearance, her untidy hair and unwashed face with mascara now streaked across her cheeks because of crying. The few steps from her house to the police car seemed to last longer than any other steps she had taken in her life. Although she knew she was innocent, she felt embarrassed in front of the crowd and ashamed that she had brought this on her parents.

She knew that they would be subjected to malicious gossip for weeks to come. For anybody who had ever held a grudge, or felt envious of the Quinleys, it was now payback time.

The sight of the over inquisitive mob soon refuelled Bill's anger and Julie heard him, first arguing with the police officers, and then shouting abuse at the intrusive audience. 'Have you nothing else better to do? Get back in your houses and mind your own bleedin' business! Our Julie's innocent and she's better than the bleedin' lot of you put together. Now go on, piss off!'

His shouts were interspersed by Betty's uncontrolled sobbing. Not one of the crowd flinched. Julie had no doubt that her father's spectacle had added to their entertainment. It occurred to her that she had never before seen her father so out of control, never seen her mother so upset, and her neighbours had never before seen Julie looking anything less than immaculate. For her it marked the beginning of a prolonged descent.

Suddenly, Julie caught sight of her younger sister, Clare, heading towards her. She could hear her astonished voice repeating to her friends, 'It's our Julie!' As she became nearer, she shouted, 'Julie, what's happened, where are they taking you?'

A policeman rushed in front of Clare, preventing her from making any contact with her sister, and Julie was bundled into the police car. As she repositioned herself on the rear seat, Julie could hear her younger sister's frantic screams and, while the officers tried to restrain Clare, she shouted, 'Get off me, leave me alone, that's my sister, you can't take my sister!' It was all too much for an eight year old to take in.

The police car began to drive away. Julie heard her father shouting at the crowd again. 'I hope you've enjoyed your morning's entertainment. Now bugger off home the lot of you!'

She turned to see her mother trying to comfort Clare as the Quinley family stepped back inside their defiled home.

Inside the police car Julie tried to put aside her feelings of sorrow and despair in an attempt to pull herself together. She needed to remain calm in order to tackle this situation. But despite knowing she was innocent, she felt degraded and helpless.

She eased open her handbag, aware of Sergeant Drummond's observation. Julie took out a mirror and held it in front of her face. Her reflection echoed the way she was feeling about herself. She removed a tissue and used her own saliva to dampen it so that she could wipe away the remains of stale make-up. Having achieved that, she set about brushing her hair.

Sergeant Drummond turned towards the officer driving the police car and quipped, 'Look at that, her friend's just snuffed it after a night out with her, and all she can think about is what she looks like!'

Julie tried to ignore the caustic comment. She needed to remain as composed as possible under the circumstances. For Julie, looking good meant feeling good, and she knew that it would help to give her the strength to get through this ordeal. In complete defiance of Sergeant Drummond's remark, Julie continued to work on her appearance, adding a little blusher and lip-gloss.

She then attempted to think about her situation logically. *"Yes, they had spiked Amanda's drink with shorts. There was no point in denying that. Chances were the police would find out anyway and that would only make matters worse. But what about the drugs?"*

She thought about whether there had been any time when somebody could have given drugs to Amanda, but decided that it was impossible to account for everybody's whereabouts throughout the entire evening. She had been too drunk herself for one thing.

As thoughts of Amanda flashed through her mind, she could feel her eyes well up with tears again, but she fought to maintain control. "*I mustn't let them get the better of me*," she kept repeating to herself. Then she remembered the inspector's words when he had said, '*possible* drugs overdose.' "*So, there's a chance that no drugs were involved anyway*," she thought, on a positive note. Then her spirit was further dampened by the realisation that, if there were no drugs found there was no possibility that anybody else was involved. That could mean only one thing; that Amanda's death was purely down to her and Rita having spiked Amanda's drinks with various shorts throughout the evening.

Julie's thoughts turned to Rita, and she wondered whether the police had taken her in for questioning too, as she must have been the 'one other' to whom the Inspector had referred. She thought about the surly inspector, convinced that he was going to give her one hell of a grilling once they got inside the station. "*But I can't have killed Amanda*," she reasoned to herself. "*She was starting to come round a bit when we left her.*"

As she pictured her friend's face the last time she had seen her, Julie fought once again to contain her tears, as she went through the events of last night in her mind.

Chapter 2

Friday 20th June 1986

It was Friday night, the big night out of the week. Julie was sitting at her dressing table putting the finishing touches to her hair and make-up. When she was satisfied that she had achieved the desired result, she pouted her lips and kissed her reflection in the mirror, saying, 'you're gonna knock 'em dead tonight – you sexy beast.' She was disturbed by the sound of a, 'tut tut' coming from the doorway of her room. It was her mother, Betty.

'Julie Quinley, I don't know. You get dafter by the minute. When you've finished dolling yourself up, Rita's downstairs waiting for you.'

Julie took no offence at Betty's comments as she was accustomed to their friendly banter. She turned in her chair, gave her mother a beaming smile, then dashed across the room and planted a kiss on her cheek, saying, 'Here I go, don't wait up!'

She headed downstairs to find Rita in the hallway. As they greeted each other, Betty passed them on her way to the living room. Julie stepped away from Rita, allowing her mother to pass. As she did so, she noticed what Rita was wearing. "*My God, she's really gone to town this time!*" she thought, observing Rita's white lycra mini skirt, low cut red top and towering, white stiletto heels.

'You look nice Rita,' she commented politely.

'Oh thanks,' Rita replied, preening herself.

Julie then heard the sound of voices coming from the living room. She put her fingers to her lips, motioning Rita to keep quiet as she led her towards the living room door while they listened in on Bill and Betty's conversation.

'She's at it again, is she?' Bill asked.

'Aye, she's only kissing the bleedin' mirror now. I swear she gets more puddled by the minute that girl,' replied Betty, in an amused tone.

Julie looked at Rita and managed to stifle a giggle as she heard her father grumble, 'I can't understand it me, young women out till all hours of the night up to God knows what, and with all these dubious characters hanging about.'

'Yes, I know your feelings Bill, you have mentioned it once or twice.'

'Well, she's twenty years of age for God's sake! She should be married with a family now, not stuck in some nightclub getting drunk, with a load of riffraff!'

Julie held up her hand for Rita to see as she formed the shape of a mouth opening and shutting, in imitation of her father's familiar complaining.

'She'll have plenty of time for settling down when she's had a bit of fun and built up a career for herself,' Betty replied. 'A lot of women don't even think about having children until they are in their thirties these days. Anyway, she's got her head screwed on the right way. She won't do anything daft.'

'Huh,' was Bill's response, followed by silence.

Julie and Rita backed away. Julie then opened the front door and they stepped out into the street, shutting the door as quietly as possible so that Julie's parents would be unaware of their eavesdropping. As soon as they were outside, they gave in to uncontrolled laughter.

'I bet your mam was a right one in her day!' giggled Rita.

'She might have been, given half a chance.'

Julie thought about her mother and the tale she had told her many times about her married life. Times had been hard for Betty when she got wed and their finances were fully stretched after Julie's birth. Therefore, they decided to postpone extending their family until they could afford it.

When Julie was in school, Betty found herself a job in a store in order to bring in some extra income. After a few years of being stuck at home, Betty was a bit apprehensive at first, but she soon settled in and made lots of new friends. This in turn improved her social life and she began to relish her newfound freedom. After that, there never seemed to be an appropriate time to have more children.

However, as Betty reached her thirties and sensed her biological clock ticking away, the desire grew to extend her family before her time ran out. This resulted in the birth of Clare, twelve years Julie's junior, and now a likeable, sweet girl of eight.

Although Betty was immensely proud of both her daughters, at times she regretted not doing more with her life, and every time Julie thought about her mother's lack of achievements, she was determined not to make the same mistakes.

As Julie and Rita made their way up the street, on the way to their friend Debby's house, the familiar clickety clack of high heels reverberated on the pavements.

Julie's home was in a street full of three bedroom semis in a Manchester suburb. Many of the houses looked dreary and run down, a result of the poverty in the area. The home of Bill and Betty Quinley, however, was one of the more presentable houses in the street. The front garden was well tended and baskets of bright blooms hung at either side of the front door.

Julie's sister, Clare, and her friends, who were playing further up the street, paused in their play as Julie and Rita approached. For a group of eight year olds, the image of Julie and Rita dressed to go out was a sight to behold, and they gazed in awe as the two older girls walked by.

'Bye our Julie,' shouted Clare.

'Bye sweetheart. I'll see you in the morning and don't forget to be a good girl for mam and be in at eight o'clock.'

'I won't,' said Clare, full of respect for Julie who she saw as a role model.

Julie couldn't help but swell with pride as she sensed the idolatry glances of the young girls, and caught snippets of their conversation on passing.

'Wow Clare, I wish I could go out all dressed up like your Julie, wearing make-up and everything!'

'Our Julie lets me wear her make-up sometimes.'

Julie turned to Rita and they smiled at each other on hearing these childish comments. They looked an oddly matched pair: Julie, tall and elegant, and Rita, who was just a year older than Julie, smaller, brasher and louder in every sense of the word. Julie, although slim, was also curvaceous and well proportioned. Her features were sharp but nonetheless attractive.

She usually opted for the sexy but sophisticated look, and tonight she was wearing a shortish pale blue skirt with a matching fitted jacket, which bore the popular shoulder pads of the eighties. She wore the customary white stiletto heels and had a white leather handbag to match. Her make-up was subtle and served to define her striking features, and her blond hair was naturally wavy.

As they rounded the corner at the top of the street, Rita opened up the conversation, by talking about her day at work, which was at a food factory.

'Me and Debby were talking to Charlie at work today. He's a card! He told us this joke…What's white and slides across the dance-floor?' Then, pausing for effect, she added, 'Come dancing,' the double entendre being a reference to a popular TV dancing show around that time. 'Well, that was it! We couldn't stop laughing after that. The slightest thing set us off.'

They both laughed at this and Julie replied, unwittingly. 'Oh I wish I worked somewhere like that Rita. It sounds as though you have a great time.'

'Why not?' Rita replied enthusiastically. 'I can let you know when there's any vacancies. You should get a good reference from your place and you'll soon learn the ropes. There's not much to it really and I can put in a good word for you so it won't matter if you haven't got any experience.'

Julie was a bit taken aback by this as deep down she saw herself as being a bit above factory work, but she didn't quite know how to put her thoughts into words without offending her longstanding friend. So she replied with caution.

'I'd love to, but I don't want to waste my qualifications.'

'Come off it Julie, what's a couple of 'O' levels? Besides, if you decide you don't like it at the factory, you can always go back to office work. Anyway, you're a bloody receptionist for Christ's sake. You're hardly gonna qualify for the High Achievers Award, are you? I mean to say, I earn more than you do.'

Julie resented Rita's views concerning her choice of career, but tried not to show it. Despite her resentment, she appreciated Rita's open and frank manner, which she had been grateful for in the past, so she maintained a cautious approach.

'It's what it can lead to that matters. I could do a course in computers or something.'

'Like as if. You're too busy enjoying yourself to stick a college course. Besides, I could do a course in computers, come to that.'

Julie didn't wish this to escalate into a full-blown argument but felt that she must assert herself, so she replied, 'You haven't got the 'O' levels or the office experience.' Then, realising that she was now becoming a bit confrontational, she tried to lighten the conversation by joking, 'Anyway, the talents always a bonus.'

Rita, however, was not so easy to pacify. 'Come off it. All men who work in offices are bloody wimps! You can't beat a bloke with a good trade. That's what my dad says and it's true.'

'What's the use of a good trade if there's no work around for them?'

'Oh that's just temporary. They'll be all right now we're getting over the recession. It's all down to that bleedin' Maggie Thatcher anyway.'

'Well while all your blokes with a trade are still busy looking for work, there's blokes being promoted at our place.'

'Yes blokes, exactly! Anyway, Vinny's a builder isn't he and there's nowt wrong with him?'

Knowing the mood that Rita was in, Julie guessed at what was to follow, and she was reluctant to discuss the subject of her boyfriend Vinny.

'Yes, he's all right, I suppose.'

'But?' prompted Rita.

'Well, I just wish he had a bit more ambition, that's all.'

'You know your trouble Julie? You don't know when you're lucky. Vinny's gorgeous. Loads of girls fancy him. I wouldn't kick him out of bed myself! He's got his own place, and he's good between the sheets, from what you've told me.'

Julie smiled, amused at her friend's audacity. 'Well he does know which buttons to press and when to press them, but there's more to life than sex you know Rita.'

'Oh yeah? Well when you find it let me know, and I'll have a double helping,' Rita quipped.

As Julie laughed, she turned to Rita and said. 'Let's stop being so bleedin' serious! It's Friday night for Christ's sake! We're supposed to be enjoying ourselves, not putting the world to rights.'

Rita decided that she had made her point anyway, so there was nothing to be gained in pursuing the matter. 'Yeah, you're right Jules. Come on, let's go for it.'

They carried on walking for a few moments before Julie asked Rita, 'What time are we supposed to be at Debby's house?'

'Dizzy Debby? Oh I said it would be about seven by the time we got there.'

'Don't be rotten. She can't help being a bit slow at times.'

'It's all right, she's used to being called Dizzy Debby. It's her nickname at work. Anyway, there's an offy on the way so we can grab some booze and have a few before we go and meet your friends. Eh, I tell you what Julie, we'd better make sure we give your friend Amanda a good time, seeing as how it's her birthday night out.'

'Don't worry, we will,' replied Julie with a smile.

When they reached Debby's house, it was Debby who answered the door and led them straight up to her bedroom. Her home was in complete contrast to the one that Julie had just left, and the décor was shabby and dated. Julie recoiled as they passed the bathroom and smelt the pungent aroma that emanated from it. She looked at Rita for her reaction, but Rita didn't respond. Julie wondered why; could it be that Rita was used to it so it didn't bother her. "*No*," she chided herself. "*Rita's home might be a bit untidy, but it was certainly a lot cleaner than this one.*"

Julie could see that Debby was excited about the forthcoming night out and was anxious to get started. When they entered her bedroom she noticed Debby already had three half pint glasses ready and the sound of Luther Vandross was blasting out of the stereo.

'Don't your parents mind you having your music that loud?' asked Julie.

'No, they have the bloody tele so loud, they can't hear it anyway.'

'Mine are as bad,' said Rita. 'Ever since my dad came home from the pub with that dodgy VCR he's been like a bleedin' kid with a new toy.'

The girls seated themselves and began to pour the cans of lager. Julie pretended not to notice the greasy marks that covered the glasses. She inwardly cringed on observing Debby's choice of clothing, accessories and make-up, but was too considerate to comment. Everything about Debby was overstated, from her fluffy bright blond hair to her fashion sense. All of her clothes were in vivid colours, uncoordinated and clung perilously to her large breasts and rotund hips.

The girls settled down with their drinks and began to discuss music, fashions and other topics of mutual interest. At eight o'clock, in a more animated state than when Julie and Rita had arrived, they set out, giggling, towards the nearby bus stop in order to make the trip to the city centre which was just a few stops away. When they got off the bus they had a short walk to the pub where they had agreed to meet two of Julie's workmates, Amanda and Jacqueline, at eight thirty. While they were walking along, they spotted two policemen just ahead of them.

'I think it's time we had a bit of fun!' said Rita.

Chapter 3

Friday 20th June 1986

When Julie, Rita and Debby entered the Downtown Bar it was packed with trendy club-goers and the sound of Madonna was blaring through the speakers. The girls began, undeterred, to make their way through the crowds. Julie noticed Amanda and Jacqueline standing at a table in the corner and waving. As they approached the table, Julie saw the look of scorn on Jacqueline's face, which alerted her to Rita and Debby's appearances. Their tight tops and short skirts were in contrast to the sharply tailored suits that Amanda and Jacqueline wore.

Amanda greeted them enthusiastically, her smile enhancing her pleasant features, while Jacqueline managed to force a wry frown. "*She's just as bad outside of work,*" thought Julie. She had always been at a loss to understand Amanda's friendship with sulky Jacqueline, but she put it down to the fact that she was the only person in Amanda's department who was of a similar age. Apart from that, Amanda saw the good in everybody, and was sometimes dominated by Jacqueline who was her supervisor. Julie's relationship with Jacqueline was one of tolerance with Amanda acting as a buffer between them.

Julie was not about to let Jacqueline's scornful expression spoil her evening, however, and she put all thoughts of her aside while she recounted her recent experience.

'You'll never guess what's just happened to me?' she asked.

Noting the anticipation on Amanda and Jacqueline's faces, she continued. 'Well, we were just on the way here when we noticed these two coppers in front of us. Rita fancied a bit of mischief so she dared me to pinch one of their bums. Well, having had a few drinks, I was feeling a bit brave. So I thought, yeah, why not? As soon as I did it, I wished I hadn't have bothered. This policeman went bloody mad, said I had committed an offence and all kinds.

'Then, him and his friend had a chat, trying to decide what they should do with me, and the other one said there was no alternative but to take me down to the station and charge me. I nearly died, thinking about the look on my poor mam's face when I had to tell her what had happened. So, I tried to talk them round, telling them that we were only having a laugh and we didn't mean any harm. The first copper said that nevertheless it was a very serious offence and not to be taken lightly, and I thought, "*Oh Jesus, I've done it now!*"

'Then, I noticed the big smirk on the other one's face. They were only having us on weren't they?'

'Aye, it looks like they were the ones that had the biggest laugh when they saw the terrified look on your face,' added Rita, laughing.

'Your pranks will get you into trouble one of these days Julie, you mark my words,' said Jacqueline haughtily.

The other girls joined in the laughter until Julie realised that in her excitement she had forgotten to introduce everybody. 'By the way,' she said, nodding towards her two friends. 'This is Rita and Debby,' and pointing to the other two, she added, 'and this is Amanda and Jacqueline.'

'Hiya Mandy, hiya Jackie,' Rita greeted in an over-familiar tone which was resented by Jacqueline.

'It's Jacqueline, actually,' came the frosty reply.

'Oh, pardon me for breathing!' said Rita.

Julie, sensing the tension between the two girls, decided to divert everybody's attention by asking if anybody would like a drink. Jacqueline and Amanda politely refused while Rita and Debby decided to accompany Julie to the bar.

'What the bloody hell's wrong with misery guts? Are her knickers too tight up her arse or what?' asked Rita as soon as they were out of earshot.

'Oh take no notice, it's just her way,' said Julie.

'Well I'm glad I don't have to bloody work with her anyway. Honestly Julie, I don't know how you stand it working in an office. There's some right miserable cows.'

'I don't work with her Rita; I'm on the switchboard. Anyway, they're not all like her. Amanda's a great laugh. She might look all prim and proper, but just wait till she's had a few drinks and you'll find out what she's really like.'

'I can't wait!' said Rita.

They ordered the drinks and made their way back to the table occupied by Jacqueline and Amanda. As they approached, Julie noticed Amanda look up with a smile aimed at Rita. Noting the soft drinks that the girls were carrying Amanda asked, 'Are you lot not bothering having a drink then?'

'Give over, course we are!' replied Rita, as she took a seat at the table with her back to the bar. Then she pulled a small bottle of whisky from her handbag, and surreptitiously poured a good measure into her glass of lemonade, adding, 'but I serve bigger measures than they do in here and a bloody sight cheaper as well!'

Julie, Debby and Amanda laughed while Jacqueline displayed a half-hearted smirk.

As the girls started to make conversation, both Rita and Jacqueline found that, despite their initial reservations, they agreed on many topics. In spite of Rita's exaggerated use of the word 'Jacqueline', and Jacqueline's overzealous observation of Rita and Debby's dress and behaviour, they got along quite well. They shared a lot of the same views and opinions, especially relating to Amanda's boyfriend. However, the manner in which they each expressed their opinions differed.

Amanda had opened up the conversation by stating that she would have to be home at 1 o'clock otherwise all hell would be let loose.

Rita, at a loss to understand the reason for this, asked, 'Why, what's the problem?'

Jacqueline was quick to point out, 'It's her boyfriend; he's the jealous and possessive type.'

Jacqueline and Julie were used to hearing Amanda's constant complaints about her boyfriend, Les. They were also resigned to the way in which, when challenged as to why she stayed with him, she replied, 'He's not so bad really', or 'He does have his good points.'

However, Rita, on learning all this afresh, commented in typical Rita style. 'Look, you're not tied to him by a ball and chain. You can do whatever you want, so tell him to piss off!'

'I can't do that,' Amanda replied. 'I live with him.'

'Well he must have something going for him then to make you go home so early. Is he loaded or just good between the sheets?' asked Rita.

Amanda appeared embarrassed. 'He has his own business, well a few actually, but I'm not with him just for that.'

'Must be good in bed then,' Rita nodded and Julie laughed at her effrontery.

'All men are a bit demanding though, aren't they?' replied Amanda.

'Yes, they're all the same,' said Jacqueline.

Jacqueline didn't have much experience with men. She had been brought up in a sheltered environment by a domineering father. He had terrorised her mother for years, and Jacqueline had witnessed his use of mental cruelty. According to him, any liaison with the opposite sex outside of marriage was a sin. So Jacqueline had been unable to have intimate relationships with men until she was old enough to leave home.

By that time she found it difficult to relate to them on both a social and a physical level. Consequently, her relationships usually lasted a matter of weeks. This didn't stop her from trying though, and she hid her lack of experience behind a façade.

'They're all bastards!' chipped in Debby, and Jacqueline was forced to agree.

'Well, we all seem pretty much in agreement there,' announced Julie, laughing.

'Yes, all after one thing and if they don't get it they're soon off,' stated Jacqueline, to which Rita replied, 'Yes, and even when they do get it, they soon bugger off when they've had their fill,' which brought uproarious laughter from the other girls except Jacqueline who displayed a subconscious look of disapproval.

As they were celebrating Amanda's birthday, the girls decided to make the most of it by going on a pub-crawl, followed by a nightclub.

When they reached the second pub, which was situated upstairs from the Downtown bar, Jacqueline was filled with excitement as she noticed a man, who she termed an "old friend" standing at the bar. She excused herself and dashed over to greet him, to everybody's surprise.

The other girls looked at each other in silence, which was broken by Rita, saying, 'Well girls; looks like we'll have to carry on without her.' Then, turning towards Debby and Amanda, she continued, 'I tell you what, why don't me and Julie go to the bar and get the drinks in while you two go and find a table?'

Julie guessed that Rita was up to mischief when she noticed how keenly her eyes followed Amanda and Debby as they went in search of a table. When Rita was sure they were out of earshot she whispered to Julie. 'Do you think Amanda will notice if we add a little something to her drink?'

Julie giggled, 'Oh Rita, you bugger. Go on then, go for it. It is her birthday tomorrow when all said and done. I've never seen Amanda when she's paralytic but she's funny enough after a few drinks. It should be a good laugh. Just put one measure of vodka in to start with. It's the hardest to trace, but don't let that bloody Jacqueline know or there'll be hell to pay.'

They then joined Amanda and Debby at the table, and adopted serious expressions as they awaited Amanda's reaction to her drink. It wasn't until Amanda had taken a couple of mouthfuls that she commented. 'There's something funny about this drink. It doesn't taste like Bacardi and Coke at all; in fact, it tastes really strong.'

Julie was quick to respond. 'Eh, that's happened before in here. I don't think they wash the glasses properly. Do you remember that drink you had once Rita, the one that tasted of Pernod?'

Rita managed to suppress a giggle. 'Oh yeah, I do. I took it back didn't I?'

She then looked around at the bar area, and when satisfied that she had achieved a suitable effect she continued. 'Mind you, you're wasting your time in here tonight, it's mobbed. It took them ages to serve us. You'd be there forever trying to get it changed.'

'Oh it doesn't matter,' said Amanda.

'Well, I tell you what we'll do,' added Rita. 'We'll drink up quick in here and then head for The Boardrooms 'cos I don't fancy queuing up half the night and then drinking from dirty glasses into the bargain.'

'What about Jacqueline?' asked Amanda. 'She doesn't look as if she'd be too happy to leave this pub.'

'Oh she'll be all right. The Boardrooms is only over the road. If you tell her where we're going, she can always follow later if she wants,' assured Rita.

Julie and Rita downed their drinks straightaway setting a pace that the others felt obliged to follow. They then stood up, Rita stubbed out her cigarette and they headed towards the door.

Whilst Amanda was talking to Jacqueline, Rita whispered to Julie, 'Right, we can't pull that stroke again in the next pub or she'll suss us, so what I think we should do is this …me and Debby will go to the bar while you drag Amanda off to a table. Then, instead of putting something else in her drink, we'll just order her a double Bacardi with plenty of Coke. She's already had one dickey drink so she shouldn't tell the difference. Then, we'll see how she goes on with that and we can always nip to the loo together to decide our next move.'

'Oh Rita,' said Julie, laughing, 'you make it sound like a military operation.'

They didn't notice that Amanda had returned until they heard her say, 'What's this about a military operation?'

'Oh erm, Rita was just planning our pub crawl,' Julie replied.

They were relieved to hear that Jacqueline wasn't going to join them until later, as this gave them more opportunity to carry out their deception.

They all settled at a table in the next pub and awaited Amanda's reaction as she tasted her drink. 'That's more like it,' she commented, after taking her first mouthful. Rita and Julie managed to stifle a giggle.

When they had been in the Boardrooms for about ten minutes, they noticed Jacqueline enter hand in hand with her "old friend". She left him by the door as she made her way towards them. As she looked at Amanda, she announced, 'He's offered to take me for a meal. Do you mind?'

'Not at all,' Amanda replied. 'You go and enjoy yourself.'

For the first time that evening a smile lit up Jacqueline's face as she turned and walked away from them.

'Just be careful that he doesn't want you for afters!' shouted Rita, teasing. As soon as Jacqueline was out of earshot, she announced to the others, 'Well girls, if she's copped tonight, there's hope for all of us!'

Julie, embarrassed by Rita's outburst, said, 'Rita, don't be so mean, and don't forget, she's Amanda's friend.'

'Oh don't mind me,' remarked Amanda. 'I admire Rita's frankness, after all, there's no point pretending Jacqueline's a stunner when we all know she isn't. I say good luck to her. I hope she hits it off with him, if you know what I mean.' Then she burst into uncontrolled laughter and giggled. 'Mind you, it would be a first, according to rumour.'

Julie and the others looked at each other in astonishment. For Amanda that was a very scathing comment. All of a sudden the realisation hit Julie – the spiked drinks were having an effect and it looked as though they were about to see another side to Amanda. Following this encouragement they continued to mercilessly spike Amanda's drinks with shorts at every opportunity, adding a little more as Amanda grew progressively drunker. As the evening continued, Amanda became bolder than Julie had ever seen her.

On one occasion, she noticed a small hole in Debby's tights, and could not resist the temptation to stick her finger in the hole and work it further. This brought about peals of laughter from Julie, Rita and Debby, who soon retaliated. In no time at all they were tearing the tights from each other, dashing about under tables in order to entrap their victims and unable to contain excited squeals of amusement.

By the end of the evening Amanda had sung several popular songs, danced on tables and acted a total fool. In terms of entertainment, the girls had got a good return on their initial investment of a few spiked drinks.

Chapter 4

Friday 20th June 1986

As it approached closing time in the pubs, they tried to decide where to go next. Rita and Debby were keen to go to a wine bar, which stayed open until 2am and usually had a live band on stage. Julie, however, had reservations.

'I think we should get Amanda home. She's really plastered now,' she said. 'Look at the state of her! She's thrown up three times and knocked a drink over!'

Rita and Debby looked at Amanda who was sitting with her head tilted to one side and remains of vomit smeared around the outside of her mouth. She was muttering incomprehensibly, and giggling to herself.

'Oh she'll be all right, we'll get her to drink some water to sober up,' replied Rita, refusing to be discouraged.

'I'll go and get it,' volunteered Debby. They didn't realise that she had spotted a man who had been chatting to her earlier.

After a few minutes Julie and Rita grew tired of waiting for Debby to return from the bar.

'What the hell's she up to?' asked Rita, standing on tiptoes in order to see through to the bar. 'I should have guessed! She's copped off. The dizzy cow's probably that busy being chatted up that she's forgotten all about the glass of water! I'd better go and get it my bleedin' self!' With that she stormed off in the direction of the bar.

Rita soon returned and busied herself with trying to get Amanda to drink as much of the water as possible.

'Not so fast!' insisted Julie. 'You'll have her throwing up again.'

Rita, however, ignored Julie's comment while she made sure that Amanda finished the pint of water. She then rushed off for another one. When she returned, she said to Julie, 'That bleedin' Debby's still at it you know. I suppose it's the last we'll see of her tonight.'

Julie surmised that Rita was probably feeling a bit envious as she and Rita were being faced with the possibility of accompanying Amanda home.

After drinking two pints of water, Amanda remained extremely drunk. Julie attempted to appeal to Rita's more caring side by insisting that they see Amanda safely home. 'There's nobody more disappointed than me Rita, but we can't leave her in this state', Julie cajoled.

'Oh, all right then', Rita conceded. 'I suppose I'd never live with myself if we just shoved her in a taxi and something happened to her, and she's in no fit state to go anywhere else.'

'Good on you Rita, you're a pal', said Julie.

'Oh think nothing of it', replied Rita, glancing at her watch. 'Besides, if we get cracking now, we might just make it somewhere else after all.'

Julie couldn't resist a smile. 'You don't give in, do you? You bugger.'

They virtually carried Amanda from the pub, with her arms slung around each of their shoulders, propping her up between them. As they passed within a metre of Debby, they looked at her, and, before she had chance to say anything, Rita shouted, 'Don't tell us, you're going to the wine bar! Well I hope you have a better bloody time than we're having.' Pausing, she then added, 'Oh, and Debby ... don't do anything I wouldn't do!'

When they arrived at the taxi rank, they were disappointed to see that a large queue had already formed. While they were waiting they tried to find out Amanda's full address, but this was proving difficult. However, eventually they succeeded. After about half an hour, they reached the front of the queue. By this time, Amanda's condition had improved a little. They surmised that this was perhaps because the water was now beginning to have an effect.

By the time they arrived at her home, she was starting to liven up again and had burst into a chorus of, 'Show me the way to go home.' This was much to the annoyance of the taxi driver who had been reluctant to carry them at first, due to Amanda's state. After paying the taxi driver, they got out. Rita asked him, 'Will you wait a minute for us while we get her to her door?'

'You're joking, aren't you?' replied the taxi driver. 'It's Friday night, and I'm not missing any fares while I'm sat here buggering about with you lot!'

'Oh never mind,' Julie said to Rita, 'Sod him, we'll ring another from Amanda's place.'

'Yeah,' shouted Rita, 'Sod you, you miserable old git!'

The enraged taxi driver sped off, leaving them standing on the pavement outside Amanda's home.

Rita tried not to let this put her off as she turned to Amanda and said, 'Come on then Mandy, get your key out, then me and Julie can be off once we know you're all right.'

Amanda began fumbling about in her handbag, but after a few minutes of searching, it became apparent that the keys were not to be found. Rita sighed. 'Is *he* home?'

'It depends if he's back yet,' slurred Amanda.

Amanda and Les's flat was one of several contained in a large Victorian house. Julie looked on the nameplate at the front door and saw that the flat was on the first floor. She realised that in order to get Les to answer the door, he would have to come out of his flat and down a flight of stairs. Julie winced at the thought of disturbing Les at this time of night. Knowing his reputation for moodiness, she guessed that he wouldn't be pleased, especially when he noticed the state Amanda was in, but, she thought, if it has to be, then it has to be! 'We'll have to ring the doorbell!' she suggested.

Amanda stepped towards the door. Unfortunately, her state of intoxication did not give way to subtlety, and as she hammered at the door, shouting, 'Let me in sweetheart!' Julie felt that she could probably be heard several blocks away.

After a few minutes of shouting and ringing the doorbell, the door was yanked open and the enraged form of Les appeared.

'Just what the hell do you think you're playing at? You'll wake the neighbours up with that racket!' he shouted.

Amanda attempted to calm him down by throwing her arms about his neck and mumbling words to the effect that she loved him and didn't mean to wake him up.

He was quick to notice her drunkenness and this further angered him. 'Just look at the bloody state of you!'

Julie tried to placate him. 'I'm sorry, she's had a few too many. We got a bit carried away with it being her birthday, but she's come to no harm, and we made sure she got home safely.'

'Come to no harm?' he stormed. 'Look at the bloody state of her – she's out of her head! Anyone could have taken advantage of her.'

'I'm OK love,' muttered Amanda. 'Don't shout at them, they're only trying to help.'

'If they were half decent friends, they wouldn't have let you get like this in the first place. Now get inside! I want you as far away from this pair of slags as possible.'

Before Julie or Rita could say anything in their defence, Les had pushed Amanda into the house, and slammed the door shut.

'I don't suppose there's any chance of you ringing a taxi for us?' Rita shouted sarcastically.

'The bastard!' shouted Julie.

'Twat!' muttered Rita.

Rita surprised Julie by asking, 'Eh, do you think she'll be all right with that bastard or what?'

'Oh, I think so,' replied Julie. 'From what Mandy tells me his bark's worse than his bite. He must have something going for him, she seems happy enough. In fact, some mornings she walks in work as high as a kite with a bleedin' big smile on her face! I think he's just worried in case she loses her inhibitions and buggers off with somebody else. She'll soon get round him. I bet they'll be bonking within half an hour.'

'Oh, that's all right then. Right, how about our bit of fun, Jules? Are we going to get this bleedin' taxi into town or what?'

'Are you joking Rita? It's half past bloody twelve. God knows what time it'll be by the time we flag a taxi down on the main road - that's supposing we can find it!'

'I knew it was a bloody daft idea to take her home! Not that we got any thanks for it. If that bastard of a boyfriend of hers would have let us phone a taxi from their place, we could have been on our way to town by now.'

Julie was tempted to mention that it was their fault for getting Amanda drunk, but she thought better of it. Then Rita, who was now extremely vexed, added, 'Right, I tell you what, we'll go out clubbing tomorrow night instead.'

'Too late,' Julie responded. 'I've already arranged to go out with Vinny.'

'Out where?'

'Oh, he's taking me to the Bella Vida for a meal, didn't I tell you?'

'No you bleedin' didn't. The Bella Vida? That's a bit pricey isn't it? I thought it was usually a curry down Rusholme, then back to his place for a bonk. Could this be getting a bit serious by any chance?'

'Well, put it this way Rita; I wouldn't go ordering your wedding hat yet.'

This flippant remark helped to lighten the atmosphere between them, and Julie added, 'No, I told him I wouldn't be seeing him tonight, so he asked to take me out tomorrow instead and offered to take me for a meal. Well, I wasn't going to look a gift horse in the mouth, was I?'

'Are you sure he hasn't got an ulterior motive Julie, you know, he isn't going to pop the question or anything, is he?' Rita teased.

'Christ, I hope not, otherwise I'm not going!'

They both laughed.

The discussion continued and they finally agreed that they would go for a drink on the Sunday evening instead at their local, the Flying Horse. After a few minutes they found the main road and set about the arduous task of catching a taxi at 20 minutes to one on a Saturday morning.

Chapter 5

Saturday 21st June 1986

When the police car screeched to an abrupt halt outside the police station it jolted Julie back to the present. The police officers marched her into the station where she was thoroughly searched, then introduced to the custody sergeant by the name of Miller, a gaunt, diligent man, who seemed in awe of the inspector.

Inspector Bowden outlined the circumstances of her arrest to Sergeant Miller who then asked her several questions and filled in the appropriate boxes on his custody sheet. He explained procedure to her including her right to a solicitor, her right to have someone informed and the necessity to take a urine sample in order to test for drugs. She tried to protest but was soon hushed by Inspector Bowden who bellowed, 'Be quiet and listen to what the custody sergeant has to say! You'll have ample opportunity to speak for yourself later.'

Julie opted to have a duty solicitor attend the interview, but waived her right to have someone informed. She figured that her parents already knew anyway, and Rita would probably be in the same position that she was in at the moment. Besides, if she did ring Rita, she feared that her motives might be misinterpreted.

She didn't think about Vinny; she hardly had time to think at all as Inspector Bowden rushed her through the process, eager to deal with her as soon as possible. Sergeant Miller complied with his demands as he didn't wish to offend the inspector.

Julie was then handed back to Sergeant Drummond, the female arresting officer, who led her to an interview room and advised her that they had to wait until arrangements for collection of the urine sample were made. Then she would be interviewed.

The time spent waiting seemed a lifetime although it was no more than a couple of minutes. Julie felt clammy and uncomfortable. She was conscious of Sergeant Drummond watching her all the time, and her heart was beating so loud she thought the sergeant must be able to hear it and sense the fear that surged through her body. She tried to look away from Sergeant Drummond, occupying herself by studying the bare, neutral walls, and picking out odd flaws in the paintwork, but always there was the disconcerting sensation of being watched. Like a fly drawn into a web, she constantly needed to check whether she was still being observed, but each time she caught her eye she felt increasingly uncomfortable.

Eventually the custody sergeant entered the room accompanied by a female officer who, he explained, was authorised to take a urine sample. Julie was taken away, thankful to have escaped the watchful eye of Sergeant Drummond, but dreading what might lie in store for her next.

The officer carried out the procedure with the minimum of fuss, but it didn't lessen Julie's shame and embarrassment. She then informed Julie that she would now be taken back to the interview room. Julie felt as though she was on a factory conveyor belt; being forcefully transported through the various painful stages of her own destruction, wanting to call a halt to the whole thing but powerless to do so.

When Julie entered the interview room for a second time, she was met by the fierce glare of Inspector Bowden accompanied by his sidekick Sergeant Drummond. Seeing the expression on his face, Julie knew that her initial assumption was about to be proved correct; he was going to give her one hell of a grilling.

For the next twenty-four hours the irrepressible Inspector Bowden and Sergeant Drummond conducted interviews at spasmodic intervals, breaking occasionally for food and refreshments at the insistence of the custody sergeant, Miller, who took great delight in ensuring that the correct procedure was being carried out, and meticulously recording the information on his custody sheet.

Throughout the interview periods the interrogation was relentless, with the two officers asking her the same questions repeatedly in the hope that she would crack and give something away. Part of Inspector Bowden's interview technique was to ask a series of quick fire questions in his most commanding tone, without pausing, so that Julie felt bewildered and unable to say anything in her defence.

Julie had been supplied with a duty solicitor, a small, balding, meagre looking man in his late fifties. Although a complete stranger to Julie, she had presented her case to him and he had done his best to advise and support her. However, against the might of Inspector Bowden and Sergeant Drummond, their joint pleadings were pitiful.

During the repeated interviews Julie had suffered a range of emotions. She had shouted, argued, cajoled and, at one point, broke down in tears and almost begged for mercy. She felt sheer frustration at her inability to convince the two officers of her innocence.

In the late evening Inspector Bowden switched emphasis. The new scenario that he presented to Julie took her by surprise.

'On her return home Amanda Morris boasted to her boyfriend about the drugs which she had taken whilst in your company,' he said.

'We didn't take any drugs!' snapped Julie. 'We don't go in for that sort of thing. We're just normal girls out to have a good time, that's all.'

'Normal, Miss Quinley? *Normal*, do you say? Do you call running around ripping each other's tights off, *normal*? Do you call being asked to leave a certain establishment, because you were dancing on the tables, *normal*? Do you call having to accompany your friend home, due to her severely drunken and drugged up state, *normal*?'

As the inspector asked each question, his voice took on a more aggressive tone, laying much emphasis on the word 'normal'. Perversely, what had seemed hilarious to Julie the previous evening, now seemed ridiculous and immature when described by Inspector Bowden. She cringed with embarrassment.

The intervals between questioning were just as traumatic for Julie. She spent her time in a sparse cell that contained a narrow bed with one shabby blanket and no pillow. In one corner of the cell was a washbasin with a pot placed underneath it. The bed was hard and uncomfortable and she felt cold. There was a dank, musty odour, interspersed with the smell of urine.

She was unable to sleep; partly because of the discomfort, but also because of her state of mind. A couple of times she had awoken after a few minutes, shivering, both from the cold and from fear. Her dreams had been disturbing; she had dreamt of death and her own persecution. In one dream she had been tried for murder, and the jury had laughed. She could hear them whispering amongst themselves, "she's not normal", "her behaviour isn't normal" and the foreman sneered at her as he announced the verdict "guilty". Julie felt despair as the judge passed sentence, and heard herself scream. When she woke up, she could still feel the tension in her muscles especially her throat, which felt sore and dry.

The small, bare cell offered no escape from her nightmares. Each time Julie awoke, she recalled the full horror of the situation as she took in her surroundings.

Eventually Julie gave up on sleep and sat upright on the bed. There was nothing to keep her occupied except her own thoughts, which were almost as tortuous as the dreams. She kept seeing the pained expression on her mother's face when the police had made the arrest, and her father's look of anger and humiliation. As much as Julie hated the present situation, she dreaded returning home.

Her mind turned to Rita. Had she been arrested as well? She was presumably the "*one other*" to whom Inspector Bowden had referred. How was she coping? Knowing Rita as she did, Julie assumed that she would be giving the police a good run for their money. "*What if Rita had given drugs to Amanda while I was at the ladies?*" she thought, but she pooh-poohed the idea. "*Rita might be flirtatious and brash, but she's far too level-headed to do anything so stupid.*"

Julie wished that she hadn't let Rita persuade her to lace Amanda's drinks with shorts. "*But it's too late now!*" she thought. "*The damage has already been done.*"

***

Saturday 21st June 1986

Inspector Bowden strode towards the door of Detective Chief Inspector Marshall's office, stopped and knocked loudly.

'Come in!' shouted the DCI.

Inspector Bowden entered and saw DCI Marshall seated behind his enormous desk appearing affable and relaxed as usual. However, Inspector Bowden knew that under his pleasant, rotund exterior, the DCI harboured a hidden depth and determination that was underestimated by those who lived to regret it.

The DCI pre-empted Inspector Bowden by asking, 'How is the investigation coming along inspector?'

This caught Inspector Bowden a little off guard, changing the scenario that he had rehearsed in his mind. However, he still felt certain that his words would make an impact on the DCI, and bring about a positive response to his request.

'Very well, sir,' he replied. 'In fact, that's the purpose of my visit, to confirm that we will be taking the suspects to court to request a three day remand in the cells once the 72 hours is up.'

Inspector Bowden thought that by giving DCI Marshall the impression that a three day remand had already been agreed, he could pressure him to make a request at the Magistrates' Court.

DCI Marshall, however, was well rehearsed in responding to pressure and Inspector Bowden presented very little threat to him. He let out a jaded sigh before replying in a patronising manner. 'Now then Inspector Bowden, let's take this one step at a time, shall we? Firstly, before we even think about taking anybody to court, you need the superintendent's agreement to hold the suspects for the initial 72 hours.' He paused for effect, and watched Inspector Bowden squirm before he continued. 'At this point, Inspector Bowden, it has not yet been decided whether we will be holding them that long.'

As Inspector Bowden tried to respond, the DCI raised his voice an octave while placing his right hand in front of him, indicating that he hadn't finished speaking. 'Secondly, Inspector Bowden, before we reach a decision, there are a couple of matters that we need to consider. Perhaps you could help me by answering the following questions?'

Again he continued before giving Inspector Bowden a chance to speak. 'How are the suspects shaping up? Is there any sign of them confessing or do they still maintain their innocence?'

'Oh they'll admit it all right. They've got to in the end. It's obvious they're guilty.'

'That,' boomed the DCI, 'does not answer my question! Have the suspects actually admitted anything?'

'No,' Inspector Bowden was forced to concede.

'Very well then; how about our other enquiries? Have any of the team come up with anything? Have any witnesses come forward to say they saw anything untoward take place?'

'Yes sir, as soon as the suspects told us which bars they'd visited we sent some officers straight there to question the public. A few of the staff from the Portland Bars remembered their raucous behaviour from last night,' Inspector Bowden volunteered, 'and a barman even saw them pouring vodka into one of Amanda Morris's drinks before handing it to her.'

'Raucous behaviour is not what killed Amanda Morris, inspector, and if our suspicions prove correct, and there were drugs involved, then a witness to a drink spiked with vodka is simply not good enough! Am I correct in assuming that no drugs were found on either of the suspects or in their homes?'

'Yes,' replied the inspector. 'But Amanda Morris's boyfriend says she boasted to him about the drugs she had taken while in the company of the suspects, sir.'

'Are you referring to Mr Leslie Stevens?'

'Yes sir.'

'A man with a previous record, I believe.'

'Yes sir, but not drugs related, just driving offences, and petty theft when he was an adolescent.'

'Nevertheless, it makes him an unreliable witness. What about the urine samples?'

'No trace of drugs sir.'

'Very well. Under the circumstances, I feel that I have no alternative but to recommend to the superintendent that we release the suspects due to lack of evidence.'

As Inspector Bowden began to make desperate protestations, the DCI added, 'That will be all inspector! You may leave my office.'

Inspector Bowden, realising that he was wasting his time by pleading any further, retreated from DCI Marshall's office, feeling temporarily defeated.

***

Sunday 22nd June 1986

In the early hours of Sunday morning Sergeant Miller entered Julie's cell.

'Go and collect your things, you're going home,' he instructed.

'Why, what's happened?' she asked.

'Never mind, just do as you're told and do it quickly before the inspector changes his mind!'

Julie obliged. She was unaware that Inspector Bowden had been compelled to release her following his meeting with DCI Marshall.

In a neighbouring interview room Rita had also undergone stringent questioning from one of Inspector Bowden's colleagues, and this interview hadn't yielded any results either. So Julie left the police cells feeling a mixture of emotions; relief that she was no longer in custody, but anxiety about the reception that she would receive when she arrived home.

Throughout her time spent at the police station, the one person who Julie had not given any thought to was her boyfriend, Vinny. In the midst of her ordeal, it had escaped her mind that she had arranged to meet him at the Bella Vida restaurant at 8pm on Saturday evening.

Chapter 6

Vinny entered the Bella Vida just before 8pm. He was feeling a combination of nervousness and excitement as he thought about his plan to take his relationship with Julie to a higher level of commitment, and toyed with the small package inside his jacket pocket. He was dressed smartly in a pair of beige Chino trousers, a pale blue and beige striped shirt and a navy blue jacket. Vinny had made a special effort for this evening, which he hoped would be a memorable one. However, although he had arranged to meet Julie inside the restaurant at 8pm, there was no sign of her. *"Oh well, I am a bit early,"* he thought, and he took his seat at the table for two and waited patiently.

While he anticipated Julie's arrival, his mind became absorbed by thoughts of her. He had known Julie for most of his life. When he was eleven they began to attend the same secondary school; Vinny had recognised her as the well-presented and attractive girl who lived a few streets away. Even at that age there was something about her that made her stand out from the crowd. She later admitted to him that until she saw him at secondary school, she wasn't aware that he existed.

That didn't surprise Vinny as he had been the quiet type. All through school they didn't have much to do with each other. They were in different classes for one thing. Julie was in one of the top classes whereas Vinny was midstream.

He had always liked her and when he reached the age where girls became a major obsession, Julie was top on his list of desirables. He'd never had the courage to approach her though. Although good looking, he wasn't cool enough to be considered a heart-throb, and he thought of girls like Julie as being well out of his league. In a school of over a thousand pupils, Vinny saw himself as just one of hundreds of ordinary boys.

After leaving school he noticed her the odd time in the street or at the bus stop and they would acknowledge each other with a polite nod of the head. He still didn't have the courage to ask her out until a couple of years after they had left school.

He was in Saturdays nightclub with some of the lads when he spotted Julie and Rita only yards away. His heart began to race on catching sight of Julie, immaculately dressed and oozing sensuality. He couldn't help but stare.

Rita was the first to react, and unfortunately, she seemed to be taking his staring as a sign of encouragement.

He noticed them deep in discussion; a discussion that seemed to concern him as Julie also began to look in his direction. To his surprise she submitted a pleasing smile, which he returned. He could feel his face flushing and he reacted by turning away. Mentally he scolded himself as he knew that she would interpret this as a lack of interest. He turned back, thrilled that she was still watching him, and this time he managed to hold her gaze until she and Rita responded by approaching him.

His first impulse was to panic. "*Jesus, Julie Quinley's coming over. What do I do, what do I say?*" he thought. He was tempted to walk away, but he knew that if he did he would miss his chance to impress her. So he stayed, and smiled avidly as Rita opened up the conversation.

'I thought it was you,' she began. 'We haven't seen you in here before. Is this going to become a habit?'

He noticed her initial use of the word "I", subconsciously excluding Julie, and wondered if they had approached him on Rita's account. The situation then presented him with more challenges; how to talk to them without making a fool of himself, and at the same time let them know that it was Julie he was interested in and not Rita.

He fumbled for words, staring shyly at the two girls and aware of Julie's eyes on him. It took a few moments before he replied, but when he did he seemed to do OK. By turning towards Julie and addressing his reply to her, he made it obvious that she was the one he was attracted to. 'It's my first time here,' he said, 'but I might just make it a regular thing.'

Once he had broken the silence they began to make small talk, discussing mutual acquaintances, school memories and careers. He occasionally eyed Rita, trying to keep her a part of the conversation out of politeness, but the person who he addressed most of his comments to was Julie. As soon as Rita sensed his disinterest, she slipped out of their company and found somebody else to chat up, leaving him alone with Julie. The prospect no longer daunted him, however, as the conversation was now in full flow and he felt that they were getting along well. The four pints of lager that he had drunk also helped.

It was obvious that Julie was attracted to him and he couldn't believe his luck. In fact, he was so eager that he couldn't help but get tongue tied now and again. She seemed impressed when he revealed that he had bought his own house. That didn't last long though when he told her that it was in the next street from his parents, and that he still went there for tea most evenings.

As the night progressed and the alcohol loosened Vinny's tongue, he confessed that he remembered her from as far back as about the age of seven, even before they went to the same school. He had always admired her from a distance but hadn't done anything about it as he had thought she would not be interested in him. As he put it, 'brainy girls didn't go out with lads from his class.' As soon as he uttered the words he felt foolish and inadequate.

When he plucked up the courage to ask Julie on a date, she delighted him by saying yes. That was two years ago, and they were still no further forward than they had ever been. Vinny wondered why; there seemed to be an aloofness to Julie that he couldn't penetrate. He felt that even now she didn't regard him as her equal. But that wasn't good enough for Vinny. He wanted more from the relationship than just a casual acquaintance. Maybe with a ring on her finger everything would be different, and if she turned him down, well that would prove that she didn't think that much of him anyway. What he would do if that situation arose he wasn't quite sure, but at least he would know where he stood, and the more he thought about it, the more he knew that it was something he had to do.

By the time it reached 8:20, the waiter had asked Vinny twice if he would like to order, and Vinny had explained that he was waiting for someone. It was now becoming evident, even to the waiter, that that someone was not going to show up. The waiter fussed around a nearby table, straightening knives and forks and flicking imaginary bits of dust off the tablecloth. Now and again he cast a sidelong glance in Vinny's direction, as though awaiting a decision.

Vinny had already glanced at the menu several times and had long ago decided which dishes he would like to order. His stomach rumbled in anticipation. As he tried to occupy his time during the lengthy wait, he gazed around the restaurant at happy couples tucking into their meals. Some looked back and, to Vinny, it seemed that everybody in the restaurant knew that he had been stood up.

Eventually it became obvious to him that there wasn't much hope of her turning up this late in the evening. After taking one last glance at his watch, he stood up, sighed and nodded towards the waiter before he left the restaurant feeling downcast and very humiliated.

His first thought was to return home, but he decided that there was no point in sitting there brooding. So he made his way to his local pub where he knew he would find his friend Pete, amongst others.

When Vinny walked inside the pub he knew it was a mistake. His clothing looked out of place in the surroundings of his local, so it became apparent to everyone that he hadn't intended to stay there for the entire evening.

'Where you off to mate?' asked an acquaintance called Danny.

'I'm not off anywhere, I've already been,' Vinny replied.

'Well you're soon back aren't you?'

Vinny sighed as he made the obligatory reply. 'Let's just say my arrangements didn't turn out.'

'You've been stood up, haven't you?' asked Danny sniggering.

The crowd sitting with Danny were quick to join in the fun, as they laughed and made jibes. Pete came to Vinny's rescue. 'All right mate, do you fancy a pint?' he asked as he put his arm around Vinny's shoulder and led him to the bar.

Pete was aware that Vinny had arranged to take Julie for a meal, so when he showed up in his local a little after 9pm, he guessed what had happened.

'Take no notice of that bunch of prats. Let's go and sit over there and you can tell me about it.'

'There's nothing to tell. I've been stood up, haven't I?'

'Have you tried ringing her to find out why she didn't show up?'

'Yeah, I rang her from two phone boxes on the way here but the phone was engaged all the time. I thought about calling round to her house but that would just make me look desperate.'

'No, don't be a mug! Don't worry about it mate. It's not the end of the world.'

'Maybe not but, oh I dunno, I just don't know where I stand with her anymore.'

Vinny shook his head from side to side before continuing. 'It's not like it's just any bird, you know? I really thought that me and Julie had something good going, especially after the last time I saw her. Christ, she couldn't get enough of me!'

'Look Vinny, there's plenty of birds you can have. Why wait around for Julie? It's obvious she's not that bothered.'

'It's not just about having a shag though is it? I want more. I want commitment.'

'For God's sake Vinny, you're starting to sound like a woman!'

An uncomfortable silence descended over them; commitment wasn't a word that entered into Pete's vocabulary. Vinny withdrew the package from his pocket and showed it to Pete.

'Oh I get it,' said Pete, nodding as the realisation hit him. 'You were going to pop the question? Jesus Vinny, you have got it bad!'

'Yeah,' replied Vinny, becoming annoyed. 'Fuckin' muggins, that's me. Two hundred quid this set me back and she can't even be arsed showing up. She's probably out with that bunch of slags she hangs around with.'

'Oh, Rita the Man Eater and that blonde bird with the big tits, do you mean?'

'Yeah, that's right; all out on the cop while I'm sat in a restaurant looking like a right dick.'

'I don't fancy your chances if she's out with them two mate. I bet they've copped off already.'

'But Julie's not like them two Pete.'

'Well, maybe not, but I wouldn't trust that Rita as far as I could throw her, not after what she did to me.'

'Yeah, but you had only seen her a couple of times though, hadn't you? You'd have probably dumped her soon anyway. It's not like me and Julie, we've been together for a while now.'

'That doesn't mean to say she's not seeing someone-else behind your back though does it? They're all the same them lot; they just use blokes for what they can get. I thought that Rita was a good laugh, but she was just taking the piss, letting me take her for meals while she had other blokes on the go as well.'

'Yeah, but you were seeing someone-else as well Pete, weren't you?'

'At least I wasn't flaunting it in front of her face. I felt dead shown up when she walked in Saturdays with that bloke and just sailed right past me without even letting on. I felt like a right mug.'

'I know how you feel mate,' Vinny responded.

This prompted some sympathy from Pete who realised how carried away he had been in maligning Rita when his friend was feeling hurt. He slung his arm around Vinny's shoulder in a rough, masculine embrace. 'Look mate, don't let it worry you. There's plenty of birds you could have. If she can't be arsed, then find someone who can.'

Vinny looked down in silence and took solace in his pint of beer. Pete tried to discuss other matters in order to take Vinny's mind off the situation, but after they had drank a few pints, Vinny raised the subject again.

'I'm going to ring her and find out what the problem is.'

'She won't be in.'

'Well I'll ring her in the morning then.'

'Don't be a mug Vinny, it's her that's stood you up not the other way round. If anyone should be phonin' anyone, it should be her phonin' you.'

As Vinny began to recall the embarrassment of sitting alone in the restaurant while the waiters whispered amongst themselves, his disappointment turned to anger.

'Yeah, you're right Pete. Why should I ring her? Stuff her!'

Having made his decision, Vinny removed his jacket, rolled up his sleeves and loosened his collar. 'Right, let's get pissed!' he said.

Now that he was feeling more in tune with his environment, he spent the rest of the evening playing pool, getting extremely drunk, and trying to forget about Julie.

Chapter 7

Sunday 22nd June 1986

Julie arrived home on Sunday morning feeling exhausted, full of grief for her lost friend and terrified at the prospect of what lay ahead. She was met by Clare who was standing in the hallway looking as though she had been waiting there most of the morning. Clare announced, 'It's our Julie, mam,' casting a backwards glance towards the living room where her parents sat, but failing to meet Julie's eyes, as though afraid of what she might find there. Julie was then greeted by three anxious, expectant faces. She forced a narrow smile and said, 'I made it back home then,' endeavouring to sound nonchalant.

Her mother stepped forward and threw her arms around her. 'Oh Julie love, I'm so glad to see you! I've been worried sick, thinking that you wouldn't be coming home.'

Julie replied, in an attempt at flippancy, 'Don't be daft mam, they can't hold me without evidence! They had to release me.'

'God help us when they do find the bloody evidence then!' said her father.

Julie withdrew from her mother's embrace and turned on her father. 'There is no evidence to find. I'm innocent, and so is Rita!' she shouted.

'Well if you were so bloody innocent, they wouldn't have been here in the first place, turning our house over, and showing us up in front of all and sundry! I always said that no good would come out of all this clubbing, staying up till all hours...'

Julie interrupted, sniping viciously at her father, 'Don't you start! I've had enough with those bastards, interrogating me, day and night, accusing me of things I haven't done, and now even my own father won't believe me! What kind of a father is that anyway?'

Bill pounced forward, with his hand raised. 'Don't you dare speak to me like that!'

Before he could manage to strike, however, Betty wedged

herself between Bill and Julie. 'Leave her alone Bill! This isn't helping matters. Julie, get up to your room!'

Julie did as she was told to the sound of her father's voice berating her, 'You're no daughter of mine! Out till all hours, with a load of scum, getting drunk, involved in murders, MURDERS, I say!'

As soon as Julie reached her room and shut the door, renewed tears filled her eyes. She found it hard to accept that a night out had resulted in such a travesty; her friend dead, the hostility of her own father, the guilt and shame which she had brought on her family. She needed to convince her parents of her innocence, but what could she say to reassure them? Her father had never approved of her lifestyle. He was old-fashioned and always would be. He was also a bit of a male chauvinist. If he knew half the things that she and her friends got up to then she would sink even lower in his estimation. How could she explain to him that they were only meant to be having a laugh?

A recurring thought began to trouble her. It was of Inspector Bowden, ridiculing her and her friends' behaviour, and she could feel her cheeks burn with embarrassment. She could see the similarities between her father and the inspector – two of the old school, with their 'women should be at home, tied to the kitchen sink' philosophy. Her mind was in a quandary. She thought that in some ways perhaps they were right; her life was just one useless, time-wasting mess. Maybe she should find herself a husband and have a family, instead of running around and acting the fool.

Julie lay down on her bed but, once again, sleep eluded her. She was too upset at her friend's death, and her father's animosity towards her. He had always been so supportive of her in the past, even though he didn't approve of her way of life. She felt that she had let him down, and his anger unsettled her. Julie hadn't seen this aspect of her father's personality before, and what she had seen in the last twenty-four hours had shocked and disturbed her intensely.

Suddenly the bedroom door opened and Julie tensed in anticipation, expecting her father to walk in, but it was Clare. Her younger sister walked towards the bed. She seemed ill at ease, and hesitated before she spoke, 'Julie ... I just came to say... well, that, I believe that you haven't done anything wrong. I don't care what my dad says!'

Julie reached her hand out towards Clare but she seemed to shrink away from her. Wanting to reassure her little sister, Julie stood up and flung her arms around her. She could feel Clare beginning to relax in the comfort of her embrace. They wept in each other's arms and it was a while before Julie spoke, 'Thanks Clare; that means a lot to me. I haven't done anything wrong. I was just in the wrong place at the wrong time, that's all.'

After Clare had left the room, Julie still couldn't sleep so she took a long awaited shower. She stood beneath the powerful spray for ages, letting the hot water flood over her and scrubbing at her skin as though trying to purge herself. She didn't realise just how hard she had scrubbed until she emerged from the shower, with patches of her flesh red and slightly sore. Julie dressed soberly, wearing no make-up, subconsciously attempting to prove to her father that she was still his innocent little girl.

As Julie made her way downstairs, her stomach churned at the prospect of encountering her father's wrath again. She wanted to call Rita, to find out if she too had been arrested. Julie needed to confide in someone with whom she could identify at this dreadful time.

Inside the living room Bill peered over the top of his newspaper, then pulled it upwards, signifying that he didn't want to look at her. She stepped gingerly towards the telephone and then trembled with shock as her father bellowed, 'And don't be gabbing on there for ages either! It's me who pays the bloody bills in this house!'

Shocked by his manner towards her, she replied, timidly, 'I won't dad.'

As soon as Rita answered the telephone, she responded to Julie's unease, 'Listen Jules,' she said, 'they put me through the ringer as well, but don't worry about it! We know we've done nowt wrong, so them bastards can fuck off! I tell you what though, I'd love to find out who *did* give drugs to Amanda!'

'So would I,' said Julie. 'That's if there were any! It might have just been too much drink!'

'Maybe, but I doubt it. Anyway, I can tell you're feeling upset at the moment, so why don't we go out tonight and have a few drinks, and a chin wag? Maybe you'll feel a lot better then.'

'Oh, I don't know,' said Julie, thinking what her father's reaction might be to the news of another night out.

Rita guessed that Julie was having difficulty speaking openly on the phone. 'Can't you talk?' she asked.

'Not really.'

'All right, give me one word answers then. Are you having a hard time at home, because of what's happened?'

'Yes.'

'Has your old man had a go at you?'

'Yes,' replied Julie, almost in a whisper, afraid that her father might have overheard Rita's comment.

'You might as well get away from him for a few hours then,' urged Rita. 'You've got nowt to lose have you?'

'Oh, go on then,' agreed Julie reluctantly.

'Right, great, I'll see you in the Flying Horse at eight o'clock then. Oh, and don't forget to ring Vinny,' Rita added before Julie had a chance to replace the receiver.

"*Oh My God, Vinny!*" thought Julie, and she remembered how she was supposed to have met him the previous night. She had been so preoccupied by her troubles that she had forgotten about him until now. She knew that it was a bad time to ring and explain, while her father was within earshot, so she decided to do it later.

Julie ventured into the kitchen to see what sort of a reception she would receive from her mother.

Betty was pottering about, busy as usual, starting to prepare the Sunday dinner. Her cheerful greeting surprised Julie. 'Hiya love, don't suppose you managed to get any sleep at all, did you?'

'No, mam.' Julie skirted around Betty before continuing. 'Listen, I'm really sorry about all the trouble I've caused you and my dad. I swear mam; I've not done anything wrong! We just had a few drinks and a laugh, that's all. All right, maybe Mandy had a few too many and we had to take her home. But we thought she was all right. She seemed to be coming round a bit when we left her.'

Her anguish was such that her words came out in a rush until eventually, unable to continue, her voice broke and she succumbed to tears.

Betty stopped what she was doing and dried her hands, taking Julie in her arms. Forgetting any attempts at bravery,

Julie was transported back to her childhood, wanting her mother to shield her from all the guilt and pain of the last 24 hours. As she laid her chin on her mother's shoulder, she gave way to uncontrolled tears and felt her legs weaken beneath her.

Betty tried to reassure her. 'Listen love, try not to worry, I believe you. I bet somebody else was giving her drugs when you were too drunk to notice, eh? It'll all come out in the end, mark my words!'

'It doesn't change the fact that she's gone though, does it?' sobbed Julie, 'and my dad hates me for it; he thinks I've done it!'

'Does he 'eck. He knows you're innocent just as much as we do. He's just suffering from hurt pride, that's all. He's worried about what the neighbours think. Anyway, you know he's never liked the idea of women going to clubs, and this just gives him a good excuse to get on his high horse again.'

'I'll stop going out then mam, I will. I'll do anything to get things back to how they were!' said Julie, her voice beginning to tremble with emotion.

'You bloody well will not, you'll get on with your life! Just give him a few days and he'll come round, you'll see. In fact, get yourself out tonight girl. I'll have a word with him and see if I can get him to ease off you a bit.'

'Oh thanks mam,' said Julie, hugging her mother tightly.

'It's all right Julie love. I can tell what you're going through, but nobody should be punished just for having a good time.'

Julie, now feeling more at ease, helped her mother to finish preparing dinner. She was relieved to know that her mother was supporting her and trying to make things easier with her father.

Once Julie had finished helping her mother, she returned to her bedroom where she struggled to banish memories of her last meeting with Vinny from her mind, feeling that they were inappropriate under the circumstances.

However, grasping at a source of comfort in the midst of her troubles, she gave in to thoughts of the previous weekend. She had gone back to Vinny's house with him after going out with her friends. Recalling how precious those moments had been, she lay back on her pillow and cast her mind back.

Chapter 8

The last time Julie saw Vinny was the previous weekend. She had awoken at about 10am on Saturday morning to find Vinny snoring gently beside her. Julie was reluctant to disturb him straight-away, so for a while she lay still, immersed in her own thoughts.

She was feeling quite serene and content after a night of passionate lovemaking. Vinny always had this effect on her. It was just as she always said to Rita, Vinny knew "exactly which buttons to press and when to press them." For Julie, it was one of the most satisfying aspects of their relationship.

Her mind wandered back to the previous night and how Vinny had coaxed and caressed her in the most intimate of places, until she was completely relaxed. Then, he had contin-ued to kiss and stroke her, teasing, knowing what she wanted but refusing to give it to her until she had almost begged him. When she felt as though she could bear the anticipation no longer, he had entered her at just the right moment, sending her body into uncontrolled spasms of sheer pleasure.

When they had both reached their climax, they lay in each other's arms, spent and truly gratified, until Julie drifted off to sleep.

She knew that once he awoke, their lovemaking would continue until well into the day, with only brief interruptions while they rested or made conversation, until their increasing hunger for food forced them to rise. With this realisation, she took the opportunity to go and make herself a drink before settling back into bed beside Vinny.

As Julie clambered into bed her movement disturbed him. Once Vinny had awoken to the knowledge that it was now Satur-day morning and Julie was in bed next to him, his initial reaction had been precisely as she had foreseen, to her immense delight.

Afterwards, when they had lay still for a while, Julie asked, 'How's Pete; is he still pining after Rita?'

'Is he 'eck! Rita's nowt special you know; girls like her are ten a penny.'

'Well she put him in his place anyway.'

'Not really, he wasn't that bothered. He was seeing somebody-else as well.'

'That doesn't surprise me! He's always been the same.'

'Well you can't blame him after what Rita did.'

'He was only bothered because she dumped him before he got a chance to dump her. It must have made a change for Pete to see a girl give him the run-around instead of the other way round.'

'It was the way she did it Julie, flaunting that bloke in front of him. She was just after what she could get and as soon as she thought Pete had sussed her she was off looking for her next mug. I think she's a right tart! I'm surprised you knock around with someone like her.'

'Look Vinny, what annoys me about fellas like Pete is that they think it's all right for them to do it, but they don't like it when the shoe's on the other foot. I say good luck to her.'

'I'm not getting into an argument about those two again. I'll go and make us something to eat,' said Vinny as he jumped out of bed and headed towards the kitchen.

While Vinny was cooking, Julie decided to take a shower. As she stood under the water, she looked around the bathroom at the décor, which was stylish and contemporary. This never failed to impress her. For a man he was very fastidious. He had obviously put a lot of time and effort into decorating and furnishing his home and the results were impressive. He did have very good taste and knew how to make the place seem homely and yet fashionable at the same time.

When she emerged from the bathroom, she could smell the tempting aroma of grilled bacon, and they were soon tucking into bacon sandwiches and chatting about work and family. When they had finished, Julie offered to wash the dishes, and then declared that it was time she got home. As usual, she waited for Vinny to approach her regarding any future arrangements.

'Will I see you in the week then?' he asked.

'Oh, I'm sorry Vinny but I'm really busy.'

'All right, what about the weekend?'

'Well I'm out on Friday for Amanda's birthday, but Saturday would be nice.'

'Ok, I tell you what then,' he said, taking hold of her hands. 'As I won't be seeing you all week, why don't we have a special night out? I'll take you for a meal if you like.'

'Yes, that would be lovely, Vinny.'

'Right, how about the Bella Vida then?'

'The Bella Vida! That's a bit posh isn't it? Are you sure you can stretch to that?'

'No problem. I want it to be a really special night,' and he rose from his seat and put his arms about her.

By the time Julie left Vinny's house and set off for home, she felt as though she was walking on a cushion of air.

***

Sunday 22nd June 1986

As Julie recalled the special time that she had had with Vinny the previous weekend, she couldn't help but feel bad about last night. While she had been at the police station, Vinny had probably been sat alone in the Bella Vida waiting for her to show up. Of course it wasn't her fault; how was she to know that she was going to be arrested? But maybe she should have rang him from the station when she had the chance.

She treasured her moments with Vinny. He made her feel so happy. She knew he loved her; he demonstrated that every time they were together. Vinny's problem, though, was that he had difficulty putting his feelings into words. He was the same in his working life. He was good at his job, but he worked too hard and for little thanks.

Julie was forever asking him why he didn't look for a better job or try to get a qualification to enhance his prospects, but he didn't seem concerned. "*If only he had a bit more get up and go!*" she thought. "*Then we could really start to get somewhere.*" As long as he continued to display such complacency, however, she had no intentions of settling down with him.

"*He's not so bad though. He might be uneducated and appear almost uncouth at times, but he is good to me, and he always makes me feel special when I'm with him. In fact, he bloody well pampers me."*

She thought once again about how much Vinny had been looking forward to their night out at the Bella Vida. *"I'll ring him and explain as soon as I get a chance,"* she told herself.

***

Sunday 22nd June 1986

The family ate their meal in silence. Julie toyed with her food. She could sense the anger still emanating from her father, and this caused her to feel ill at ease. Bill rushed through his food and, as soon as he had finished, he scraped his chair back and announced that he was going for a walk. When he had left the table, the others exchanged knowing glances and each breathed a sigh of relief.

As soon as she had eaten as much as she could manage, Julie took the opportunity to make her long awaited phone call to Vinny, while her father was out of the house. His angry reaction surprised her when he asked, 'What were you doing last night that stopped you from turning up at the restaurant?'

Equally angry, Julie retaliated, 'What was I doing? I'll tell you what I was doing! I was stuck at a police station all night, getting the grilling of my life. That's what I was doing!'

Vinny was stunned by this statement and, when he spoke, Julie could sense that he had mellowed slightly towards her. 'What do you mean, at a police station? What's happened?'

Julie explained the events of the weekend to him, adding that she had been to hell and back in order to enlist his sympathy. Her ploy seemed effective, for he then replied, 'I'm really sorry to hear that. Still, try not to worry. If you know you've done nothing wrong, then you'll be all right. In fact, they wouldn't have released you if they'd had anything on you. Tell you what, why don't I see if I can re-book the restaurant for tonight, and try to cheer you up a bit?'

Julie replied tentatively, knowing that Vinny was about to receive another blow to his pride. 'I can't, I've arranged to meet Rita. You see, they arrested her too, and ...'

Before she had a chance to finish her sentence, Vinny's fury was re-ignited and he stormed at her, 'I might have bloody well known! You put everyone before me. To hell with you then! If you can't be bothered about me, then why should I bother about you?'

When he slammed down the receiver, Julie was shocked. In the last couple of days she had seen so many extreme behavioural changes in the people close to her that it was all becoming a bit too much for her to absorb.

***

Sunday 22nd June 1986

They met in the foyer of the Flying Horse. Julie had already been standing there for about ten minutes, having arrived early. She had been anxious to leave her home as her father had returned, bringing the tense atmosphere back with him. She had not put her usual effort into her choice of clothing. Somehow, her heart wasn't in it, but she couldn't help noticing that Rita had, once again, gone to extremes in order to get herself noticed. They exchanged a faint smile and headed straight for the bar.

No sooner had they seated themselves, than Julie spotted Lindsey Pilkington making her way towards them. She instinctively knew that this wouldn't be a pleasant encounter. Lindsey was trouble with a capital T and Julie had done her best to avoid her for years. If ever there was any aggravation going on in the local pubs then you could almost guarantee that Lindsey and her friends would be at the heart of it. As soon as Lindsey reached their table she asked, 'What's this about you Julie, being dragged off by the police?'

'Oh here we go,' said Rita. 'It hasn't taken the vultures long, has it?'

'I was only asking!' replied Lindsey, defensively.

'It doesn't matter, Rita,' said Julie. 'They're all gonna want to know sooner or later anyway. I expect we're flavour of the week at the moment.'

Julie explained the events of the last two days to Lindsey. Once Lindsey was satisfied that she had heard all there was to hear, she went to join her own friends. Julie and Rita watched in dismay as Lindsey recounted the tale to a group of avid listeners.

'Never mind,' said Rita. 'It'll soon blow over. It's just a seven-day wonder, that's all.'

The girls then settled down and began to exchange comments about their time spent at the police station and the events sur-rounding their arrest.

Rita had also been subjected to a rigorous interrogation. However, she had received a better reception on returning home. 'Well,' she said laughingly to Julie. 'It's not as if they're not used to the coppers round at our house. My dad was halfway over the back gate before he realised they hadn't come for him. They were all dying to find out what had happened and my dad says that the cops have always had it in for our family, anyway, so I shouldn't let 'em get to me.'

Julie outlined her home situation to Rita, and the conversation she had had with Vinny. Rita offered a few words of reassurance, and these might have comforted Julie, if it hadn't been for the repeated interruptions they had to endure.

Rumours of their arrest were spreading, and they were faced with a constant stream of locals stopping at their table in order to quiz them. That in itself was bad enough, but Julie was disconcerted by the witty comments which she received, such as, 'Hiya Jailbait, how're you doing?' These tasteless remarks were becoming increasingly tiresome as the evening wore on.

Rita advised Julie to, 'put a brave face on, and don't let them know you're bothered,' but she found the situation very trying. Rita encouraged her to stay until the end of the night as part of their act of defiance and, as usual, Rita's resilience amazed Julie. She seemed to react to the taunts with indifference and didn't give any indication whatsoever that the situation bothered her.

The end of the evening brought mixed feelings for Julie. She was relieved to be leaving the Flying Horse but, when she thought about returning home, she dreaded the anticipated response from her father. Luckily, everybody had gone to bed when she reached home. The house was quiet and peaceful so Julie took the opportunity to sit down for a few minutes and collect her thoughts before going to bed. Unfortunately, however, as soon as she began to contemplate her circumstances, she found herself, once again, immersed in a flood of tears.

Chapter 9

The Manchester offices of Belmont Insurance Company were situated on King Street, which was at the heart of the city centre and housed many of the top financial institutions. The building itself dated from the Victorian era and was a tall, magnificent structure. Anybody arriving at Belmont's Manchester offices could not fail to notice the building's impressive architectural design. In contrast, the interior was very modern.

Like the other offices of the Belmont Insurance Company, the Manchester office conveyed the overall image that the company wished to portray; from the outside, long established, sturdy and reliable, and from the inside, forward thinking and technologically advanced. Belmont Insurance also had a good reputation for looking after its staff and, as one of its employees, Julie enjoyed many of the perks on offer. All in all, when compared to many of her other friends, she felt that she held a very privileged position. Rita and Debby might earn a bit more than her but they had to work long, tiring shifts in a hot factory. They had few promotion prospects, less holidays than Julie and no sick pay entitlements.

Belmont Insurance opened for business at 9am, but Julie liked to arrive early so that she could grab a cup of coffee, settle herself in at the switchboard and observe the arrival of the rest of the staff. She normally enjoyed this time of day when many of her friends and associates would stop for a chat on their way to their respective departments. It also gave her a chance to impart confidences with her friend Norma who shared switchboard duties.

Norma was forty-seven and had grown up children of her own. She and Julie had a good friendship, which had got off the ground from the day Julie had joined the company as a trainee switchboard operator at the tender age of just sixteen. Norma had interminable patience, was a natural teacher, and was more than willing to take Julie by the hand and show her all there was to know. Under Norma's wing Julie was soon able to get to grips with the job and, because of her pleasant nature, she quickly became acquainted with many other members of staff.

With the passing of time, Norma and Julie found they were very much at ease in each other's company, and could confide in each other regarding their private lives.

This Monday morning, however, was different from any other Monday morning, and Norma was surprised to see Julie sidle up to her desk at one minute past nine.

'Morning Julie, I'd just about given you up for dead,' she exclaimed.

Julie shuddered at the irony of Norma's words. 'Is Jacqueline in yet?' she asked.

Norma sensed that something was wrong. 'Yes, she stormed in ages ago, and muttered something about you not showing your face.'

Norma registered Julie's reaction, and asked, 'Have you two had a barney then?'

'Oh, it's worse than that!' said Julie. She took a deep breath and uttered the chilling words that still sounded alien to her:

'Amanda's dead.'

'Jesus Christ! What's happened?'

Julie began to relate the sorry tale but found herself getting choked up and was unable to continue.

'It's all right, take your time,' said Norma.

After she had composed herself, Julie continued, stopping to take deep breaths each time her voice became shaky. When she had finished, Norma leant over and covered Julie's hand with her own in a reassuring gesture. 'I'm so sorry Julie, Amanda was such a lovely girl! She didn't deserve to die like that. I'm surprised to see you still in work.'

'I had to Norma. I didn't feel like it, but people are blaming me and I couldn't let them think I'd gone into hiding, could I?'

Norma nodded sombrely, then added, 'Look, we'd better catch up on a few calls and then we'll have a bit more time to talk about it.'

Julie did as she was instructed but, at the same time, she wondered if this indicated a rebuff by Norma. However, she needn't have worried as, once they had cleared the backlog of calls, Norma turned to Julie and said, 'Right, now we can talk. Listen Julie, you're going to have to face Jackie you know? As far as I'm concerned you're innocent! It doesn't matter what Jacqueline, high and mighty Bartlett thinks, you know you're innocent and I know you're innocent! You've been brave enough to come into work today, but you've still got to face her. Get up to that canteen at lunchtime, and show her that you're not running away! You've got nothing to hide, remember, so don't let everyone think you have.'

'Right, I suppose I better had,' conceded Julie. She knew that Norma was right, but she wasn't looking forward to seeing Jacqueline. 'I just wish I knew why Amanda died! It can't have been just because of the drink, but until I know otherwise there'll always be that doubt in my mind.'

Norma surprised Julie with her angry reaction. 'Now you listen to me Julie Quinley! People don't usually die from having a few too many drinks. You said yourself that she was coming round a bit when you left her. I reckon someone's been giving her drugs somewhere along the line but you can't be held responsible for that! Anyway, it'll all come out in the wash, you mark my words, so don't you go worrying yourself.'

Julie felt better knowing that she had Norma's support and for the rest of the morning she carried on with her work. She tried to take her mind off things but the thought of facing Jacqueline wouldn't go away. She told herself that perhaps Jacqueline would understand, and that it wouldn't be such an ordeal after all, but she knew that this wasn't likely.

The only time when her thoughts deviated from her dread of facing Jacqueline was when insurance salesman, Mike Marston cheered her up by putting in an appearance.

'Morning ladies,' he greeted them as he strode to the counter.

Julie's face was immediately transformed, the worry lines melting away as she smiled radiantly at him.

Mike, aged 28, was a real smoothy. Tall, dark and handsome, he exuded charm, and most of the women he came into contact with couldn't fail to be impressed. Julie was one of those women. They had flirted outrageously during the last few weeks and Julie had waited for the moment when he would ask her on a date.

'How are you feeling this morning Julie?' he asked.

'Fine,' she lied, not wishing to put him off by confiding in him about her atrocious weekend.

'How about you?' she asked.

'Great, a bit worse for wear though,' he grinned as he suppressed a yawn.

'Really, what have you been up to then?'

'Oh this and that, you know; too many late nights, too much rich food and too much to drink.'

Julie laughed and, feeling encouraged, he continued. 'You know my trouble, I can't say no.'

'Really?'

'Yes, if the company's right, and there's fine food and wine on offer, then I'm just a sucker for a good time.'

Seeing that he had hit the right cord with Julie he sidled up to her and whispered. 'If an attractive young lady was to ask me for a good time out, then I would be powerless to refuse.'

Julie beamed as she replied, 'If it's a lady you're referring to then shouldn't it be you that's doing the asking?'

He was amused at her effrontery. 'Consider yourself asked,' he quipped. Then, without giving her a chance to reply he added, 'Name the time and place, and I'll be there. Give me a ring and let me know.'

He then vanished just as slickly as he had appeared.

'He's a bit cocksure of himself, isn't he?' commented Norma. 'He didn't even give you a chance to say no.'

'That's because he knew I'd say yes.'

'So you're going to ring him then?'

'Course I am, I've been waiting for him to ask me out for ages.'

'I thought you had a boyfriend.'

'Jesus Norma, you're beginning to sound like Rita. I am seeing Vinny, but it's just a bit of fun, that's all; it's not like I've made my marriage vows or anything.'

'Just be careful, that's all Julie. By all accounts he's a bit of a ladies man, and I don't want you getting hurt.'

This comment prompted Julie's curiosity. 'What's been said about him?' she asked.

'Well, you know he used to work at Leicester branch, and I've heard he broke a few hearts there. He's ruthless when it comes to business as well. He's won the top salesman award for the last two months running, and from what I've heard he's heading straight to the top and will do anything to make sure he gets there.'

'Well there's nothing wrong with having a bit of ambition. I like to see ambition in a man. And as for breaking hearts, he's not even been out with anybody at this branch.'

'He has only been here two months Julie, give him a chance. You might be his first victim, that's aside from anyone he's been seeing outside the company of course.'

'Most men like to sow their wild oats. He's just waiting to meet the right one, that's all.'

'Well suit yourself Julie, but don't say I didn't warn you. I think you've got enough on your plate at the moment without the likes of Mike Marston adding to your troubles.'

Julie ignored Norma's comments. She really fancied Mike. He was a man who was going places and she would accept his offer to take her out; in fact she couldn't wait. She knew about his reputation, and knew that she was running a risk by going out with someone like him, but the attraction she felt towards him was too strong to fight. Anyway, she decided, she *was* only going on a date. What harm could that do? It might even lead to something. Men like him usually settled down eventually, and why shouldn't she be the one to tame him?

She thought about Vinny. She did feel a bit bad about that but told herself that she shouldn't do. Julie hadn't promised Vinny a long-term commitment so he shouldn't expect one. And as she began to dream about Mike with his air of cool sophistication, Vinny's rugged simplicity paled into insignificance.

She was so excited that she temporarily forgot about her problems, but they soon re-emerged, and as she watched the clock approach 12, she knew that there was one problem that she had to deal with straightaway. Norma wished her luck as she picked up her handbag, ready to make her way up to the canteen.

Chapter 10

Monday 23rd June 1986

As soon as Julie walked into the canteen she could sense the antagonistic atmosphere. She gazed towards the table where Jacqueline and her friends were sat and noted the way in which the girls around the table glared back at her. Her first thought, before entering the canteen, had been to walk over to Jacqueline and speak to her. However, when she caught sight of the hostile glances that she received, she changed her mind. Instead, she approached the counter and placed her order.

She couldn't concentrate on selecting her food, as she was too preoccupied. She therefore chose the first item on the list, which was Shepherd's Pie. Julie then walked over to a table and took a seat. It was the first time in years that she had sat on her own in the canteen and Julie suddenly felt very self-conscious.

It was difficult trying to appear casual and avoid looking over at Jacqueline's table. Julie's natural curiosity caused her to glance at the group of girls. She made several attempts to look elsewhere but found that her eyes kept straying back towards that table.

After a couple of minutes, she felt compelled to gaze in that direction once more as she heard a loud scraping sound followed by a lot of commotion. It was Jacqueline, dragging her chair back as she stood up and made some angry announcement which Julie couldn't quite hear. Julie's heart sank as she realised that Jacqueline was heading in her direction. In no time at all she was standing over Julie, looking down at her.

The onslaught from Jacqueline was so sudden that Julie didn't have a chance to defend herself. 'I don't know how you've got the bloody nerve to show your face in here after what you and your friends have done! I knew that you were a bunch of common tarts, but now I know that you're even worse. You're not fit to be seen on the sole of my shoe! Amanda was a lovely girl. She was too good to have a friend like you, and now she's gone. Well I hope you're all proud of yourselves, you murderers! The sooner you're behind bars Julie Quinley, the better off we'll all be.'

Jacqueline emphasised this last point by prodding Julie in the shoulder. As Julie opened her mouth in an attempt to defend herself, Jacqueline turned on her heel and stormed back towards her own table. By now the attention of the whole canteen was focused on Julie and Jacqueline.

Jacqueline, noting this attention, stopped and announced to everybody, 'Yes, you heard right, Julie Quinley and her friends are murderers! They killed Amanda Morris, by getting her pissed senseless, and the police think that one of the sly cows even gave drugs to Amanda as well. That seems to be their idea of fun. Now that hard faced bitch is sat there large as life when she should be behind bars!'

As the scandal reached the ears of the onlookers, a hush descended on the room. Julie looked up, and noticed the shocked faces staring towards her. She was speechless and powerless to defend herself. What could she say that would make any difference? The damage had already been done, thanks to Jacqueline.

In a feat of immaculate timing, Mrs Stubbs, one of the canteen staff, appeared at Julie's table with her lunch and slammed it down on the table as she announced, 'There you go, and I hope it bloody chokes you!' She then walked away.

Julie's first reaction was to flee from the room, but Norma's words kept echoing inside her head and she told herself, "*If I run, everyone will think I'm guilty.*" She knew that she had to see it through. "*I'm going to eat this bloody pie if it kills me,*" she said to herself. "*I've got to try to act as normal as possible; I mustn't let them get to me.*"

Consuming the meal was a struggle. Julie had never before realised that eating could take such an infinite length of time. Her muscles were tense and she found it a tremendous effort to swallow each mouthful. Her throat was so constricted that she felt as though she would choke. Occasionally, she raised her head and glanced around the room just to let people see that she wasn't about to bow down in shame.

She could sense eyes watching her, but every time she looked up, they quickly diverted their gaze. This caused her to become even more self-conscious. She felt as though her every movement was being noted; the shaking of her hands, the way she struggled to swallow – her face becoming more flushed with each agonising gulp, the way she shuffled uncomfortably on her chair.

A piece of pie then became lodged in her throat and she lifted her drink so that she could attempt to swill it down. Unfortunately, the cup slipped from her shaking hand. She quickly grasped at it and managed to steady the cup on the table, but not before some of the contents had spilt onto her food.

As she replaced the cup, Julie heard somebody clear their throat and a couple of people coughed, as though indicating a break in the tension. She couldn't face going to the canteen staff for a cloth to wipe up the mess, so she searched her bag for a tissue. Julie only succeeded in clearing up part of the drink with her tissue, so she had to face eating the rest of her meal with her plate swamped by liquid.

She had managed to gulp down the lump of Shepherd's Pie while her mind had been drawn to other things, and this had encouraged her to devour a few more forkfuls. However, she was still only two thirds through the pie, and was beginning to struggle once more. She knew that she mustn't leave her food uneaten, as this might suggest that she had rushed away, unable to face people any longer.

When Julie reached the point where an acceptable amount remained, she arranged her cutlery so that it concealed the biggest lumps of food. She then stood up and pulled back her chair as calmly as she could, in defiance of her rapidly beating heart and clammy hands. Julie then walked from the canteen with her head held high.

When Julie reached the reception area, she almost broke down in tears of relief now that her ordeal was over. 'Jesus Norma, that was hell!' she announced.

'Cheer up Julie, you've got the worst of it over with. Things can only get better from now on!'

Unfortunately, however, Norma's words couldn't have been further from the truth. Later that afternoon the manager asked to see Julie in his office and she returned to the reception area after about ten minutes.

'Well?' asked Norma.

'He wanted me to take some time off with full pay until the heat dies down a bit.'

'Oh well, at least things should have improved by the time you come back. It won't be flavour of the month anymore. How long has he given you?'

'I'm not doing it Norma.'

'Really, why not?'

'What, and let them all think that I'm guilty? You must be joking!'

'I can understand your point I suppose. What did you say to him?'

'Exactly what I've just told you.'

'Well I doubt whether they can force you to take time off and they probably won't bother trying. They'd be frightened of the consequences after that carry on with John in motor department.'

As Julie stared at her blankly, Norma continued, 'You know, the one that took them to a tribunal.'

'Oh yeah, I'd forgotten about that.'

They were then silent for a short while until Norma added, 'Well I just hope you'll be able to handle it Julie, but you know I'll be here to support you.'

'I know, thanks Norma,' Julie replied as she replaced her headphones.

**

Monday 23rd June 1986

Julie returned home from work on Monday evening. As she put her key in the front door she was full of apprehension. She was relieved to find, however, that her father's attitude towards her had improved a little. Julie noticed that his attempts at civility were, for him, a struggle and she guessed that her mother must have had a few words with him. Instead of the friendly banter that she had sometimes had with her father in the past, he remained polite, treating her like a stranger.

This caused her almost as much distress as his anger had done the day before. As she listened to her father asking her to, 'pass the butter please', as opposed to, 'give us the butter Julie love', she knew that her relationship with her father was in a sorry state, and she wondered if they would ever recapture the affinity which they had once shared.

At work the next day, there was no sign of improvement. People who had always greeted Julie with a friendly 'hello' when they arrived at work now ignored her. Some made deliberate attempts not to gaze in her direction. Others stared venomously at her, causing her to feel ill at ease. Some did still say hello to Julie, but she guessed that the news mustn't have reached them yet.

Although Norma insisted that Julie should venture up to the canteen again, she couldn't face it, and instead, she found herself wandering around the shops during her lunch hour. The situation seemed to worsen as the week wore on and Julie was tempted to take some time away from the place, but Norma persuaded her not to. Throughout the week Norma had remained a tower of strength to Julie, and without her Julie did not know what she would have done.

Chapter 11

Detective Inspector Bowden received a fax on Wednesday indicating the preliminary findings of the post mortem. It would be a few weeks before he received the detailed pathology report, but the fax, which had been rushed through to him at his insistence, did give an indication as to the cause of death. He sat sipping his cup of coffee while slowly digesting its contents.

Sergeant Drummond, observing that he was giving the piece of paper his full attention, asked, 'Is it the post mortem sir?'

'Um,' he grunted in response.

She didn't interrupt him further, knowing that he would relate the contents of the fax to the rest of the staff as soon as he was ready. Inspector Bowden believed in following a chain of command and preferred his subordinates to remain subordinate.

After a couple of minutes Inspector Bowden stood up and took a deep breath, expanding his chest and pulling his shoulders back, like a soldier on parade.

'Sergeant Drummond, I'm going to see the DCI. Can you take all calls please? It shouldn't take more than a few minutes!' He then took another deep breath and fixed his face with a stern expression as he prepared to do battle.

Inspector Bowden knocked on the door of DCI Marshall's office and was summoned inside.

'Ah, Inspector Bowden,' said the DCI. 'Any news?'

'Yes, as a matter of fact there is sir,' replied Inspector Bowden as he handed the preliminary report to DCI Marshall.

He allowed DCI Marshall a few minutes to read the contents of the report before he began his entreaty. He knew that the bullying tactics he employed on subordinates and suspects wouldn't gain him much ground with the DCI.

Although DCI Marshall was not outwardly dominant, he followed his own stringent set of rules, and if anybody attempted to step outside those rules, he would assert his authority calmly and resolutely. A well-educated and intelligent man, he made Inspector Bowden's furious outbursts seem like an infant's tantrums, and Inspector Bowden often left his office feeling impotent and dejected by his lack of influence.

The DCI forced Inspector Bowden to wait several minutes while he read the report and then re-read some of the more pertinent details. Inspector Bowden recognised the enforced wait as part of a well-used ploy to make him feel ill at ease. It would also give DCI Marshall some time to prepare his response, which was bound to disagree with Inspector Bowden's reaction to the report.

Eventually he lifted his head and looked towards Inspector Bowden with eyebrows raised in an inquiring motion.

'I want to charge them sir!' said Inspector Bowden.

'On what grounds?' DCI Marshall countered.

'The amphetamines. It's obvious, isn't it? Amanda Morris died of a drug and alcohol overdose, proving that they must have given her amphetamines that night as well as alcohol.'

'Steady!' said the DCI as he raised his hand to silence Inspector Bowden. 'I do not doubt that the victim died of an alcohol and amphetamine overdose. That matter is not in dispute. However, there is no proof that either of the two suspects gave amphetamines to the deceased prior to her death. We have already discussed this point.'

'They must have given her the drugs! They were with her all night, and they could have slipped some speed into her drink at any time.'

Inspector Bowden waved his hands about in agitation.

'Tell me, Inspector Bowden,' the DCI continued, 'were both suspects searched at the time of arrest?'

'Of course they were …sir.'

'And were their homes searched?'

'Yes sir!'

'And were any drugs found?'

'You know there weren't, but that doesn't mean to say …'

'In that case, Inspector Bowden, there is no proof that the drugs found in Amanda Morris's body were put there by either of the suspects. Furthermore, both of the suspects have a clean record and no history of drug abuse. So, until you find further evidence, inspector, we will not be able to charge them! Now then, what about other lines of enquiry?'

The inspector raised his eyebrows inquisitively. 'I'm referring to Mr Leslie Stevens. He has a record, hasn't he?'

'Well yes sir, but not drugs related. I don't think it's him. The man was distraught! Besides, Amanda Morris was already intoxicated by the time she reached home, and a search of his flat showed there were no drugs on the premises.'

'Very well, I suggest you continue digging then until you come up with some hard evidence inspector and that means covering all angles, not just the easy ones.'

Inspector Bowden retreated looking very downhearted and embarrassed. He noticed Sergeant Drummond watching him return to his desk, and flashed her a warning look to discourage her from asking any questions until he was ready to discuss the case.

After a few moments Inspector Bowden broke the silence, 'Come on sergeant, we're going!' he ordered.

'Where to sir?'

'To interview more witnesses. We need more evidence. The DCI refuses to see the obvious outcome of the post mortem as concrete evidence!'

'So there were drugs then?' asked the sergeant.

'Oh yes, there were drugs all right; speed! One of the buggers must have slipped it into her drink. So, what we need to do now is find some evidence that links Julie Quinley and Rita Steadman to the drugs. You and I both know that they killed Amanda Morris; we just need to prove it!'

***

Wednesday 25th June 1986

Inside the Portland Bars Inspector Bowden made a beeline for the barman, and produced his identity card. He needn't have bothered. The barman recognised him immediately. He had experienced his interview techniques in the past, and he guessed what the inspector's visit was about.

'I've already spoken to one of your officers and I've got nothing more to say!' he announced as Inspector Bowden approached the bar, accompanied by Sergeant Drummond.

'Well, let's see if we can have another go at jogging your memory then?' the inspector replied, while he gestured towards an empty table. The barman followed, not wishing to upset the inspector.

'I believe that you saw Julie Quinley and Rita Steadman pouring vodka into Amanda Morris's drink,' prompted Inspector Bowden.

'No, I didn't say that,' the barman interjected. 'I saw two girls at the bar pouring a vodka into someone's drink. I don't know whose drink it was. I don't even know if those are the girls you're talking about, but your officer seemed to think they fitted the description.'

'Can you be sure that it was vodka they were pouring into the drink?'

'Yeah, sure.'

'How can you be so sure? It could have been anything they were putting in!' fumed Inspector Bowden.

'No, it was definitely vodka; they bought it here at the bar.'

'Right, fair enough. Can you be certain then that they didn't put something in the glass as well as vodka?'

'Not that I noticed. As soon as they put the vodka in they were off.'

'And what were their reactions while they were pouring the vodka?'

'They just seemed to be having a laugh. I guessed that they were playing a trick on someone ... oh I would have stopped them but the bar was very busy that night and I was serving my next customer.'

The barman was completely taken by surprise when Inspector Bowden made a quick grab at his lapels and hoisted him up from his seat. 'You'd better not be keeping anything from me!' he threatened. 'If I find out that our suspects obtained their drugs from here then I'll have your head on a plate!'

The barman winced. 'You won't find any drugs in here; you know that from the last time you raided us.'

The inspector released him and threw him back against the chair. 'Come on!' he shouted to Sergeant Drummond. 'We're wasting our time here.'

Chapter 12

Wednesday 25th June 1986

After interviewing witnesses at the Portland Bars Inspector Bowden and Sergeant Drummond headed for Les's flat. The inspector's approach was a little more sympathetic in this case as Les was the boyfriend of the deceased. Nevertheless, Inspector Bowden was still determined to extract as much information as he could.

'You reported the death of your girlfriend, Amanda Morris,' said Inspector Bowden, consulting his notebook. 'I believe that she returned home in an extremely intoxicated state following a night out with some friends. Can you tell us about the night that Amanda died?'

'Yes,' said Les. 'I woke up hearing a terrible commotion. Mandy was shouting and banging on the door. It wasn't like her to carry on like that.'

His voice trailed away, and he paused, trying to regain his composure and clearing his throat before continuing. 'I was angry with her for waking me up and I was worried about what the neighbours might think, so I shouted at her when I answered the door ...'

Les's voice broke again and between sobs he uttered, 'I'm so sorry for shouting at her like that. How was I to know it was the last time I'd see her alive?'

'It's OK, take your time,' said Inspector Bowden.

Eventually Les continued.

'Mandy was in a terrible state, and there were two girls with her. I recognised one of them from the place where Mandy works ...well, worked, but the other one looked like a real scrubber. I blasted them off for getting her in such a state. Then I slammed the door on them. When they'd gone I had a few words with Mandy but she was too drunk to take any notice. So I helped her get ready for bed, and that was that.'

'What about Amanda's mention of drugs?' asked Inspector Bowden.

Les stared blankly at him for a few moments before replying. 'Oh that, yeah, she was rambling on about something her friends gave her. She said it gave her a real buzz. I didn't know what she was going on about at the time. It's only later that it clicked.'

'Did it not occur to you that she might need medical attention?' asked Sergeant Drummond while Inspector Bowden glared at her. Evidently, he didn't want anything to detract from his line of questioning.

'No not really, I just thought that she'd be all right after a good night's sleep.'

Les's sobbing conveniently returned. 'I'm sorry,' he wept. 'Maybe I should have got help but I had no idea; I've never dealt with anything like this before.'

Inspector Bowden, regardless of his emotional state, seized the chance to progress the interview further. 'Did Amanda say what it was that they had given her?'

'No, she was just rambling on about taking drugs. I didn't know whether to believe her. She wasn't making a lot of sense.'

'Did she say what form the drugs had taken – powder, tablet, injection?'

'No, sorry,' muttered Les.

'OK, thank you for sparing us some of your time,' said Inspector Bowden and they then left Les's flat.

As soon as they got outside Sergeant Drummond said, 'They can't have slipped it in her drink when the two of them went to get served if Amanda Morris took the drugs knowingly. Besides, it's a bit risky doing it at the bar in full view of the staff, isn't it?'

'Well perhaps they got her drunk first then encouraged her to take drugs. The poor girl probably didn't have a clue what she was doing! Either way, it still makes them guilty. They got her drunk, they supplied the drugs and they got her to take them when her judgement was impaired. I know their type; they think it's fun to take advantage of a poor innocent girl.'

'I see your point sir but shouldn't we have searched Leslie Stevens' flat again in case uniform missed something? He has got a record when all said and done, and he did seem a bit vague when you asked him about Amanda's reference to drugs.'

'Don't be ridiculous! Why should we want a more thorough search of his flat when we already know who the culprits are? Just because he has a record for speeding offences and petty theft does not make him guilty of murder. I'm surprised at you sergeant! You could see the state he was in. The poor man's devastated! You ask yourself how that compares to the state Julie Quinley was in when we took her to the station. More concerned with putting her make-up on from what you've told me.'

'Well yes, I suppose you're right there sir,' the sergeant conceded.

'There you go then,' Inspector Bowden asserted. 'Besides, there's countless witnesses as to the drugged state Amanda Morris was in before she even set off for home.'

'Yes, sir.'

'See sergeant, you've got a lot to learn yet. All the evidence is there. You've just got to be able to find it.'

'Yes, sir,' Sergeant Drummond replied again, and didn't pursue the matter further.

They got inside the car. Sergeant Drummond took the driving seat and asked, 'Where to now sir?'

'Back to the suspects. We have to keep up the pressure! They might let something slip.'

***

Wednesday 25th June 1986

As soon as the officers had left his flat Les slumped down on his sofa. The interview had got to him. His sense of impotence enraged him and he took a swipe at the empty cups on the coffee table. They flew across the room, landing in fragmented shards.

Mandy was gone and there wasn't a fuckin' thing he could do about it! Why? Why did shit always happen to him? All his life he'd had to settle for second best. Brought up in a stinking hovel with a useless drunken bitch of a mother, he'd got sick of seeing countless strangers come and go. The jovial ones, the cocky ones and the downright nasty ones! It was common knowledge in the street where he'd lived that his mother would go with anyone for a few drinks. By the time he reached his teens he understood the implication of having so many 'uncles' and as time passed by his resentment festered.

As he wallowed in pain and self-pity at losing his precious Mandy he recalled countless occasions when he'd borne the shame of living with such a mother. Like the time when he'd picked her up from the street. She was so drunk that she couldn't stand straight. She'd fell down in the pouring rain and when he managed to get her off the floor her clothes and hair were drenched, her face filthy. He'd had to accompany her home while she squealed with amusement like some demented caricature.

He'd left home at the earliest opportunity. From then onwards he made sure that he earned plenty by whatever means necessary, legal or otherwise. It didn't matter to him as long as he could live a lifestyle that was far removed from his childhood. He wore stylish clothes, drove smart cars and kept a nice home. Occasionally he came across his mother in some pub or other, usually drunk and staggering, but he avoided her, refusing to acknowledge her existence.

And the girls loved his flash lifestyle, but most of them were slags just like her. They'd do anything for a meal and a few drinks. Then he met Mandy who was so different. She was everything his mother and all those tarts would never be. Mandy had class; she was the prize. And now she was gone and he couldn't stand it! When his bitter thoughts threatened to overwhelm him he dashed from his flat, and made his way towards the city centre.

***

Wednesday 25th June 1986

The arrival of the police at Julie's house late on Wednesday evening turned an already trying week into a traumatic one. This time they interviewed her at home, advising her that they had received the preliminary results of the post mortem indicating that Amanda died of a drink and drugs overdose.

'Tell me,' Inspector Bowden asked Julie, 'how long have you been taking speed?'

Julie stared at him, incredulous. 'What are you talking about?'

she asked. 'I've never taken speed in my life or any other kind of drug.'

'How often do you visit the Portland Bars?' Inspector Bowden persisted.

'I don't know. What's that got to do with anything?'

'Come now Miss Quinley, you must have some idea of how often you go there.'

'I don't know, most weekends I suppose. It all depends.'

'Depends on what Miss Quinley; on whether you want to obtain drugs?'

'No, not at all. We don't go there for that. It's just one of the pubs we go to. It all depends where everybody fancies going. Sometimes it might be there, sometimes it might be one of the other pubs.'

'And how long have you been frequenting these pubs?'

'A couple of years I suppose.'

'Well then, Miss Quinley, I'm sure you're aware of the problem in the past with a former member of staff at the Portland Bars who was a known drug dealer.'

Julie's mouth fell open in shock. 'I had no idea!' she said.

'Come off it! You've been going in there every week for a couple of years and you had no idea about the availability of drugs? Yet you were seen putting something into Amanda Morris's drink. Do you expect me to believe that?'

The interview continued unabated and Julie responded to the questions with a flat denial, until her father burst into the room. 'Look you lot!' he shouted, 'She's told you she's not given drugs to the girl and no amount of bullying is going to get her to change her mind. Now bugger off out of my home, and leave my daughter alone!'

The officers exchanged glances. Detective Inspector Bowden then stood up and calmly replied to Bill, 'All right Mr Quinley, I think that we were just about through with our questioning for now anyway, but I can assure you of our return just as soon as we have gathered further evidence. Now goodbye and good day!'

Detective Sergeant Drummond took her cue and fell in line with Detective Inspector Bowden as he left the house.

Julie was flabbergasted by this reaction from her father and didn't know whether to thank him for defending her. She was saved from having to make a decision however as her father exited the room just as quickly as he had entered it.

Julie took the opportunity to phone Rita. She wanted to forewarn her of the police detectives' imminent appearance, but was surprised to find that Rita had already received a visit and she reacted to the encounter with her usual air of indifference. Julie tried to emulate Rita's display of calm, but it belied the panic that she felt inside. 'Yes, you're right Rita. They can't do anything to us without proof.'

'That's right Julie, so stop worrying and let's try to carry on as normal. I think we should go out Friday night. After all, moping about isn't going to bring Amanda back, is it?'

Although Julie was amazed to hear Rita talk like this, she allowed herself to be persuaded into going to the Flying Horse. It was the last place that she wanted to meet in view of the fiasco of the previous Sunday, but she reasoned that as her own strength of mind was very much in abeyance at the moment, she should let Rita lead her by the hand and do whatever she thought was right. She also felt that people had to be faced and now was as good a time as any.

'By the way Rita,' said Julie, 'I'm supposed to be going out tomorrow night as well, but I don't know if I'll bother after the way I've been feeling.'

'Who with?'

'Well, you remember that dishy salesman I told you about called Mike Marston?'

'Yes', Rita replied.

'He's asked me out at last. Bloody typical isn't it; I've been wanting him to ask me out for weeks and then he goes and does it when I'm feeling like a bag of shit.'

'What about Vinny?'

'Oh, here we go. What about Vinny, Rita?'

'I thought you were supposed to be seeing him.'

I am, but I'm only going on a date with this guy. There's no harm in seeing Vinny in the meantime till I see how things work out.'

'Oh, I get it, good old Vinny will always do as a back-up eh?'

'It isn't like that Rita. Me and Vinny aren't serious. Besides, I've got loads of time for settling down. Who wants to be married at my age?'

'Well try telling him that; you might find he has a different point of view. Anyway, it's up to you. Maybe this bloke's what you've been looking for, and if he isn't, then at least you'll have got it out of your system.'

Julie said goodbye to Rita, but continued to think about the predicament she was in. She didn't really want to finish with Vinny. If he'd had a bit more get up and go he might have been the perfect man but he was just too complacent at times. She did think a lot of him though and, while on this train of thought, Julie came to the decision that she should ring him and try to sort out the mess that they had made of their previous telephone conversation.

She was relieved when Vinny accepted her apology in earnest, and even offered her an apology too. Julie arranged to see him on the Saturday night, delighted with his change of heart, and determined to continue her quest to carry on a normal life.

Chapter 13

Thursday 26th June 1986

Julie had been undecided about her date with Mike right up until the last minute. There were so many reasons that she thought she shouldn't go.

Firstly, there was Vinny. She felt as though she was being disloyal to him but really there was no reason why she should. She was a free agent with no ties. That was the way her relationship with Vinny had always been. They'd agreed as much from the outset. However, she couldn't help feeling that Vinny's views had changed since then and no matter how much she told herself that she was doing no wrong, she still felt guilty. She hadn't promised Vinny any commitment, but she knew that if he ever found out that she had been on a date with someone-else, he would be hurt.

Secondly, she was bothered by Norma's words of warning although these didn't concern her as much as her feelings of guilt about Vinny. She knew about Mike's reputation but it was something that she chose to ignore. Julie refused to spend her time worrying about what might happen. She recalled the old saying, 'nothing ventured, nothing gained', and decided that it was appropriate. If she didn't go out with Mike then she might spend the rest of her life regretting it.

The third reason why Julie felt she shouldn't go out was because of her present state of mind. She felt bad that she was going out so much and enjoying herself when Amanda had just died, but she convinced herself that Amanda wouldn't want her to sit at home moping. Anyway, it would be a good way to take her mind off things and she couldn't afford to miss this chance. Men like Mike were few and far between and now she finally had the prospect of going on a date with him. Just the thought of him sent a tingling sensation through her body.

In addition to all of these concerns, Julie was feeling nervous. Mike was in a separate league to the men she usually went out with. Most of her previous boyfriends had been a disappointment as they hadn't had the vision to see beyond their own little worlds. But Mike was different. He was sophisticated, educated and had travelled. He was interesting, amusing and probably came from a different background to hers. His family might even be loaded for all she knew.

Julie finally decided that she would go on the date. To hell with her concerns! After all, wasn't this the opportunity she had been waiting for?

***

Thursday 26th June 1986

They met in a pub near work, one that they were both familiar with. Mike had offered to pick Julie up from her home but she had declined. She preferred not to let her parents know who she was going out with. Julie had had enough grief from Rita and Norma about seeing Mike and didn't relish having to explain the position to her parents as well. She also preferred not to let Mike see the area where she lived just yet as she didn't want to give him any cause to go off her before they had even got to know each other. For the same reason she had decided not to tell him about the events of the previous weekend. There was nothing more likely to send a man running than the thought that he might be dating a murderer, she thought.

Julie figured that Mike would soon find out about what had happened. It was unavoidable as the news was spreading through the office like wildfire. She knew that he hadn't been in the office much this week as he had a diary full of customer visits, so the chances were that he hadn't heard the rumours yet. "*Fine,*" she thought. "*I'll leave off telling him for now and cross that bridge when I come to it.*" At least that way she would have a chance of him getting to know her without any pre-judgement.

Mike looked even more gorgeous outside of work than inside. His appearance was less formal but still smart. He wore a pair of slacks and a very fetching shirt, and she could tell that he was freshly showered and shaved. As he approached her she caught a whiff of his expensive aftershave. They made small talk, complimenting one another on their appearances as they drank. Then, when they had finished their first drink he guided Julie out of the pub and into his car.

'Come on, let's go!' he suggested.

'Where are we going?' she asked.

'Wait and see, it's a surprise, but I just hope you didn't have a big tea before you left home.'

Julie smiled and relaxed in the comfortable seat of his shiny new Ford Sierra while they headed out of the city, and in the direction of the Cheshire countryside. Mike flicked a switch on his state of the art stereo and the sound of Motown classics filled the car.

After about a half hour drive, they stopped at a beautiful restaurant. It was an old building, surrounded by greenery and with a small stream flowing towards the rear. Julie stepped inside the restaurant and was pleased to find that it was full of old-world charm, affluently decorated, and with an abundance of knick-knacks dotted about the place. There were toby jugs, and brass ornaments and plates, many of which appeared to be antiques. The atmosphere was tranquil, and, as soon as they entered, a waitress showed them to their seats.

Julie was a little taken aback to find that she couldn't under-stand much of what was on the menu. It was either in French, or, otherwise, it contained dishes that she had never heard of. She guessed that this was all aimed at making the place much more upmarket than your average restaurant. For a while she struggled through the descriptions grasping at vague recollec-tions of her 'O' level French vocabulary. She didn't want to appear ignorant and unsophisticated in front of Mike.

'I'll start with the escargot,' she announced, opting for a word that seemed vaguely familiar and attempting to sound confident in her choice.

Mike looked puzzled. 'Are you sure?'

"*Oh damn!*" she thought. "*I've hit a no-no. I must have re-membered 'escargot' for the wrong reasons.*"

It was only by thinking of the most undesirable French dishes imaginable that she recalled the meaning of the word that had been bothering her for the last few minutes. "*No wonder it rang a bell.*"

'It's bloody snails isn't it?' she blurted out and then became embarrassed at her little outburst.

Mike found her embarrassment hilarious and it was a while before he could control his laughter enough to respond.

'I didn't think you were a snails type of girl myself,' he teased.

'I'm not, I just forgot what it meant, that's all.'

'Don't worry,' said Mike, covering her hand with his. For some he may have appeared patronising, but Julie saw it as kindness, and was thankful when he offered to translate the entire menu for her.

Julie made her choice, opting for soup followed by a mushroom starter and chicken in a creamy garlic sauce for the main course, and declaring emphatically that there was no chance of her wanting a sweet after so many courses, let alone the cheese and biscuits. She mistakenly thought that this might make her appear more ladylike.

'I'm sorry, I didn't mean to embarrass you Julie.' Mike said. 'I've known women who had excellent etiquette but it doesn't make them any better a person you know? I like you for yourself and if I can show you a bit of the high life, then why not? There's no rules about who can come in here Julie.'

Once the chore of choosing her food was out of the way, Julie began to unwind and enjoy herself. However, when the food arrived she regretted her decision to waive the sweet. The courses were minuscule and so decorative they appeared almost too good to eat. However, she didn't gasp in wonder, but tried to act as though this type of meal was an everyday occurrence for her as she tucked into the mouth-watering works of art with gusto.

Mike was the perfect gentleman throughout the evening. He pulled her chair from beneath the table for her, opened doors, and allowed her to choose the wine. He was also good company and during the exquisite meal he regaled her with tales of his exploits. She hadn't laughed so much in a long time.

Julie was sorry to reach the end of such a perfect evening. Despite her earlier decision not to mention Amanda's death, she found herself opening up to him, such was the calming effect that he had on her. During a break in the conversation she happened to comment on how nice it was to have such a good time after the lousy time that she had had recently. Then, before she could help herself the whole story came tumbling out.

'I'm sorry to hear that,' said Mike.

Julie missed the note of irony in his voice and the way in which he switched the subject, telling her about the recent loss of his aunty and how it had affected him. She merely thought that this was Mike's way of sympathising with her.

At the end of the meal there was no awkwardness about who paid for what. Mike just settled the bill, no questions asked, and they headed back to his car.

He insisted on taking her home even though she tried to refuse, embarrassed by the prospect of letting him see the area where she lived. She was also relieved, however, as he knew that she lived with her parents so he wasn't expecting anything from her in payment for her evening's entertainment.

When they arrived outside Julie's house Mike didn't comment. He just gave her a chaste goodnight kiss, and told her how he had enjoyed their evening together and how much he was looking forward to seeing her again. Then he left it at that. The whole experience had helped to cheer Julie up at just the time when she needed it. She couldn't wait for him to ask her out again.

***

Friday 27th June 1986

'Something's put a smile on your face,' said Norma when Julie arrived for work the next morning.

'It's about bloody time!' said Julie. 'The rest of this week's been hell.'

Despite Julie's other worries, she couldn't resist telling Norma about her night out and what a great time she had. She detailed the restaurant, what they had to eat, how Mike had been the perfect gentleman, and added that he hadn't even expected to drag her back to his flat afterwards.

'You were wrong about him you know,' Julie stated. 'He's a lovely man. If he'd have been the womaniser that people say he is then he'd have had me back to his flat in a flash.'

'Don't count your chickens. Maybe he's trying to win you over before he does the dirty on you.'

'Thanks very bloody much Norma. Spoil my day, why don't you?'

'Sorry,' said Norma. She didn't say any more. She didn't need to. Each of them already knew what the other was thinking.

Chapter 14

Friday 27th June 1986

Friday night arrived after a trying week at work for Julie. Rita and Debby called for her, and they walked to the Flying Horse together. In many ways this was like any other Friday night; the three of them dressed to impress, the make-up, the heady scent of perfume, the excited chatter as they made their way down the street. Julie knew deep down, however, that this wasn't just an ordinary Friday night. So much had changed in the last week.

Although they were trying to carry on as normal, it was the little things that gave it away; the way Rita had insisted on calling for Julie instead of meeting her in the foyer of the Flying Horse, for example. Julie knew that Rita recognised her need for support but Rita didn't want to mention it outright. Then there were the uncomfortable breaks in the conversation, especially from Debby, who couldn't fail to mention previous good nights out in an attempt to cheer Julie up. Unfortunately, those good nights had been when Amanda had still been alive. Any oblique references to Amanda's presence last time they had all been together caused Dizzy Debby to stutter with embarrassment and Rita would then try to change the subject.

When they arrived at the Flying Horse, Rita turned to Julie and said 'Well, their seven days are almost up. Let's see if they've found something else to gossip about, eh?'

Debby turned to Rita with a look of confusion on her face.

'Seven day wonder,' Rita explained, but to no avail. 'Oh, never mind!' said Rita, frustrated, 'Let's just get in and get a bloody drink, shall we?'

The fact that this Friday night was different from others became even more apparent when they entered the pub. They noticed the tense atmosphere straightaway. Numerous pairs of eyes stared at them and then gazed away as they approached. At the bar backs were turned against them. People whispered in corners.

'Stuff them all!' said Rita, raising her voice. 'They haven't got a bleedin' clue!'

She looked antagonistically around the room, challenging those present to say something, but was met by a stony silence. Julie and Debby looked at Rita beseechingly. Julie took a few steps away from the bar area hoping that Rita would follow; to her relief Rita eventually did. They chose to sit at a table that was positioned along the outer perimeter of the room in a quiet part of the pub.

'I can't understand it' said Julie, dismayed, 'I thought they were our friends.'

'Just goes to show then, doesn't it?' replied Rita, loudly. 'It's at times like this when you find out who your friends are, isn't it? Sod 'em all, they're nowt but a bunch of arseholes if you ask me!'

Julie pleaded with Rita to keep quiet. 'I don't want any trouble Rita, I've had enough this last week.'

'All right,' conceded Rita. 'Let's just ignore them.'

The three girls tried to pretend that the atmosphere didn't exist but it was impossible to disregard it. When Debby suggested that they go elsewhere, even Rita agreed.

As they left the pub they could hear the sound of Lindsey Pilkington's voice shouting, 'That's right, bugger off! Can't you see we don't want the likes of you in here?'

Before Julie and Debby had a chance to respond, Rita was back inside the pub, turning over chairs and anything else that stood in the way of her and Lindsey Pilkington. Within seconds she was on top of Lindsey, clawing at her face and yanking at her hair like a madwoman.

Lindsey's friends were quick to react with three of them tugging at Rita in an attempt to drag her off Lindsey, and shouting malicious insults. In the ensuing clamour caused by Rita's threats, Lindsey's terrified screams, and the shouting of Lindsey's friends, Julie struggled to make herself heard.

'For God's sake Rita, leave it!' she yelled. 'It isn't worth it.'

Either Rita couldn't hear her or she was too consumed with rage to notice, but she continued to tear into Lindsey while Lindsey's friends tried to pull Rita off. Julie looked at the scene desperately, noticing Debby standing beside her, appearing helpless and pathetic with her jaw hanging low. By now it was becoming evident to Julie that attempts by Lindsey's friends to drag Rita off were half-hearted. They were more intent on inflicting injuries to Rita in vengeance for those she was inflicting on Lindsey.

'Come on!' Julie ordered Debby, and without thinking of the consequences she dashed towards the group of girls and began to pull at Rita, at the same time trying to coax her away. She took a few blows to her head and shoulders, but luckily Debby had come to her aid and, because of Debby's size, she had more luck with prising Rita from Lindsey.

Julie then became aware of a number of things simultaneously and it was difficult to take it all in at once; Rita's furious expression, the clumps of hair hanging about Rita's shoulders, Lindsey's swollen and bloody face, the fact that Lindsey was no longer surrounded by her friends and the sound of male voices. Then Julie noticed the reason that Lindsey's friends had retreated; a group of men, including the landlord, were approaching them and looking like they meant business.

'Come on now girls, turn it in!' bellowed the landlord.

Julie raised her hand towards him and the other men, 'It's all right, we're going,' she assured them.

'Well don't bother coming back; you're all barred!'

It took all of Julie and Debby's efforts to extricate Rita from the scene and get her outside the pub. Eventually Rita realised that no matter how much she struggled, there was no way Julie and Debby were going to let her back inside.

'Jesus Rita, you could have got us all a fuckin' good hiding,' Julie cursed. 'It's lucky the landlord stepped in to stop them. Let's get away from here quick before they decide to bleedin' follow us and finish the job off.'

'Julie's right,' said Debby. 'Jesus Rita, what the fuckin' hell got into you?'

Rita refused to calm down, and it took their best efforts to haul her away from the pub while she continued to shout threats at Lindsey Pilkington. 'You cheeky bitch! I'll have you, don't you bleedin' worry!'

It disturbed Julie to note that Rita had completely lost her composure, and had just displayed the troubled emotions that must have been eating away at her ever since their arrest. The only difference between her and Rita was that Rita had kept her emotions under wraps; until now that is.

'Jesus!' Julie exclaimed when they had all calmed down a little. 'I think I preferred it when I was at bleedin' work!'

'What do we do now?' asked Debby.

'We're goin' to town to have a bleedin' good time, same as we always do!' said Rita as she brushed the clumps of hair away from her shoulders and re-arranged her clothing.

Rita spoke forcefully and the other two were not prepared to argue with her, so they went along with her demands. As far as Julie was concerned, however, she would have been happier to go home and try to forget that this night had existed.

Their one consolation when they arrived in the city centre was that very few people knew about their backgrounds and, despite the fracas in the pub, the physical evidence was minimal so they felt accepted as part of the throng.

After having a few drinks in the pubs, they made their way to Saturdays nightclub. Debby, undeterred by the evening's events, managed to find herself a companion in record time while Julie and Rita decided to have a few more drinks to drown their sorrows. For the rest of the evening they caught occasional glimpses of Debby, which wasn't unusual as she made a habit of latching onto someone of the opposite sex at the earliest opportunity whenever they went out.

Once Julie and Rita had bought their drinks, they sat down for a chat.

'I can't believe that carry on in the Flying Horse,' Julie said to Rita. 'What got into you?'

'I don't know. I suppose I just got sick of people treating us like a piece of shit. Anyway, don't worry about it. They'll soon get over it, especially when we're proven innocent. They'll all be up our arses then!'

'Will we be proven innocent though Rita? What if the police never find out who drugged Amanda?'

'Something's bound to come up. Anyway, even if it doesn't, they've got nothing on us! Innocent till proven guilty, don't forget.'

'It doesn't change the way people are towards us though, does it Rita? It's hell at work at the moment! Jacqueline had a right go at me in the canteen the other day.'

'Why, what did that cow say?'

'She accused us all of being murderers, in front of everybody as well.'

'So what did you say?'

'Nothing, how could I? A canteen full of people were all watching me.'

'So what? That's all the more reason why you should have set the record straight.'

'You don't know what it was like Rita; you don't work there.'

'I don't care. I'd have told that Jacqueline what I thought of her and no messing! I knew she was a cow.'

The girls didn't speak for a few minutes until Rita interrupted their silence by announcing, 'Look who's just arrived; it's Vinny.'

'Oh yeah,' said Julie.

'Well don't look so overexcited, will you?'

'What's the big deal? I'm seeing him tomorrow night! Anyway, the way things are at the moment, I've got enough on my mind without thinking about men.'

'Suit yourself,' said Rita.

Vinny had already spotted them and was making his way through the crowds. When Julie realised that he was within earshot, she discontinued her conversation with Rita for fear of being overheard. Instead, she turned towards him and smiled.

Before he had a chance to talk to her, however, Rita rose from her seat and stepped in his direction. She adopted a seductive stance with hands on hips, breasts protruding forwards to their best advantage, and head and shoulders cocked back with her body swaying from side to side.

'Hi Vinny,' she greeted. 'What brings you here tonight? We haven't seen you for a while.'

Without waiting for a response she continued. 'Mind you, need I ask what brings you here?' and she nodded her head in Julie's direction. 'Well, I just hope she's up for it, because if she isn't I know of a few likely candidates who would be glad of the chance,' she said, fluttering her eyelashes.

Vinny, totally embarrassed by this blatant proposal, was anxious to make himself scarce so he turned towards Julie and said, 'I'll see you tomorrow,' then dashed away.

As he made his way back towards his group of friends, Rita shouted after him, 'See you around, big boy,' and then looked at Julie with a mocking grin on her face.

Julie was furious and made no attempt to hide her anger as she fumed, 'Just what the hell do you think you're playing at?'

'Oh just a bit of fun Julie, that's all. Keep your hair on!'

'Fun, is that what you call it? Playing up to him more like! I'm surprised you didn't just ask him to give you one there and then!'

'Oh give over Julie; I only wanted to embarrass him for a laugh, that's all. You do remember what laughing is, don't you?'

'Stop being so bleedin' sarcastic, I don't mind a laugh as you well know but I do mind when somebody flirts with my boyfriend! Anyway, I'm surprised you can have a laugh after what's happened.'

'Oh lighten up Julie! What's happened has happened and you aren't going to change anything by walking around with a face like a wet weekend. Anyway, I thought you weren't that bothered about Vinny. You seem more interested in that fella from work.'

'I'm still going out with Vinny, and just because I've been on a date with someone-else, it doesn't give you the right to snatch Vinny from under my nose!' Julie's voice began to falter as she continued. 'I just can't stop thinking about Amanda and you're carrying on as if nothing's happened. How do you do it Rita?'

'By taking my mind of it, that's how Julie,' Rita replied. 'There's a lot of bad things happened to me in my life and if I let them get to me I'd have cracked up a long time ago. You've just got to get on with life Julie and try not to let things get to you.'

'That's easier said than done!'

'I know, it takes practice. I haven't forgotten about Amanda and I never will. But I'm buggered if I'm going to let it mess up the rest of my life, and neither should you!'

Julie managed a faint smile as Rita continued. 'We haven't done anything wrong Julie; we've got nothing to feel guilty about! Somebody gave Amanda drugs. It wouldn't surprise me if it wasn't that cow Jacqueline. She's probably giving you a hard time so she can cover her own tracks. If I were you I'd give her what for!'

'You're not me though, are you?'

The two girls gazed at each other in silent acknowledgement of their differences in character until Rita broke the silence by taking Julie's hand and saying, 'Come on Jules, no hard feelings, eh? Let's go and have a dance, cheer ourselves up.'

Despite her efforts to cheer herself up, however, Julie failed and she ended the evening extremely drunk and downhearted. She couldn't remember how she got home but recalled falling into bed in a drunken stupor. She slept for the next ten hours. It was the best night's sleep she had had for the last week. However, she did not wake up feeling refreshed. She woke up with a dry throat, a blinding headache, and feeling both physically sick and sick at heart.

Her thoughts were troubling her. She was amazed at Rita's resilience and couldn't help but think that if Rita had recovered so well from such a traumatic week, then maybe she could have recovered just as well from the guilt of being Amanda's killer. Instead of feeling upset, worried and ashamed as Julie did, Rita was reacting with indifference interspersed with periods of anger and aggression. Were those the reactions of a guilty person perhaps? Or, worse still, a murderer? Could Rita have slipped something else into Amanda's drink without anyone knowing about it? But how would Rita get hold of drugs? Her sister, of course; she did go around with some pretty dodgy characters. But why would Rita want to do it? Bitterness? Resentment?

Apart from that there was the way that Rita was so quick to blame Jacqueline. It seemed that every time they discussed Amanda's death, Rita tried to point the finger of suspicion at Jacqueline. Did she genuinely suspect Jacqueline or was she trying to divert attention?

Then Julie mentally chided herself for thinking in such a way. The events of the last week must have taken their toll if she was beginning to suspect her best friend who she had known for years.

Chapter 15

Vinny was pleased to see Julie on Saturday night. When he opened his front door, he had a beaming smile on his face. As she stepped inside he showered her with compleents. 'You look gorgeous tonight love. I like your blouse, is it a new one?'

Julie guessed that this was Vinny's way of cheering her up and trying to make up for their argument of a few days ago. She returned his smile, attempting to appear relaxed.

He offered her a drink. Julie had only just recovered from her hangover from the previous night's overindulgence, and now had a very dry throat. The thought of sharing one or two bottles of wine with Vinny didn't appeal. What she would have preferred was a long, cool, refreshing glass of water. However, she didn't want to spoil Vinny's plans for this evening, so she accepted the proffered glass of wine.

'Well, where did you get to last night?' she asked.

'Pete met this bird he fancied and we ended up going to another club so that he could be with her. He was like a little lamb following her everywhere. I left them to it in the end and came back here. I think I was a bit in the way. From what he told me today he'll be seeing her again.'

'He sounds keen.'

'Yeah, he is.'

Then Vinny changed the subject. 'It was a good match today. We won 3 –1.'

The subject of football had never appealed to Julie but she feigned interest. 'Oh that's good.'

Julie downed her glass of wine, which made her thirstier. 'Vinny, would you mind if I had a glass of water?' she asked. 'I'm a bit dehydrated from last night.'

Vinny obliged. 'Good night then, was it?' he asked.

Julie was unable to disguise her shock at such a question and it was now impossible to retain her polite, relaxed façade. 'You haven't got a fuckin' clue have you?' she asked vehemently.

Vinny, in his ignorance, was stunned. He couldn't understand what he had done to provoke such an attack but he didn't wish to get into yet another argument. Vinny had planned a lovely evening for them both, an evening of relaxation, drinking, chatting and ultimately, seduction.

He replied cautiously. 'What's the matter love, what have I said?'

'We were drowning our bleedin' sorrows,' Julie snapped back. 'A friend of ours has just died, remember, and we've had the bad luck to have been accused of killing her!'

Vinny raised his hands in mock surrender, 'OK, I'm sorry, I didn't think.'

Then he paused for a moment, giving further thought to the situation before continuing. 'Look Julie, I know you've had a hard time of it, and in my own way I'm trying to cheer you up and take your mind off things, that's all.'

Julie replied, stonily, 'Some things just won't go away.'

Vinny's response was to take Julie in his arms and stroke her hair, 'It's OK. Things will get better, I promise you.'

'Well, that's you and Rita that seem to think so. I just wish I could feel that confident about it.'

'Don't mention Rita to me! You should have heard the stick I got from my mates about the way she was carrying on last night. Rita the Man Eater they call her. How do you put up with a friend like her?'

'She's all right really. It's all just a big laugh to Rita, her way of taking her mind off things. Pete's just got a downer on her because she dumped him.'

'It's not just Pete, Julie; all the lads think she's a tart.'

'Oh yeah, and where do you think they've got that idea from? Pete, of course! Leave Rita alone. From what she tells me she's been through a lot. That's probably why she's like she is.'

'Well I'd watch her if I were you!'

'Why, is she a threat?'

'Not with me she isn't; I wouldn't touch her with a barge

pole! Besides, I'm happy with what I've got,' he said, as he planted a kiss on her cheek.

After a few minutes of comforting Julie and feeling her become more relaxed in his arms, Vinny placed his hand under her chin and turned her face up towards his. He then kissed her passionately on the lips and she responded. He ventured further, undoing the buttons on her blouse.

Julie could feel Vinny becoming aroused but she was unable to respond. Usually the touch of his hand on her breast would send shivers down her spine and a tickling sensation in her stomach, but now all she felt was irritation. She tried to persuade herself that she would enjoy it once she got in the mood, but it was hopeless. The dark thoughts that tormented her mind also negated her bodily sensations. She felt cold, indifferent and unresponsive. Eventually she decided that there was no point going further and she struggled free of Vinny. 'It's no good Vinny, I can't.'

'Why not, I thought you were up for it?'

'Well I'm not. I can't explain it Vinny, I just don't feel in the mood tonight.'

'Well,' he replied, becoming angered at her rejection. 'There's nowt like leading me on and then dropping me, is there?'

'I wasn't trying to lead you on Vinny! I thought that if we carried on I might come round to it, but I can't. I'm not in the mood tonight, that's all. What's wrong with that?'

Vinny was reduced to silent contemplation. Julie, his Julie, had changed during the last week and he was finding it very difficult to come to terms with her alter ego. He didn't attempt to make further conversation, fearful of upsetting her again. Instead he sat drinking his wine and flicking through a newspaper that had been lying on the coffee table.

Julie was also in a state of contemplation. She didn't want to be here. She wanted to be on her own, moping and miserable. Vinny's behaviour was annoying her and she knew that it was unfair to take her feelings out on him.

She decided that it would be better for them both if she left. 'Vinny, can you order me a taxi please? I want to go home.'

'I don't want you to go home Julie. You don't need to go

home!' Vinny pleaded. 'It's OK, we don't have to have sex if you don't want. We can just watch a film or something. I just want you to be with me Julie.'

Hearing Vinny plead in this way almost reduced Julie to tears of guilt and frustration, and she couldn't hide the emotion in her voice. 'I'm sorry Vinny, but the way I feel at the moment, I'm just making both of us miserable and it isn't fair to you.'

Vinny conceded and ordered her a taxi. As she left his home, he kissed her on the cheek and said, 'Bye love, hope you're feeling better soon.'

Julie managed a reticent smile as she walked to the taxi. 'I'll ring you when I am,' she assured.

Vinny watched as the taxi took Julie away. When he thought about their shambles of an evening, he felt anger and disappointment at himself. Why did he always have to botch things up? He knew what she had been going through and had been determined to make the evening good for her. He had hoped to take her mind off her troubles while she was with him, but he hadn't succeeded.

Vinny thought about her parting words. 'I'll ring you when I'm feeling better' was what she had meant. He understood that this was her way of telling him not to bother ringing her while she was in this frame of mind; his only choice was to wait for her call.

***

Sunday 29th June 1986

It was Sunday evening and Julie sat alone yet again in her bedroom. She had finally gained the solitude that she had craved all weekend, but it brought no comfort. Instead she was tormented once more by her own thoughts; the atmosphere of Friday night, the way she had upset Vinny, how much she missed Amanda and worries about what was to become of her and Rita. "*And if all that wasn't bad enough,*" she thought, "*I've still got work to face tomorrow!*"

She got changed into her nightshirt and as she lay in her bed she tried to prepare herself for yet another night of troubled sleep.

Chapter 16

Monday 30th June 1986

When Julie arrived at work on Monday she wasn't feeling at her best. Apart from not getting much sleep during the night, thoughts of such a terrible weekend were still fresh in her mind. Norma, perceptive as ever, picked up on how she was feeling straightaway.

'Bad weekend again was it?'

'You bet!'

'I expected it,' said Norma to Julie's surprise. 'Well, I know you Julie and you're not the sort of girl to go out and have a whale of a time after what's happened.'

Norma's sensitivity touched Julie as she replied. 'It's everywhere I go Norma. When I go out with the girls they're trying their best not to mention it, which only makes it worse. The people in our local were ready to hang us on Friday night. Rita totally lost it and attacked this silly cow who was giving us grief. And to make matters worse, I've fell out with Vinny.'

'Oh you haven't, have you?'

'Well not so much fell out as I just can't be bothered at the moment. He doesn't seem to understand what I'm going through. Nobody does. This weekend was nearly as bad as the previous one. In fact, I think the only good part of last week was Thursday night.'

Despite her stresses, Julie began to look all dreamy eyed again as she thought about her date with Mike.

'Talk of the devil,' said Norma and before Mike was within earshot, she added, 'I bet he's come to ask you for another date.'

Julie followed Norma's line of vision and watched in amazement as Mike flew past, completely blanking her.

'It's because of Amanda, isn't it?' she asked Norma, the disappointment evident in her voice.

'Perhaps not, it might have nothing to do with that. He's maybe just late for an appointment, that's all.'

'No, I'm not stupid Norma. I know what it is. He doesn't want to know me 'cos he thinks I killed Amanda.'

As Julie's face adopted a pained expression, Norma didn't contradict her or offer any further assurances about Mike.

Later that day when Norma returned from a late lunch break she brought some news with her. She broached the subject with Julie, 'It's the funeral on Thursday. There are rumours that the company will be operating with a skeleton staff and we've to tell all callers that someone will get back to them the following day due to special circumstances.'

'Oh,' was Julie's initial response. Then she followed it with, 'Are you going?'

'Not if you want to. There'll have to be at least one of us here to man the switch.'

'Oh yeah, they'll welcome me with open arms, won't they?'

'I see your point Julie, but it doesn't seem fair. You were Amanda's friend and you've just as much right to be there as anyone.'

'It's not worth it Norma. It was bad enough in the pub on Friday, and they didn't even know Amanda. Imagine what the reaction of Jacqueline and her cronies will be, not to mention that bloody Les and Amanda's family? They'll all think I'm guilty.'

'Are you sure you'll be all right here if I go?'

'Yeah, I've no choice have I?'

Norma remained silent for a few moments, at a loss as to how to respond. Finally she said, 'You look all in love. Have you not been sleeping either?'

'Not much.'

'Well we're not very busy at the moment so why don't you go and have a coffee? There'll be no-one in the canteen at this time so you won't have that to worry about.'

'Are you sure Norma?'

'Of course, go on! I'll manage'

Julie arrived at the canteen without encountering anybody. She felt relief at being able to go somewhere without facing everybody's anger and accusations. She sat there for a while staring out of the window, just her and her cup of coffee. Becoming pensive, she couldn't help but recall the dismal events of the last two weekends. When she realised how such thoughts were controlling her mind, she tried to break free of them but they wouldn't disappear. She shook her head vigorously from side to side in an attempt to banish those thoughts. Still they would not go away.

Julie realised that spending time on her own was a mistake. She needed to keep busy! That was the only way to take her mind off things. She left her cup of coffee half empty and shoved her chair back under the table, her irritation showing.

On the way back to the switchboard she stopped off at the ladies. Jacqueline was the last person she expected to see there, and Julie felt a surge of fear pulse through her body as Jacqueline and her friend halted their conversation and scrutinised her. Instead of the verbal onslaught that Julie was expecting, however, Jacqueline merely grasped her bag from the sink surround and breezed past her, saying to her friend, 'Come on, we don't want to be seen with a murderer, do we?'

Julie was dumbstruck. For some reason they had seemed anxious to get away. This was uncharacteristic of Jacqueline; Julie had expected another confrontation. She shrugged and turned towards the mirror. Shocked at the sight of her pale reflection, she spent a few moments applying make-up before entering a cubicle, where she shut the door.

And there it was! Staring back at her. Forgetting what she had come into the ladies for, she dashed out, screaming in horror.

It took Norma several minutes to calm her down, and even then, the only coherent words she could get out of her were, 'in the toilets… a cloth.'

Eventually, when Julie had calmed down enough to carry out her duties on the switchboard, Norma decided to go to the toilets to find out for herself what great terror was lurking there.

Norma was unable to spot the cause of Julie's disturbance at first and thought that maybe Julie had had another encounter with Jacqueline. It wasn't until she went inside a cubicle that she spotted the words, 'JULIE QUINLEY IS A MURDERER' emblazoned on the back of the door, in huge letters, which covered its entire length and breadth.

Norma decided to play it down. 'Honestly Julie, I thought somebody had been attacked or something. It's just some silly bugger up to a prank, that's all! Here's a cloth and some cleaner. Go and scrub it off if it makes you feel any better.' Then, realising the harshness of her words, she added, 'Those that want to believe it will believe it anyway, and those of us that don't, still don't, so try not to let it worry you!'

Despite brisk scrubbing, Julie was unable to get rid of any of the writing. Whoever put it there had used a permanent marker. She cried tears of frustration as she continued to rub futilely at the toilet door until she realised that, just like her anguished thoughts, no matter how hard she tried, it was never going to go away!

**

Monday 30th June 1986

After another difficult day Julie was relieved to arrive home. She was even more relieved when she received a phone call from Rita to say that she was calling round to see her. In her naivety, Julie believed that she was coming to cheer her up. Rita's news surprised her.

'I've been made redundant.'

'Oh Rita, I'm so sorry to hear that! As if you haven't got enough on your plate!'

'It's no big deal Julie. Factory jobs are ten a penny. Anyway, I've decided to have a well-earned rest. I'm going on holiday to Greece with Debby.'

Julie, normally so selfless, could not help but feel betrayed and her first thought was that she would be left to cope alone while Rita was away sunning herself.

'Well, aren't you going to wish me a nice time?' asked Rita.

Julie snapped to her senses. 'Yes, of course I hope you have a nice time Rita. I'm just a bit surprised, that's all. It seems so sudden!'

'Well, I didn't get a bad payoff having been there for five years, so I thought, why not?'

'What about Debby, she's only been there a year or so; how's she going to afford it?'

'She's got savings, believe it or not, always has had from being a kid. I mean, when you think about it she doesn't spend much. She only goes out once or twice a week with the girls. We share taxis, she pays for a couple of drinks and her entrance to a club. Then, she cops off with someone the minute we get inside and lets them pay, not that I blame her.'

'How will you go on if she does her disappearing act and you get left on your own when you're abroad?'

'Oh, you know me Julie, not exactly a wallflower am I? And if there's plenty of talent up for grabs, I'll be doing plenty of grabbing.'

'Oh you dirty sod', laughed Julie, momentarily forgetting her troubles.

'Anyway, what's to stop you coming with us Julie? We'll have a right laugh!'

'There's not much to laugh about at the moment Rita. Besides, how would it look at work if I took a couple of weeks off? They'd think that I can't face them!'

'Don't be daft! What does it matter what they think? A holiday will do you good!'

'No Rita, I can't go. I have to stay here and see this through. If I go away, I'll still have to face it when I come back. Anyway, what about the police; will they let you go out of the country while you're under suspicion?'

'Stuff the police! They've already questioned us twice and they've got nothing on us. I won't even let them know I'm going away. If they want to speak to me again, they'll just have to ring the bloody hotel!'

'When do you go?'

'Friday night.'

'Bloody hell! You don't waste time, do you?'

'Well, they laid us off there and then, so there was no point hanging around. Me and Debby went straight to the travel agents to cheer ourselves up. It's going to be a mad rush. I'm going out to buy some new gear tomorrow, then I'll have to get some sun lotions and all that. I can't wait!'

Julie didn't bother mentioning that Amanda's funeral had been arranged. Neither did she bother asking Rita how she was feeling after Friday night. Rita seemed so happy at the moment that she didn't want to spoil it for her. Besides, there didn't seem any need to ask as Rita appeared to be all right, and Julie was once again surprised at her strength of character.

After Rita had droned on for a while about her holiday preparations, Julie decided to change the subject.

'There was some graffiti about me on the loo walls at work today.'

'Oh yeah, what did it say?'

Julie's voice trembled as she uttered the words, 'Julie Quinley is a murderer.'

'Oh take no notice! It'll be that bitch Jacqueline and her cronies.'

'It's hard to ignore it Rita. I couldn't get it off the wall. I'll see it every time I go in there and so will everyone-else.'

'That Jacqueline's trying to cover up her own guilt by pinning it on you. The cow! I wish I could get my hands on her!'

Julie noticed that once again Rita was quick to point the finger of blame on Jacqueline, but maybe Rita was right; perhaps Jacqueline was the guilty one. It was certainly a better alternative than Rita.

'I've been thinking about that, Rita,' she said. 'Can you remember if there was any time when she was alone with Amanda?'

'That's a point! Let me think. God, it's difficult to remember now; we were all a bit pissed but she was with her before we got there, don't forget.'

'I know, but Amanda was all right then. What about later on, in the Boardrooms? I can remember us two going to the loos together when we got gabbing for ages. Did we leave Amanda on her own then or was Debby with her?'

'She was on her own as far as I remember. Debby was being chatted up by some bloke but Jackie had already gone for a meal by then.'

'What if Jacqueline hadn't gone for a meal though? She could have been hanging around, then come over and given drugs to Amanda as soon as she knew she was on her own. Then she could have disappeared before we got back, couldn't she?'

'Well I suppose so, but what would be the point of that?'

'I don't know, but someone's done it! They must have a reason, and Jacqueline is a spiteful bitch! Maybe she was jealous of Amanda, or maybe she was trying to frame us for whatever reason.'

'I suppose it's possible, but the problem is proving that she did it Julie. Don't forget, the police will have interviewed loads of witnesses from the pubs, and if anybody had seen Jacqueline go over they'd have had her in for questioning.

'It's just so bloody annoying! I know that we didn't do it, but everybody thinks we did and there's no way I can prove otherwise. I just can't make any sense out of any of it. As if it's not bad enough that Amanda's dead, without all this other hassle.'

'Julie, you're letting it get to you too much. Just ignore the bastards, or tell them to fuck off!'

'I know, but it's not easy when people who used to chat to you suddenly just blank you or give you dirty looks. Mike Marston completely blanked me today. I think he must have heard the rumours.'

'Face him with it then. Find out what his problem is instead of just stewing over it. If he's letting that stand in the way of taking you out then he's not much of a bloke is he? You're better off without him Julie. Besides, you've still got Vinny.'

'Did have,' Julie corrected her.

'You've not bloody finished with him have you?'

'Not exactly, no. I just can't be bothered at the moment and after a night out with Mike, Vinny seemed so boring.'

'Give over Julie. I've told you before, Vinny's a decent bloke, and at least he'll stand by you, not like this bloody Mike. You're living in a dream world if you think you've got something going with the likes of him. I know his type. I bet he's all smarmy and trying to show off about how clever he is.'

'Not really,' Julie defended him but lacked any argument to back up her case.

After a moment's lull in the conversation Rita declared, 'It's time I was getting off. I've got a busy day's shopping ahead of me tomorrow.'

'OK,' said Julie and, as Rita left, Julie promised to speak to her before her holiday.

'See you then,' said Rita, 'and don't forget, don't let the bastards get to you!'

Julie only managed a frown in reply. Once she was left alone again to mull over the situation, one thought dominated all others: "*Rita didn't seem at all concerned over Amanda's death.*"

Chapter 17

Saturday 5th July 1986

The call from Vinny couldn't have come at a worse time for Julie. It had been two days since the funeral and Thursday had been a particularly traumatic day at work. As Norma had attended Amanda's funeral, Julie was responsible for managing the switchboard with the assistance of an office junior who had been trained to relieve them in the event of absence.

Management had instructed Julie to tell all callers that they were operating a skeleton staff due to special circumstances and to ask them to call back the following day. This had proved challenging since many of the callers were curious about the 'special circumstances' and Julie had found it very upsetting to have to repeatedly give an explanation. There was also the odd difficult customer who insisted that he had important matters to discuss, which couldn't wait. Every time she had to mention the word 'funeral' she could feel her voice shaking and was on the verge of leaving the building on a couple of occasions.

It had also been a day since Rita had left for her holidays, and her departure was still fresh in Julie's mind adding to her feelings of fear and isolation. It was no wonder then that Julie was anything but receptive towards Vinny.

'Hi Julie, I thought I'd give you a ring to see if you're feeling any better,' he began nervously.

'Vinny, this isn't just a cold that will go away after a few days you know; my mate's dead and I've been accused of killing her! I couldn't even go to the funeral because they would have lynched me. So how do you think I bloody feel? Put yourself in my shoes. How would you feel?'

'Julie, I'm not trying to play it down. I know it must be bad. I'm just worried about you, that's all.'

'Well you don't need to be! I'm doing enough worrying on my own.'

'Don't be like that Julie; I'm just trying to help. I've left you alone for a few days to give you some space. I was hoping that things might be getting a bit easier for you by now.'

'Well they're not; in fact they're worse. The whole bloody world thinks I did it now, thanks to some bastard scrawling all over the toilet walls at work! And if that wasn't bad enough, Rita pissed off to Greece yesterday and left me to it.'

'You're joking! Some kind of a mate she is eh? I told you you'd have to watch her.'

'Stop having a go at Rita! I've told you, she's all right. I can't blame her for going away really. I just wish that I could handle it as well as her.'

'Yeah well, she doesn't have to work at the same place, does she?'

'Oh cheer me up Vinny, why don't you?' Julie replied.

'Sorry Julie. It's just difficult not to talk about it. I tell you what, why don't you come round here and I'll have a proper go at cheering you up?'

'No Vinny. I'm sorry, I'm just not in the mood.'

'Oh suit yourself then, I'll see you around!'

Julie then heard him replace the receiver. She put the phone down and stared at it for a few seconds while she thought about the conversation that had just taken place. Julie knew that she had been awful to Vinny, but there was no point phoning him back as she couldn't guarantee that she would be any nicer a second time. She was just too troubled.

The loud ringing of the phone made her jump. At this proximity it seemed to take on a life of its own. She was tempted to ignore it, but resisted. She was amazed to hear the sound of Rita's voice at the other end of the line.

'Hi Jules, how's it going?' Before Julie had a chance to respond an animated Rita continued. 'Oh Julie, you should have come. It's brilliant here, fuckin' brilliant I tell ya! The place is gorgeous, the hotel's right next to the beach, there's a happy hour every night and loads of talent.'

Julie had difficulty hearing Rita because of a commotion in the background.

'What's all that noise?' she asked.

'Oh it's just Debby having a laugh with this fella.'

'She's not copped already has she?'

'Oh aye. You know Debby, she doesn't waste any time. First night out and bang, but don't worry; I've got my eye on a really fit barman.'

There was a roar in the background.

'What was that?' asked Julie.

'Debby and her fella,' Rita replied between giggles. 'I think they approve of my choice, or maybe it was me mentioning the bang on the first night.'

A further series of roars and giggles echoed down the line.

'How are you anyway?' Rita continued. 'Oh shit, the pips are going already. See you in a fortnight Julie, and keep your pecker up.'

This brought about peals of laughter from Debby and her companion until the sound was cut off and Julie was left holding a dead telephone receiver.

She put the phone down once again and gazed towards the window at the other side of the room, feeling contemplative. It was clear that Rita and Debby were having a whale of a time with not a thought for poor Amanda. She let the tears of frustration and bitterness flow freely until they clouded her eyesight. Suddenly, as she looked towards the living room window a vision appeared.

It was a woman; a young woman, pretty with dark hair. It was Amanda. Julie watched dumbstruck as Amanda gazed back at her with a pained expression on her face, her eyes red and misty.

The vision continued and Julie was drawn to it. She stepped forward, approaching the window until Amanda's face was almost within reach. She stretched out her hand towards Amanda, but the vision died just as rapidly as it had appeared. Julie dashed to the window in search of an explanation, but the only thing she saw was her father's rose bushes swaying in the breeze. She sank to her knees and let out an almighty yell while holding the sides of her head. 'No, no!' she shouted. 'I'm going fuckin' mad! NO!'

There was nobody to hear her screams. Her parents and Clare were all out shopping. Julie didn't know how long she remained like that, shaking and sobbing uncontrollably, but it seemed like an absolute age before she calmed down and rose to her feet.

She didn't tell anybody about the vision. Julie knew it was just a figment of her imagination brought on by stress, and felt foolish discussing it. Besides, there was nobody she could discuss it with. Hadn't she already brought enough trouble on her nearest and dearest without giving them even more cause for concern? She decided to put it behind her and try to continue her daily struggle through life.

***

Monday 7th July 1986

Julie decided to confront Mike as soon as she returned to work on Monday. Even though she had enough on her plate as it was, she was determined to get some answers from him. Rita was right, there was no point in stewing over it. Apart from that, she deserved an explanation; he had promised to take her out again when all said and done.

The moment she spotted him, she asked if she could have a quiet word and led him to an interview room at the rear of the reception area. She decided to come straight to the point.

'Why have you been avoiding me Mike?'

'I haven't, I've been busy.'

'Come off it Mike! Your work doesn't stop you from saying a quick hello. Besides, I thought you were supposed to be looking forward to seeing me again.'

He squirmed uncomfortably; he wasn't going to wriggle out of this one.

'All right,' he conceded, 'I'll come clean. I think you're a great girl Julie and I'd love to take you out again, but I can't.'

'Why, is it because of Amanda?'

'Sort of.'

He grasped her hands, trying to ingratiate himself. 'I don't think you've done anything wrong Julie, but I can't ignore the rumours.'

She wrenched her hands out of his reach.

'It could damage my career Julie,' he pleaded. 'Let's just wait until everything settles down, then maybe we can go out again.'

As she stooped her head she could sense his discomfort while he awaited her reaction. 'Just go Mike. Get out of my sight!' she responded.

It was no better than she had expected, but now she knew for sure why he had been avoiding her and she wouldn't waste any more of her time on him. She didn't shed any tears. Why bother crying for something that you never really had, or was it because she had prepared herself already for what he was going to say?

When she returned to the switchboard, a few moments after Mike had sauntered past, she was relieved that Norma didn't prompt her to relay her conversation with Mike. Perhaps the expression on her face told Norma all she needed to know.

Chapter 18

Thursday 10th July 1986

Betty received the card in Thursday morning's post addressed to "Betty and Bill". It was the long awaited invitation to her niece's wedding. Betty was surprised to receive the invitation so late as the wedding was just over a week away, yet it had been the subject of conversation within the family for months. Her niece had said how lovely it would be to see them all at the church, but apologised that Clare would not be able to attend the reception as it was an adults only affair. Betty had expected, however, to see Julie's name on the invitation since the wedding had been discussed openly in front of her. She was at a loss to understand why Julie wasn't invited, but decided to ring and check, rather than just bring her along.

The reason given wasn't very convincing; they wanted to keep the numbers down due to cost, so they had been forced to leave some people off the list. Although Betty wasn't overjoyed with the situation, she accepted the excuse.

When Julie arrived home from work that evening, Betty decided to broach the subject with her.

'We've had the invite to your cousin Dawn's wedding love,' Betty began tentatively.

'Oh good, that should be something to look forward to.'

'I'm sorry Julie but they've only invited me and your father. They said that they've had to cut down on numbers.'

'You're joking, I can't believe it! Dawn's been telling me about the wedding for months. She wanted me there! What the hell are they playing at?'

'Well I can understand it in a way love,' Betty replied, attempting to calm Julie. 'Weddings are a dear do these days and I expect they've just got to cut corners.'

'That's a load of crap and you know it!' Julie yelled. 'We all know the reason I'm not being invited so why don't you just admit it?'

'Don't talk such bloody rubbish!' Bill interrupted. 'The world doesn't revolve around you and your cronies you know. People have got better things to think about. And don't speak to your mother like that!'

Julie gave a sad-eyed glance towards her mother then retired to her room. Betty could read the hurt and despair in Julie's eyes, which told her more than any words could do, and her heart cried out in sympathy.

**

Saturday 19th July 1986

It was Saturday, the day of the wedding, and also the day on which Rita was due to return from her holidays in the early hours of the morning.

'Well what do you think?' asked Betty as she swirled around in her peach, georgette two-piece outfit.

'You look fine mam,' Julie answered.

Seeing the look on her daughter's face, Betty tried to quell some of her excitement, but this was marred by Bill when he walked into the room and announced, 'You look smashing Betty love. You'll be the bell of the ball!'

Hearing a rare compliment from her husband, Betty gave a girlish giggle, unable to contain her joy. 'Go on with yer, I'm a bit old for that!'

But Bill's compliment had touched her. When the taxi driver rang the doorbell, Bill rushed to answer the door. Continuing his merriment, he shouted, 'Right ma'am, your carriage awaits!'

'You daft beggar!' Betty answered as she headed towards the front door. Before leaving the house, however, she caught sight of Julie's despondent expression.

'Are you sure you'll be all right love?' Betty asked.

'Of course I will mam, don't be daft!'

'All right, I'll see you later then, and make sure our Clare comes in on time for me won't you love?'

'Yeah, stop worrying! Just go and have a good time.'

'All right, bye then.'

Betty breathed a sigh of relief as she left the house, glad to be away from the stifling atmosphere. For the last week or so it had been like treading on eggshells. Every time she had mentioned anything connected with the wedding, Julie's face had dropped.

Betty and Bill had decided that they should go to the entire event alone as there seemed little point in taking Clare to the church and then having to return home with her prior to attending the reception. They had explained the situation to Clare and she had accepted it. Grown up parties held no interest for Clare. She would sooner go to one her friend's birthday parties where they could run around, play games and compare outfits.

With Julie though, it was a different matter. Julie would normally have been the very person that Betty would have discussed the wedding with. They would have chatted merrily about what the bride would be wearing, where the honeymoon would be, how many bridesmaids there were etc. etc. It had been difficult for Betty trying to keep her enthusiasm to herself.

'I do hope our Julie will be all right,' she said to Bill inside the cab.

'Stop worrying about her Betty! She's a grown woman and can take care of herself. It's not your fault she hasn't been invited, so stop taking it all on yourself. It's like you said, they're just trying to cut corners, that's all!'

'It's just a pity it had to be our Julie though, especially after all she's been through.'

'I know love, but it won't be just Julie. There'll be plenty of other people that haven't been invited. I bet it will only be a small affair.'

The wedding service went well. The bride looked beautiful and Betty couldn't help but shed a few tears as she watched her walking down the aisle, recalling Dawn as a toddler not so many years ago. After the photograph session, they were taken in a minibus to have a celebratory meal. As they approached the splendid five star hotel by means of its lengthy driveway, Bill turned to Betty and whispered. 'Bloody hell! They've pushed the boat out here, haven't they?'

'Yes,' Betty replied as she gazed in awe at the impressive surroundings. The hotel was set in acres of gardens with lawns stretching out for miles to the sides of the building; the grass cut to perfection and surrounded by colourful herbaceous borders.

They entered the hotel, marvelling at their opulent environment. Betty noticed the detailed cornicing, marble pillars and crystal chandeliers. As she stared about her in a trance, Bill nudged her and indicated towards the bride and groom who were preparing to meet their guests. Embarrassed, they joined the line of people.

As Betty shook her niece's hand she said, 'Ooh this is lovely! It makes me feel like royalty.'

'Enjoy it Aunty Betty,' said Dawn while the groom grimaced at Betty's lack of social etiquette. Betty shook his hand awkwardly, then she and Bill made their way towards a table lined with glasses of champagne laid on for the guests.

'I never expected a do like this!' Betty commented, surveying the surroundings.

Bill, ill at ease in such environs, replied, 'Aye, so much for cutting bloody corners!'

'Well perhaps they overspent and had to cut back at the last minute,' said Betty, defending her sister's family. 'See, there aren't many here for the meal, not as many as there were at the church.'

'I'm not surprised!' said Bill. 'I bet it's costing a bloody fortune just to feed this many!'

Several people turned round on hearing Bill's raised voice.

'Shsh!' whispered Betty. 'Don't make a show of us!'

For the next few minutes they remained silent, each engrossed in their own thoughts. Betty knew just as well as Bill did that the excuse about cutting corners wasn't a valid one. At first she had refused to see it. How could her own family turn their backs on Julie? But now, in light of what she had seen, she realised that there was only one reason why Julie hadn't been invited to the wedding.

Betty's elderly aunt Mary came to talk to them, commenting on what a lovely do it was, and telling them all about the groom's family as she pointed out who everybody was.

By the time they sat down to the meal Betty and Bill had learnt that Dawn's husband came from a family with money. His father ran his own factory, but Dawn's new husband had not followed in his father's footsteps. Instead, he had studied law at university and was now a well-paid solicitor.

During the lavish four-course meal they indulged in small talk with some of their relatives and acquaintances, but they were unable to enjoy it. They both felt out of place and disheartened at the way Julie had been treated.

As soon as they had finished the meal, Bill found them a small table in a side room. Betty noticed that there were two chairs at the table and guessed that this suited Bill as it would deter other people from joining them.

'Bill, they haven't done the speeches yet,' she said, once they were out of earshot.

'Sod the bloody speeches! It's nowt but a load of old codswallop! What's wrong with booking the local labour club, and having a good knees-up? It's a load of nonsense, all that shaking hands and drinking bloody champagne. I'd sooner have a pint anyway!'

'If that's the way they want it Bill then it's up to them. Anyway, we both know that isn't what's really upset you. It's our Julie isn't it?'

Bill paused and drew in his breath sharply before replying. 'Well it isn't right! Who are they to judge? It's not as if she's been charged with anything!'

'All right Bill,' coaxed Betty. 'I'm not overjoyed with it myself. That's supposing that it is the reason Julie wasn't invited. We don't know that; we're just surmising aren't we?'

'It's obvious Betty! Our Dawn's married into money and they don't want to be shown up by having a murderer in the family. That's the way they see it anyway.'

'Look Bill, we don't know whose decision it was. And we still don't know the real reason. You can't take it out on everybody. Besides, it might not be the reason. There's only close family to the meal, and all of those that I know are more closely related to Dawn than our Julie is. We might be reading too much into it. Let's just relax and try to enjoy it eh? It isn't every day we get the chance to live it up in a place like this, is it?'

Eventually, after a couple of drinks, Betty was relieved to see Bill begin to relax. As the evening guests arrived, they noticed a couple of acquaintances, and their conversation helped them to settle down and start to enjoy the occasion. While they were chatting, however, Betty observed the guests that were arriving for the evening reception, noting that there were many of Dawn's cousins amongst them.

When they were left alone Bill echoed Betty's thoughts. 'I wonder what their excuse is for not inviting our Julie to the evening do. The world and his wife are here.'

Betty remained silent but bore a troubled expression.

'I'm going to the gents,' Bill said, patting Betty's hand as he left the table.

Betty watched the other guests enjoying themselves while she waited for Bill. After a couple of minutes she could see him heading back towards her. Bill had remained calm for the last couple of hours so Betty was shocked to see him storming through the room with a face like thunder.

'Sup up Betty, we're going!' he shouted, banging on the table for effect.

Betty stared at him in shock.

'You heard, sup up we're going!'

Betty wasn't used to seeing Bill like this and knew that there must be a good reason for his behaviour. She quickly downed her drink, conscious of the many faces watching them as she gathered her handbag from under the table.

Aware that they were on show, Bill took the opportunity of making his feelings known as he led Betty away.

'Come on, we're going home! I'm not staying where we're not wanted for a minute longer. They can all bugger off! Our Julie's better than the lot of them put together, for all their bloody airs and graces.'

He sped through the crowd, leading Betty by the hand into the hotel lobby. As Betty watched him in astonishment, he strode up to the reception desk and ordered a taxi to take them home.

While they waited for the taxi, Betty said, 'What the hell's got into you Bill?'

Bill began to explain the conversation he had overheard in the gents amongst two of Betty's relatives. They were maligning Julie, saying she was unfit to be seen at such a function. While Bill was apologetic to Betty for having spoiled her evening, at the same time, he made it clear that he valued his daughter over and above anybody present and he wasn't prepared to put up with her being treated as an outcast. Betty knew better than to argue with him. Bill, normally a quiet man, could be quite headstrong at times.

The taxi soon arrived and Bill and Betty left the hotel. In the ten minutes that they had been waiting in the foyer, nobody had been to see them.

It was only ten o'clock when they arrived home, but Julie wasn't downstairs. They surmised that she must have gone to bed early and, as she didn't come downstairs to see why they had arrived home so early, they decided not to disturb her. Instead they settled down to watch television for a couple of hours. Betty did, however, pop her head round Julie's door before she went to bed, just as she did with Clare. Julie appeared to be sleeping soundly.

Chapter 19

Saturday 19th July 1986

Julie was led into a small room, about 6ft by 6ft. Once inside, she heard the sound of a key being turned in the lock and the jingling of the jailor's chain of keys. She ran to the door attempting to open it but it wouldn't budge. In her desperation she looked around the room for an alternative means of escape. There were windows but they were heavily barred. In between the bars, faces peered at her in amusement, jeering and shouting insults.

The room was bright, with strip neon lights lining the whitewashed ceiling. The walls and floors were whitewashed too, reflecting the brightness of the lights. As she looked around the room, the intense brilliance dazzled and stung her eyes. Her ears rang with the sound of mocking voices as they grew louder until she screamed at them to stop. But Julie's screams were met with derision. In despair she tried closing her eyes and covering her ears with her hands, but she could not escape from the noise, the blinding headache, dizziness and nausea. It was stiflingly hot inside the room and Julie started to perspire profusely.

Suddenly, the walls began to close in on her and she panicked, pushing at the walls in a futile attempt to hold them back. The voices changed to laughter; loud, raucous laughter, which echoed in her mind.

The walls drew nearer and nearer. The windows disappeared. The faces faded. And the laughter ceased. The room now became dark and ominous and Julie prepared to meet her fate. As she felt the hard stone crushing her legs, she emitted a shrill scream.

It was this scream that awoke her parents who dashed into her room to find Julie fighting for breath and sweating copiously; one clammy hand clutching her chest and the hair pasted to her forehead.

'Julie, what's the matter love? Have you had a bad dream? You frightened the bloody life out of us!' yelled Betty.

Julie's breathing had become so strained that she had difficulty replying.

'What should we do Bill?' asked Betty, beginning to get flustered.

Before Bill had a chance to answer, however, Julie had jumped from the bed, fled from the room and tore downstairs with Betty following in close proximity.

'Julie, what's wrong love?' Betty shouted in despair.

Julie struggled to force out a reply in between taking sharp breaths and swallowing hard. 'I think I'm having a heart attack or something mam! There's pains in my chest, and they're even down my left arm. I can't get my breath, and my heart's going ten to the dozen. Oh God, I think I'm gonna faint mam!'

Betty followed Julie into the living room, plumping up a cushion. 'Sit down here love, and you might feel a bit better.'

'I can't mam! It's worse when I stay still! It's better if I keep walking.'

Betty's face displayed a look of total confusion while Julie continued to dash around the room showing signs of distress but acting far too energetic for someone having a heart attack.

Fortunately, Bill strode into the room and began to take control.

'She's having a panic attack Betty. Calm down the pair of you! It'll soon pass.'

'Are you sure that's what it is Bill?' asked Betty, becoming agitated herself.

'Course I'm sure! I've seen a few of 'em in my time. You go and pour her a brandy Betty; I'll sort her out.'

Betty dashed to the drinks cabinet while Bill took hold of Julie and tried to encourage her to take slow, deep breaths, while he uttered words of reassurance.

For several minutes Julie found it difficult to settle and paced around the room in between taking sips of brandy. Eventually her symptoms subsided and the attack culminated in an outburst of tears.

'Oh mam, I thought I was dying!' she sobbed. 'Thanks for helping me dad.'

'That's all right, but if you're gonna have any more of these attacks, don't get too used to having a drink to calm you down. It's a bad habit to get into. Get yourself down to the doctors on Monday morning and see what they can sort out.'

'I will dad, thanks,' Julie muttered.

Bill returned upstairs leaving Julie and her mother to talk.

'Are you all right now love?' asked Betty.

'Yes, I'm just a bit shaky, that's all. I can't believe a panic attack can make you feel that bad! I honestly thought I was having a heart attack or something. It's a good job my dad was here, isn't it?'

'Aye, he does care in his own daft way you know Julie.'

'I suppose he does, but he's still disappointed in me, isn't he?'

'You wouldn't have said that if you'd have seen how he stuck up for you tonight!'

'What do you mean mam, what happened?'

'Oh it was a right carry on, a big posh do it was, and after them saying they had to cut corners. We knew straightaway the real reason they hadn't invited you.'

'Oh yeah?'

'Yes Julie, my own flesh and blood turning their backs on you! It shames me to say it, and if that wasn't enough your dad overheard two of your uncles having a conversation in the toilets about you.'

'What were they saying about me?'

'Oh, you know,' Betty began, 'they were talking about you being arrested, and that being the reason for you not being there, that sort of thing.'

'Go on.'

'Oh I think you've got the gist of it Julie. You don't want to hear the rest. Anyway, the point is, your father stood up to them all and told them you were better than the bloody lot of them put together, and then we stormed out.'

'You're joking!'

'I'm not love. See, I told you he cares in his own daft way, didn't I?'

This revelation succeeded in bringing a brief smile to Julie's face as her mother held and comforted her. Julie couldn't help her look of amusement as she pictured the scene that had taken place. She could imagine the horrified reactions of the other guests.

'Right,' said Betty, after a few moments. 'I'm off to bed. Will you be all right now love?'

'Yes!' Julie assured her for the second time.

Betty, however, looked unconvinced. 'You know, if there's anything else bothering you Julie, you've only got to say. You can talk to me any time.'

Julie paused for a moment, deliberating whether to confide in her mother.

'There is something isn't there?' asked Betty.

'Well, yes,' Julie admitted. 'It sounds stupid though; you'll think I've lost my marbles.'

'Don't be so daft! Come on, out with it.'

'Well, it was after Rita rang me from her holidays, you know, the day after she arrived there. I answered the phone and her and Debby sounded like they didn't have a care in the world. It started me off thinking about Amanda, and as I looked towards the window I thought I saw Amanda watching me, but when I walked towards her she was gone.' She paused a moment, gauging her mother's reaction, but when it wasn't forthcoming she added. 'There, I said you'd think I'd gone mad, didn't I?'

'I don't think anything of the bloody sort!' replied Betty. 'I was just a bit shocked that's all. It sounds to me like the pressure's been getting to you more than I realised. Oh Julie love, why didn't you tell me? I can't help you if you don't tell me, can I?'

Julie looked embarrassed.

'Now you listen to me Julie Quinley,' Betty continued. 'I want you down at that doctors on Monday. Sod work! I'll ring them and tell them you're not well, OK?'

'Yes,' Julie replied.

'Good, then get yourself upstairs when you've finished that drink, and try not to let things get to you so much.'

Betty gave Julie one last reassuring squeeze before she went to bed. Julie sat in silence for a few moments contemplating the conversation that had just taken place. A short while later she finished the brandy and dragged herself to bed feeling mentally and physically exhausted.

Chapter 20

Sunday 20th July 1986

It was the following day when Rita paid Julie a visit after returning from holiday. Rita's appearance surprised Julie. Not only was she suntanned, but she had a radiant glow about her.

'You look well!' Julie announced on seeing her. 'It looks like you've been having a good time. You'll have to tell me all about it.'

'Julie it was brilliant! You should have been there. The weather was gorgeous. The place was really nice. We partied every night and chilled out on the beach every day, and as for the talent!'

'Go on!' beckoned Julie, knowing there was more to follow. 'What's his name, how old is he, what does he do and is he good in bed?'

'Yansis, 25, a waiter and absolutely bloody fantastic!' Rita replied. 'I think I'm in love Jules, I can't stop thinking about him. I've phoned him twice already since I got home.'

'Jesus Rita, the bleedin' sun must have gone to your head,' replied Julie in surprise.

'Well Jules, sometimes it takes us by surprise when we least expect it, and he took me by surprise a few times, I can tell you,' Rita replied, laughing.

'Oh you dirty cow!' Julie responded.

They remained silent for a few moments while Julie digested the news. Then she said, 'What are you going to do then? If he lives over there, how are you going to see him?'

'Well, we've talked about that a lot. I want to go and live there. I told him I'd use my redundancy money to put a deposit down on a bar, but he was having none of it. He says he wants to do his share so he's going to see if he can raise some of the money himself. His dad's invested some money in olive trees for him apparently.'

'Bloody hell Rita, this is all a bit soon isn't it? You hardly know him!'

'It doesn't matter Julie. It feels right. I know it does! There's no point waiting around. Sometimes in life you've just got to go for it and as soon as I get the OK from him, I'm over there. There's nowt to stay here for, is there?'

'Oh thank you very much, Rita!'

'Sorry Jules, I didn't mean it like that. I'll miss you all, of course I will, but you've got Vinny and your nice family. Who have I got?'

'I'm sorry Rita; I don't mean to put a damper on things. It's just that I don't want you to make a big mistake, but if you know you're doing the right thing then I'm really happy for you.'

Julie tried to put on a brave face while she hugged Rita and congratulated her.

'Jesus Rita, I'll miss you, you know.'

Julie then shocked Rita by bursting into tears.

'Go on, you daft cow!' said Rita. 'We'll still see each other. It's not as if I'm going to the ends of the earth, is it? I'll be on the phone every five minutes, and just think of all the cheap holidays you'll be able to have.'

She then noticed the anguished expression on Julie's face and asked, 'What is it Julie; are things still bad at work?'

'Yes they are, I can't stand it anymore! I ended up having panic attacks. I'm going to the doctors tomorrow to try and get a sick note and whatever else he can give me that might help.'

'Oh Julie, you shouldn't let it get to you so much.'

'I know,' said Julie, her voice trembling. 'But that's just the way it is.'

'What about Vinny? Have you seen anything of him?'

Julie shook her head in response.

'Julie, for God's sake! He's a good guy. You can't let this take over your life. Get your act together!'

'I can't Rita. I can't explain it. I just can't be mithered when I feel like this.'

'Oh well, suit yourself,' Rita replied. 'I must be off now anyway.'

She left Julie to wallow in her self-denigration, but just before departing she turned towards Julie and said, 'Cheer up, everything will work out right in the end, you'll see.'

The news had knocked Julie sideways. She couldn't help but wonder how she was going to cope without Rita around. Under normal circumstances she would have missed her, but the way things were at the moment she felt as though she was having her life support machine removed.

The last couple of weeks had been bad enough, but the thought of being left indefinitely to face the music alone was just unbearable. Suddenly, she became wracked with guilt. How could she ever have suspected Rita? She was a good friend; she always had been. It was only now, when Rita was going away, that she realised just how good a friend she had been.

She thought about Rita's words. Maybe she should get her life back on track, give Vinny a ring and find out if she could make amends. But when she tried to decide what to say to him the prospect became daunting. What she hadn't told Rita was that Vinny had tried ringing her but she had been abrupt with him, telling him that she didn't feel like seeing him at the moment; she just wanted leaving alone.

How could she excuse her behaviour towards him and expect to pick up where she had left off? She wasn't even sure that she wanted to. What if she felt the same as she did the last time she saw him? He would take a further rejection as an insult to his pride, and where would that leave their relationship?

Finally, having resigned herself to the fact that she wouldn't contact Vinny until she was in a better frame of mind, she went over to the stereo and selected an album. As she listened to Whitney Houston's "How will I know?" she could feel the suppressed tears of frustration stinging her eyes.

***

Sunday 20th July 1986

Once Rita had left Julie's home she headed in the direction of her own house exuding an air of self-confidence following the good time she had enjoyed on holiday. In addition to her usual skimpy clothing, her suntan brought out the best in her and gave her the overall appearance of being moderately attractive.

Despite her confident air, as she strode along the road she was troubled by thoughts of Julie. She had never seen her at such a low ebb, and she feared for her friend's emotional and mental well-being. She didn't want to cause Julie any more trauma, but knew that her forthcoming plans were bound to upset her. Rita pushed these thoughts out of her mind, deciding that she had her own happiness to think of.

After Rita had left Julie in her bedroom, Betty had snatched a few quick words with her as she made her way towards the front door. The conversation was hurried and whispered as Betty did not want Julie to overhear, but the gist of it was that she was very worried about Julie as she had sunk into a deep depression and was finding it difficult to cope from day to day. Rita was at a loss as to what she could do to make things better for Julie.

***

Monday 21st July 1986

Julie sat in the dreary waiting room of the doctor's surgery surrounded by arthritic pensioners, snivelling babies and hyperactive toddlers. She was dreading seeing the doctor; she felt like a fraud. Julie wasn't actually ill, not in the physical sense anyway, but she knew, nevertheless, that things weren't quite as they should be. Besides, her parents had been so insistent about her visiting the doctor; if she let them down she feared that they might never speak to her again.

She had turned down her mother's offer to come with her, giving some meagre excuse. The real reason was that if she had a last minute panic and couldn't go through with it, she wouldn't be able to back out if her mother was there.

Julie had rehearsed what she was going to say to the doctor several times in her head, but it never sounded quite right:-

"*I think I'm having a breakdown*" – (No, too dramatic.)

"*I'm losing it doctor*" – (Losing what, you daft cow? I think you lost that years ago but we can arrange an internal examination if you prefer Miss Quinley.)

"*I'm having panic attacks*"- (What makes you say that? I don't know, my dad told me I was.)

Finally she settled on "*I'm having trouble with my nerves.*" Then at least she'd have got the condition out of the way in as few words as possible. She knew that the doctor would then prompt her to go into further detail, but she hoped that by then she would have calmed down a bit.

"*Thank God I'm seeing Doctor Frazer,*" she thought. "*At least it's better than seeing Doctor Weiller.*"

Julie had only been to see the doctor twice in the last five years so she didn't know what to expect, but she had heard about Doctor Weiller's reputation for insensitivity from her mother. Doctor Frazer, on the other hand, was a considerate 30 something female with whom Julie felt more at ease.

She was becoming increasingly tense, and every time the buzzer sounded it made her jump to such an extent that she felt sure the other patients could see her exaggerated reaction. When the buzzing was accompanied by the receptionist announcing her name, she felt the bile rise in her throat. "*Here goes,*" she thought.

'Come in,' shouted the doctor when Julie knocked on her surgery door.

Julie approached the doctor's desk and waited for her cue to begin speaking.

'Take a seat. What can I do for you?' asked the doctor.

'I've come with my nerves,' said Julie in a flurry of words. Embarrassed at her cracking voice and lack of articulation, she cleared her throat and corrected herself. 'I mean, I'm having trouble with my nerves.'

The doctor sensed that Julie was worked up and said kindly, 'All right, perhaps you'd like to explain how it's been affecting you. Take your time, there's no rush.'

'Well, I don't know where to start really. Everything's been getting on top of me. I've had a really bad few weeks. I've been getting panic attacks. It all started when my friend died.'

As soon as she began describing the situation she broke down and found it difficult to speak coherently; instead she rushed her words.

'It's all right,' soothed the doctor as she passed Julie a tissue. 'It sounds as though you've been having a rough time of it. Do you work?'

Julie could only nod in response.

'And how are you coping with work?'

'Terrible,' cried Julie. 'It's hell! They all think I killed Amanda and I can't stand it anymore,' she said between sobs.

The doctor was shocked but remained professional. She didn't probe any further, knowing that Julie was having real difficulty discussing her troubles.

'Right, I want you to take two weeks off, and I'm giving you something that will help you,' said the doctor. 'At the end of the two weeks I want you to come back and see me, then we can decide if you're still unfit for work.'

'Thank you,' said Julie as she took the prescription and sick note.

As soon as Julie got outside the doctor's surgery she felt tremendous relief, but she also felt weak and pathetic and wished that she was able to deal with her problems as well as Rita.

Chapter 21

Thursday 31st July 1986

When Rita approached number 20 Claremont Road, she wasn't thinking about Yansis or Julie as she had more immediate matters on her mind. Vinny soon appeared at the door and she abandoned her well-rehearsed, provocative pose as she stepped inside.

'Oh, hello Rita, I'm glad you could make it,' he said, smiling.

She looked up at him and replied, in sultry tones, 'I think that you and me should take up where we left off, don't you?'

Once Rita had made her way inside, Vinny shut the door firmly behind her.

So engrossed were they by their own concerns that they failed to notice the curtains twitching across the road at number 25. This was in fact the home of Melanie Butterworth, one of Clare Quinley's school friends. She had been for tea at Clare's home a few times and was used to seeing Julie there with her friends, including Rita and her boyfriend Vinny.

***

Friday 1st August 1986

The school environment is in many respects similar to other working environments in that, when a topic becomes the subject of gossip, it is discussed indefatigably for several weeks until people tire of its contents or are unable to embellish the tale further.

However, should a new element of the tale be discovered, it will re-ignite public interest in the story. Such was the case with the Julie Quinley scandal, and this latest revelation spread ferociously through the school with its libellous flames enveloping everyone in their pathway. It was only a matter of a few hours until Clare Quinley became engulfed in their fiery force and had to bear once more the consequences of the scandal to which she had become a central figure.

***

Friday 1st August 1986

When Clare arrived home from school, Julie could tell that something was wrong. Instead of the excited bustle that usually accompanied Clare, she was quiet and contemplative.

She had seen Clare behave in this way before, a few weeks ago when news of her arrest had first spread. Now, however, she thought that things had settled down so it surprised her to see Clare looking so troubled.

Julie noticed how quick her parents were to detect Clare's mood. When they tried to discuss Clare's day with her, they received monosyllabic replies. Julie wanted to find out what was troubling Clare, but she was afraid to ask in case the whole sorry subject became the focus of her family's attention once more. Her father, however, was determined to get to the bottom of things.

'What's wrong Clare love, have people been having a go at you about things again?' he asked.

Julie felt tremendous guilt knowing what the word 'things' referred to. She recalled what a difficult week Clare had suffered at school when everyone had found out about her arrest. Unfortunately, she had been so troubled with her own situation at the time that she had not given her sister the care and consideration that she would normally have bestowed on her. Bill, however, had soon settled matters by visiting the head teacher and insisting that he put a stop to the taunts.

During tea Bill continued to press Clare until she opened up to him.

'Nobody's been having a go!' Clare answered.

'Well, what is it then? Has someone said something to upset you? Who is it? Is it one of your classmates? Is it a teacher?'

'No!' shouted Clare. 'They weren't teasing me. It was just something that happened, something that Melanie Butterworth told everybody!'

On saying these words Julie noticed Clare casting a sidelong glance in her direction.

Julie's heart sank as she realised the implications. Melanie Butterworth lived across the road from Vinny. She guessed at what was to follow; Vinny had grown tired of waiting around for her and had found himself another woman. She needed to hear it from Clare first though, before she could accept the facts.

Clare spoke quietly and self-consciously, avoiding Julie's gaze.

'Vinny's got another girlfriend. Melanie saw her going into his house.'

She paused as her parents gazed at Julie in horror. Julie grew silent and let her fork drop as the words hit her.

Clare continued. 'She said it was our Julie's friend, Rita.'

Silence descended on them. For a moment nobody moved. Then Julie rose from the table leaving her plate half empty as she headed out of the room.

She had been in her bedroom for a few minutes when her mother walked in to find her with her head buried in her pillow trying to stifle the tears. Julie looked up on hearing Betty approach.

'How could she mam? How could she do that to me when she's supposed to be my friend?' Julie pleaded.

But Betty didn't offer Julie an explanation. Instead she sat on the bed beside her and took her in her arms while Julie cried incessantly, occasionally trying to speak out against the injustice of it.

Betty silenced her. 'Shsh love, it's all right,' she assured as she held her and brushed back the hair from her eyes. For Julie it wasn't all right though; she was already in a fragile emotional state and she could have done without this further upset.

That night the nightmares returned. This time Vinny and Rita were the main subjects. Julie saw them in a passionate embrace. She approached the loving couple, puzzled, but as she drew nearer to them they turned towards her, their garish and distorted faces mocking her. She felt gripped by an overwhelming anger but when she tried to shout at them her words were no more than a whisper. 'Why, why?' she asked but they ignored her and went back to their petting.

In another dream Rita was sitting with Amanda, her face taunting and menacing. It was during their last night out and Julie watched as Rita handed a white powdery substance to Amanda. Julie could see that Amanda was about to take it. She wanted to stop her but couldn't; she was just an outsider who could only observe as Amanda stared at the drug in her hand and prepared to put it in her mouth.

Julie awoke in a sweat drenched panic to the sound of her own voice screaming, 'No, no, no!' She soon took stock of her surroundings, relieved to find that she was in her own bedroom.

As Julie attempted to calm her racing heart her mother rushed into the room. 'Are you all right love?'

'Yes,' Julie tried to reassure her. 'It's just another nightmare, that's all. You go back to bed mam. I'll be all right, it's over now.'

When Betty had left her room, Julie picked up a book from her bedside table, intent on reading for the rest of the night. She knew that, in her present state of mind, there was no chance of getting any peaceful sleep.

Chapter 22

If Julie had answered the front door, Rita would never have got over the threshold. However, it was Clare who answered it so Rita found it easy to barge past a child of eight and make her way up to Julie's bedroom.

'Julie, have I got news for you!' she announced as she strode boldly into Julie's room.

'You've got a bloody nerve!' Julie shouted. 'I'm not interested in hearing anything you've got to say!'

Rita appeared shocked. 'It's important Julie!'

'It may be for you, but I don't give a stuff! You don't think I'm gonna sit here while you rub my nose in it do you? I don't want your explanations, I just want to see the back of you. Now get out of my room!' she yelled.

'What the bleedin' hell's up with you? Have you completely lost your marbles?' Rita asked, astounded.

Julie retaliated. 'Well you didn't think I was going to take it lying down, did you? I might be suffering from depression, but I've not gone soft altogether. What do you expect, a pat on the back or something? You cheeky hard-faced bitch! Just get out, go on, get back to him, and I hope you'll be very happy together.'

'Julie, what on earth's the matter? I thought we'd discussed this, I thought you were all right about me going to Greece. What the hell's got into you?'

'What do you mean, Greece? Do you mean you're going away together?'

'I told you, as soon as he gets the money, I'm going over there.'

'I'm not talking about Yansis, I'm talking about Vinny. So you can cut the pretence.' As Rita stared, dumfounded, Julie continued. 'Yes, your sordid little secret's out!'

'What are you talking about? I'm not seeing Vinny! I'm in love with Yansis. You know that.'

'Yes, that might be what you've told me, but I know what's really going on. Don't try denying it Rita; you were seen going into his house.'

Rita sighed as the realisation it her. 'I know where you're coming from now. Yes, I have been to Vinny's house, but it's not what you think, you silly cow!'

'What do you mean?'

'Julie, that lad thinks the world of you! Don't you think he'd rather have been talking to you than me? You've been such a bitch with him lately that the poor lad doesn't know whether he's coming or going. He asked to see me so that I could help him sort things out.'

'Oh I see,' Julie replied. 'He thinks you can bring the mad cow to her senses does he, and let her know what she's been missing?'

'I'm not talking about that. Now get off your high horse a minute and let me explain!' Rita continued before Julie had a chance to interrupt. 'Vinny thinks he knows who killed Amanda. He's found something out. He asked to see me about it because he was frightened of getting his head bitten off if he rang you. Anyway, he wants to try to help you get out of this mess, but if you want to find out more then you'll have to speak to Vinny about it.

'After all, it is you he's trying to help, not me. No matter what your warped mind might be thinking, we both know that Vinny wouldn't even bother giving me the time of day if it didn't involve you! And I'm disgusted at you Julie for even thinking that I would go after him behind your back. We're supposed to be mates aren't we? I might be a lot of things, but I would never do the dirty on a mate. You've really insulted me today Julie. I was trying to help you!'

Julie felt terrible. She wished that she could take back her accusations, but it was too late; she had already hurt Rita. 'Rita, I'm so sorry, I got the wrong end of the stick.'

'People see what they want to see Julie,' Rita replied coolly as she walked away.

***

Saturday 2nd August 1986

Rita's revelation had been like a lifejacket to a drowning man. Suddenly, after all these weeks of misery, there was some hope. If Vinny had found something out about Amanda's killer, then that could get her and Rita off the hook. She knew that nothing would bring Amanda back, but at least she wouldn't have to live with the guilt of Amanda's death and that would make it easier to cope.

Apart from giving her hope, Rita's words had also brought her to her senses and made her realise how useless she had become. She had been so wrapped up in her own self-pity that she had convinced herself that the whole world was against her. Instead they had been trying to help her and she had done nothing to assist. She felt so ashamed and embarrassed by her own behaviour. Finally, she decided that it was about time she plucked up the courage to ring Vinny.

When Julie walked into the living room she wasn't surprised to see her father immersed in one of his favourite pastimes of reading his paper. She hesitated at first before approaching the phone, not wanting him to overhear. But then she told herself that if she kept making excuses she would never make the call. "It's now or never," she reassured herself as she lifted the receiver and dialled the number.

As Vinny answered the telephone, Julie's heart began to race and she thought for a moment that she wouldn't be able to speak. In her agitation she rushed at the words.

'Erm, hello Vinny, it's me. I owe you an apology. I know I've been a real pain and I just wanted to say, well, that I'm sorry.'

Vinny sounded taken aback. 'Oh,' he replied. 'That's all right. I know what you've been going through. I just thought I'd leave you to it, till you were feeling a bit better.'

'I know, Rita told me. She told me about you finding something out as well.'

'Oh yes, that.'

'Yes, do you want me to come round so we can talk about it?'

'Yes, as long as you're not just coming to see me because of that.'

'Oh Vinny, I'm sorry! I did want to phone you before now but I was frightened of how you'd react after how I treated you.'

'I'd have been all right; I wanted you to ring. Anyway, you've rang now haven't you? So why don't you come round tonight if you're not doing anything?'

'Right, tonight it is, I'll see you about seven.'

As Julie replaced the receiver a surge of excitement rushed through her. She hadn't felt this good in weeks. While she was in this positive frame of mind, she decided to ring Rita next to apologise.

After a few seconds on the phone to Rita, it became apparent that Rita wasn't really hurt, but was determined to let Julie grovel for a bit before accepting her apology. Knowing that she deserved this treatment, Julie humoured Rita for a while, although she could sense that a reconciliation was imminent. Rita's words indicated her concession when she said, 'You have been a silly cow you know Julie. Fancy thinking me and Vinny were at it behind your back. As if either of us would do that to you. You know your trouble don't you? You don't realise how well thought of you are.'

'I know, I know,' muttered Julie. 'I do realise now though, and I promise I'll never doubt you again Rita.'

Julie then told Rita about her conversation with Vinny and that she had arranged to see him that evening. At Rita's request, she promised to let her know the outcome.

Heaving a sigh of relief, Julie put down the phone.

'What's been going on then?' asked her dad.

'Oh no!' she thought. Just when she was beginning to feel a lot better about things, the last thing she needed was for her dad to say something that might upset her again.

She knew, however, that she had no alternative but to confide in him if she was to have any chance of regaining his trust. After she had explained to him all about the situation with Rita and Vinny and what had transpired during her phone calls, he said, 'Well it's about bloody time things took a turn for the better! Let's hope Vinny can help you find out who really did it, but you two be careful; you don't go messing about with murderers. The minute you find anything out, you get to the police, do you hear?'

'Yes dad,' she assured.

'Oh, and Julie,' he added. 'I knew all along you were innocent. No daughter of mine goes around killing people, even if you are a bit of a boozer.'

He peered back into his newspaper, smiling to himself without giving Julie a chance to respond.

His support had been the final encouragement Julie needed and as she prepared for her meeting with Vinny, she hummed contentedly to herself. "*First Rita, then Vinny and now my Dad,*" she thought. "*I feel as though I've scored a bloody hat-trick.*"

Chapter 23

As Julie approached Vinny's house she saw the curtains twitching across the road at number 25. "*Well,*" she thought, "*I wonder what that silly little cow, Melanie Butterworth, will have to say about this at school tomorrow.*" She smiled as she thought about Clare's anticipated reaction to any quizzing from Melanie Butterworth. "*Knowing our Clare,*" she thought. "*She'll probably give the spiteful little bitch a bloody good run for her money.*"

When she knocked on Vinny's front door, she felt as though her stomach had turned to jelly. Within seconds Vinny was standing before her. He appeared like a stranger and their conversation was stilted at first. She noted his appearance; he was wearing a new shirt, which showed off his honed muscles and he looked clean-cut and sleek. A feeling of desire surged through her as she smelt the subtle but masculine scent of his body.

Without speaking he led her through to the lounge where he had placed a bottle of red wine and two glasses.

'Would you like a drink?' he asked and, when Julie didn't immediately reply, he added, 'You don't have to if you don't want.'

Remembering their last encounter, when she'd not even wanted to share a bottle of wine with Vinny, she cringed with embarrassment. 'I'd love a drink!' she responded and she smiled at him as he began to pour. She knew that she shouldn't be drinking because of the medication she was taking but she didn't want to seem difficult. She therefore decided that she would pace herself and just have a glass or two.

Julie sat down clutching her glass of wine. He took her coat from her and went to hang it up. She sensed that they were both treading carefully, and became determined to put things right between them. When he returned she tried to make polite conversation. 'How have you been?' she asked.

'Not too bad. I've missed you but, in the end, I decided that I had to get on with my life so me and Pete have been going out a lot. It's been OK I suppose.'

Julie felt an inexplicable hurt at this comment. In her naivety she had imagined Vinny sitting at home pining for her but he was tougher than she had given him credit for. She hadn't given him credit for a lot of things. Julie had been too busy chasing shadows. She thought about Mike with his slick charm. It was undeniable that he had given her a good time for as long as it had lasted but it was all a sham. She had analysed their date many times since that night and come to the conclusion that his whole conversation revolved around himself.

As soon as Mike had heard anything negative about her, he couldn't get away from her quick enough. And yet here was Vinny, strong and self-sufficient, but considerate too. Even though she had pushed him aside, he had still been there for her, allowing her the breathing space that she needed in order to sort herself out.

'There's been big changes at work,' he said. 'I've jacked in my job.'

Julie gasped in surprise, 'You're joking!'

'Yeah, I have. I got sick of them making a mug of me. Anyway, this firm called Gads Brothers asked me to work direct for them. They said that the company I worked for were incompetent and that I was the only builder who was any good at his job. So I took the offer. They've got loads of work for me, should keep me going for a while, and I'm putting a few adverts out to see if any other work comes up.'

'That's brilliant!' said Julie, astonished.

'Well you didn't think I was going to take shit from them forever, did you?' asked Vinny.

'Well, to be honest, you have put up with a lot from them.'

'I know, but it's not always easy to go out on your own you know. It's a big risk, but luckily Gads Brothers have given me the break I've been looking for. It's a bit scary though; I've still got bills to pay if anything goes wrong.'

'Give over!' said Julie. 'You'll do great. Once word gets round about how good you are, they'll be banging on your door for you to work for them.'

'Well I hope so,' Vinny smiled.

They sat in silence for a few minutes and Julie gazed around uncomfortably while Vinny got up and fiddled about with his record collection. She wanted to broach the subject of Amanda's murderer but didn't want Vinny to think that was the sole reason for her visit, especially after his comment on the phone. She sensed that Vinny knew what was on her mind but he was making her wait for the information, testing her. Julie felt an urge to keep the conversation going so that she wouldn't risk losing Vinny's confidence in her.

'You're looking well anyway,' she said.

'Thanks,' said Vinny. 'You're not looking so bad yourself. How are you feeling now anyway? Rita said you weren't so good.'

'Not too bad. It's been hard at work, in fact I've ended up on the sick, but things have got a bit better at home. My dad's been all right with me lately, so that's one good thing.' She checked herself before continuing. "*I'm rambling*," she thought. "*It's all me, me, me again. I've got to stop it. I've got to let him know how much I've missed him, how much I care.*" She didn't have the courage to speak these words, however, and she tried to disguise her discomfort as she took a gulp of her wine.

'I know it's been hard for you Julie, but I just wish that you'd have let me help you instead of turning your back on me. I've missed you, you know.'

'I know, me too,' said Julie, fighting back tears.

Vinny dashed over to her and pulled her towards him. She clung to him for comfort as the tears began to flow. Unavoidably she started to sob and felt foolish.

'It's all right, it's all right,' he reassured. 'You're here now and everything's going to be OK. I think I've found out who killed your friend and I'm going to help you sort things out.'

As much as Julie wanted to find out what he knew, she didn't speak for a few moments. Instead she took comfort in his embrace, realising for the first time that this was what she wanted more than anything; to feel his love and know that he was there for her.

Eventually, after composing herself, she spoke. 'Thanks for standing by me through this Vinny. I'm so sorry for how I've been! I don't know what came over me, I just felt as though I couldn't cope with anybody or anything. Everybody I talked to reminded me of Amanda and when I tried to take my mind off her I couldn't stop thinking about her anyway, and it was just impossible to think about anything else.'

'I know, I realise that now but I didn't at the time. I'm sorry too. So that makes us quits, eh?' he asked as he stroked her hand and looked into her eyes.

Julie smiled in reply.

'Right, so let me tell you what I've seen.' He topped up their glasses before continuing. 'Me and Pete decided to go somewhere else one night for a bit of a change. So, we went to the Hacienda. We'd heard loads about it so we thought we'd give it a try.

'We'd just got our drinks and were having a wander round when I saw this guy in the corner, and I said to Pete, "I know him from somewhere", but I couldn't place him at first. Pete said, "Have you seen what he's doing?", and when I looked I saw him taking notes off people and giving them a small package, then they'd disappear to the toilets. We couldn't believe it, all these bloody student types, and he's there flogging drugs as large as life. I couldn't stop thinking about it for ages. I've never seen anything like that in the clubs we go to. Then it dawned on me where I'd seen him.'

He paused for effect as Julie stared open-mouthed at him in anticipation.

'It was at a works do with you. He was with your mate Amanda. Right slimy git he was as well. Thought he was bleedin' rockerfella.'

'Do you mean Les?'

'Yes that's right; that was his name.'

'Jesus!' said Julie. 'Then it could have been him that gave Amanda the drugs, after me and Rita left her with him.'

'Yeah, that's what I thought.'

'We'll have to go to the police Vinny and tell them what you've seen. Will you come with us and speak to them?'

'Course I will. I told you, didn't I? I want to help you.'

For the remainder of the evening they chatted amicably. It seemed that this revelation had lightened the atmosphere between them and Julie felt able to relax once more with Vinny. When he couldn't resist her any longer and chanced making an advance, she willingly responded.

Chapter 24

Sunday 3rd August 1986

Julie stood outside the café in the pouring rain. The downpour was so heavy that even her umbrella couldn't protect her as large droplets splashed against the ground and ricocheted against her legs. She was ten minutes early so she knew she'd have to wait. The thought of sitting inside occurred to her but she didn't want to miss them; the occasion was far too important. After a couple of minutes Vinny arrived.

'What you doing stood out here? You'll catch your death of cold!' he announced.

'I didn't want to miss you.'

'Don't be daft, I'd have found you. Come inside and we can keep a lookout for Rita through the window.'

Julie allowed herself to be led inside but she insisted on sitting as near to the window as possible. While Vinny went to order two cups of coffee, Julie tried to peep through the heads of the customers so that she could catch a glimpse of Rita walking through the door. Before long she was rewarded with a view of her friend who strode towards their table as Julie waved.

The other customers were soon aware of Rita's arrival as she noisily pulled out a chair and plonked herself down on it.

'Jesus Christ, you could have picked a better bleedin' day!' she declared. 'What's all this about anyway? You were like the bleedin' secret service on the phone.'

'Shsh,' whispered Julie as she noticed an elderly couple on a neighbouring table watching them avidly.

Just at that moment Vinny reappeared carrying a tray containing two cups of coffee and two cakes. 'Hi Rita, what do you fancy?'

'Well seeing as how they don't sell what I fancy here, I'll settle for a coffee,' she replied.

Vinny swiftly headed towards the counter, his cheeks beginning to flush.

'You rotten sod!' said Julie. 'You know how you embarrass him.'

'I know,' giggled Rita. 'That's why I do it.'

When she had finished laughing, Julie began to explain to Rita why she had asked her to meet her and Vinny.

'I couldn't give too much away on the phone,' she said. 'My dad was earwigging and I'd rather they didn't know too much at the moment; not until things are sorted out anyway. I don't want to build their hopes up.'

Having gained Rita's fixed attention, she continued. 'Vinny's told me all about that bloody Les dealing drugs and we've decided to go to the police. I thought it would be better not to meet at Vinny's; you never know who's watching.'

She stopped and looked upwards to see that Vinny had returned, carrying Rita's cup of coffee and a cake. 'I was just telling Rita what we've decided to do,' Julie added. Julie and Vinny looked towards Rita for a response to their proposition.

'Suits me,' Rita replied. 'I'll come with you but I don't think you'll get anywhere with them bastards.'

'It's got to be worth a try though,' said Julie.

'Oh yeah, it's worth a try but like I said, I don't think we'll get very far. It's too hard to prove he was dealing drugs for one thing, and that's if the coppers can even be bothered to go and check it out. As far as they're concerned, we killed Amanda.'

Julie became aware of the people sat on nearby tables who were now focusing on their conversation. Although Julie had deliberately chosen a café that was located miles from their homes, she was taking no chances.

'Quiet,' she said, to which Rita shrugged her shoulders in defiance.

'I agree with Julie,' said Vinny. 'It's got to be worth a try, and if we get nowhere then we'll have to decide our next move.'

'Hear, hear,' Julie affirmed. 'I'm not giving up now, not when we've found out what that bastard's up to and we're getting the blame!'

'Right, sup up and let's go down to the station then! There's no time like the present,' said Rita.

***

Sunday 3rd August 1986

Inspector Bowden was going through one of his pacing sessions. These often occurred when he was trying to solve a crime and he would stride up and down the office, throwing out ideas to his subordinates in the hope that they would latch onto some vital clue that might tie up the case.

'Think about it Sergeant Drummond!' he commanded. 'We have a motive of sorts. For starters, the suspects were drunk and out to have a good time, and as part of that good time they wanted to see Amanda Morris make a fool of herself.'

He began to tick off each point on his fingers.

'Secondly, we can place them at the scene of the crime, which I believe to be the Portland Bars, where they were seen putting something into Amanda Morris's drink.

'Thirdly, the Portland Bars did have a previous problem with a former member of staff who was a known drug dealer, and the suspects have frequented this establishment for the last two years.'

He was just about to discuss the evidence given by Leslie Stevens when a uniformed officer approached him.

'We have Julie Quinley, Rita Steadman and an unknown male in reception waiting to see you sir,' he interjected.

'Thank you,' said Inspector Bowden as he rubbed his hands together in glee. He then turned towards Sergeant Drummond. 'Well, well, it looks like we might have the final piece of the jigsaw. My guess is that they've come to confess; probably can't live with it on their consciences any longer.'

'What about the man, sir?' she asked. 'Who do you think he is?'

'Probably a solicitor.'

He marched out of the office door and into the corridor.

***

Sunday 3rd August 1986

Julie was the first to notice Inspector Bowden approaching. How could she fail to recognise his stern demeanour? Even the sight of him sent a shiver down her spine as she recalled the night she had spent in the cells and the torment of his unrelenting interrogation.

He didn't speak to them; he didn't need to. For most people a mere sign given by Inspector Bowden would be enough to summon them into action. That sign was a nod of his head towards an interview room as he carried on walking. They followed behind.

Inside the interview room Julie saw a table with four chairs, two on either side. The inspector sat on the far side and nodded towards the two chairs opposite him. Vinny stepped aside allowing the two girls to be seated, and then looked inquisitively at the inspector for an indication as to where he might sit. The inspector touched the empty chair on his side of the table, pushed it slightly and then nodded towards the two girls.

Julie guessed that Inspector Bowden thought he was too high and mighty to move the chair for Vinny, and preferred to leave him guessing. She had become used to his tactics by now, and watched as Vinny obliged by placing the chair next to hers before sitting down.

'To what do I owe this pleasure?' asked Inspector Bowden.

Julie spoke with animosity. 'We have some information that might assist with your enquiries.' She emphasised the last four words in a parody of police procedure.

Julie then watched the expression on the inspector's face change from smug to confused.

'Carry on!' he instructed.

Before Julie had a chance to continue, Vinny spoke. 'I've seen Amanda Morris's boyfriend dealing drugs.'

Inspector Bowden adopted a blank facade and did not speak, forcing Vinny to carry on. Julie noticed Vinny fiddling nervously with his zipper before he continued. "*The bastard's got to Vinny as well,*" she thought.

Vinny took a defensive line. 'I think he must have given Amanda the drugs that killed her after she got back home that night.'

'Steady!' commanded the inspector. 'Where is your proof that he was dealing drugs?'

'I saw him doing it in a nightclub.'

'That does not count as proof. It is merely your word against his.'

Rita, who had remained uncharacteristically silent until now, suddenly spoke. 'It's up to you to find the bloody proof; that's your job isn't it? Vinny's just telling you what he's seen.'

'Do you really expect me to take the word of one of your associates?' Inspector Bowden asked.

'He's my boyfriend actually,' Julie replied, 'and he doesn't lie, and we're not murderers either.'

Rita stepped up the argument. 'I bet you've not searched his bloody flat, have you? You'll find plenty of drugs there if you bother to look.'

'Mr Stevens' flat was searched when he reported the death of Amanda Morris, and my officers found nothing. Therefore Mr Stevens isn't a suspect. We only have your word that he is involved in drugs.' The inspector nodded towards Vinny, 'And I find it all too convenient that you have found a suspect at just the right moment when it might enable you to divert attention from yourselves. However, that tactic will not work I'm afraid especially as all the evidence so far points in your direction'

He emphasised this last sentence by pointing at Julie and Rita in turn.

'You bastard!' shouted Rita.

'If you're not careful, I will arrest you for disturbing the peace.'

Julie nudged Rita and beckoned her to be quiet.

'Now then,' Inspector Bowden resumed. 'I had hoped that you had seen sense and that you had come here to make a confession. However, if you persist in denying your guilt, we will have to find another way to prove it and that will be only a matter of time.'

'You're bluffing,' Rita yelled. 'You haven't got a bloody thing on us. How can you have? We haven't done nowt!'

Julie could see that Rita was beginning to lose control and she herself was also becoming angry. She rose from her chair and slammed it back towards the table. At the same time she grabbed Rita's arm. 'Come on, we're going! We're wasting our bloody time Rita; he doesn't believe a word we say.'

'I'm not leaving here till he takes us seriously!' shouted Rita, but Julie could see that it was a lost cause and she sought Vinny's help as they led Rita away from the interview room and out of the building.

'Well, what now?' asked Vinny. As both girls glared at him, he raised his hands in mock protest. 'Sorry, don't blame me, I tried.'

'Come on, we're not waiting around here,' said Julie.

'I feel like getting pissed out of my head,' said Rita.

'Let's go and find a pub then and maybe we can decide what to do next,' said Julie.

Chapter 25

Sunday 3rd August 1986

It was a popular pub and was difficult to find a quiet table where they could have a discussion without being overheard. After a good look round they spotted a table in the corner where they would be out of earshot of the many regulars who were dotted about the place.

'Are you all right for time Vinny?' asked Julie.

'Yeah, fine.'

'What about you Rita, can you spare the time?'

'Oh yeah, I've got nothing important on today. Anyway, we're here to sort this out and that's what we're going to do.'

'OK, well I've got an idea to put to you both.'

Vinny and Rita listened as Julie began to outline her plan.

'I think we should find the evidence ourselves. It's no good catching him in the act at a nightclub. We've already done that and the police won't believe us. But if he is dealing drugs then you can bet your life that his flat's full of them.'

'I hope you're not thinking what I'm thinking,' said Rita.

'Dead right! I think we should break into the flat. It's the only way to find the proof we need.'

'Oh yeah, and what do we do with it then?' asked Rita. 'Go to the police and tell them we just happened to stumble across it in Les's flat? They won't believe us and, even if they do, we'll end up getting arrested for breaking and entering.'

'I've thought of that. We're going to make sure that the police find the drugs themselves.'

'How?' asked Rita and Vinny in unison.

'Well, first we have to break in and make sure the drugs are there. Then, we'll start a fire in another room. Just a little one, but we'll do it near the window where it can be seen. After I've legged it from the flat we'll call 999, report a fire, and leave the drugs where the firemen can see them when they go in to put the fire out. They'll have the police there in no time.'

'Jesus Julie, have you gone off your bleedin' head or what?' asked Rita. 'What if he catches you in the act? You don't want to go messing about with him. He's a nasty bastard! Anyway, you're going to make yourself more ill the way you're going on.'

'If he's a drug dealer he probably spends most of the evenings dealing in pubs and clubs. We trace his movements first and when we're pretty sure that he's likely to be out for a while, then we'll make our move. What's the alternative Rita? Letting him go free will make me more ill. Once we've got him arrested I can finally hold my head high.'

'Julie's right,' Vinny added. 'We need to make sure that the police find evidence of him dealing drugs. Then maybe they'll take us seriously and start questioning him about how Amanda died. But I won't have you doing it Julie. It's too risky and you're in enough trouble already. I'll do it.'

'No you won't! I'm not getting you in trouble as well. It's my problem and it's up to me to sort it.'

'Any problem of yours is my problem as well Julie. I'm doing it and that's that!'

Julie and Rita were stunned into silence by Vinny's unusual display of authority until Rita broke the silence by saying, 'Right, me and Julie will act as lookout then. When do you want to start tracking him?'

Now that they had all reached agreement about their course of action, they spent the next couple of hours planning their surveillance operation, which was to commence the following weekend.

***

Monday 4th August 1986

Julie was filled with trepidation when she returned to work after being off for two weeks. Although she was feeling more positive due to the recent turn of events, and the anti-depressants that her doctor had prescribed, she didn't know if she felt ready for work. "*But,*" she thought to herself, "*If I keep putting it off I'll never be ready. It's better to face up to it and get it over and done with.*"

She arrived early, determined not to hide from anybody. She had decided to brave it out and let them know that she had no reason to go into hiding or to feel ashamed of herself.

Norma was already there and her enthusiastic greeting was encouraging.

'Hello stranger, nice to see you back! How are you feeling? You look a lot better than you did.'

Julie had been in contact with Norma by telephone over the last two weeks and told her that she intended to return to work, but Norma had advised against it. 'Wait a bit longer, let the dust settle,' she had said. Julie therefore surmised that Norma was surprised to see her back and was doing her best to make her feel welcome.

'I feel a lot better,' said Julie, 'although I don't know if I'll still be saying that by the end of today.'

'Well Julie, it certainly can't get any worse, can it? You might even find that a few people have mellowed towards you since you were in work last. I've made sure that I've told your side of the story to some of them anyway.'

'Has everyone been talking about it then?'

'A few, but what do you expect? It's not an everyday occurrence is it? But don't let that bother you Julie. If anybody says anything, you just make sure you tell them the truth, and if they don't want to believe you then sod them!'

Julie changed the subject, not wishing to dwell too much on the unpleasantness that was sure to surround her once the employees of Belmont Insurance Company began to arrive for work.

'We think we've found out who really did it anyway Norma.'

Norma's jaw dropped. 'You're joking!'

'No, really! A lot has happened in the last few days Norma.'

Julie then told Norma all about Les's drug dealing, and their visit to the police. Finally she told her about their plan to set up the evidence for the police to discover, adding that they had, in fact, already begun to watch Les's flat.

'Jesus Julie, you're going to end up in a lot more trouble if you're not careful!'

'What's the alternative?' asked Julie, but before Norma had a chance to respond the first of Belmont's employees arrived.

Julie was greeted by scowls and tut tuts from the three women as they approached the lift.

The situation was repeated for the next half hour until the last of the staff entered the building. Eventually Julie switched off and stared right through them as she continued to answer telephone calls.

At lunchtime she left the building and walked around the shops so that she wouldn't have to eat in a hostile environment. Julie was relieved when she visited the ladies, however, as somebody had taken the trouble to scrub the graffiti from the walls, leaving just a vague shadow of the words that had once dominated the cubicle.

At five to five, to Julie's relief, Rita arrived in reception. Julie was delighted at Rita's show of support and they left Belmont Insurance Company together.

'How did it go then?' asked Rita.

'Bad enough but don't worry Rita, they won't get to me this time. I can't wait till we prove that bastard Les guilty; they'll all be licking my arse then, wont' they?'

'Yeah they will, and you just keep thinking that whenever it gets you down.'

'I'll be all right Rita, honestly. It helps having Norma to talk to. I was telling her about Les, and she thinks we should ...'

'You what?'

'I told her about Les dealing drugs. What's wrong with that, Rita?'

'What else have you told her?'

Julie's reply took the form of a guilty expression on her face.

'Jesus Julie! You haven't told her that we're going to break into his flat have you?'

'It's all right Rita, Norma won't tell anyone.'

'Well let's hope she bleedin' doesn't otherwise we're all in the shit! You want to be careful Julie. We still don't know if it was Les that killed Amanda. It might just be a coincidence that he's a drug dealer. That Jackie could still have done it.'

'I think the odds are on Les, Rita. It's just too much of a coincidence. Besides, you're bound to suspect Jacqueline; you're not exactly her number one fan are you?'

'We'll see,' said Rita, '...but just you be careful in the meantime.'

***

Friday 8th August – Tuesday 19th August 1986

For the next couple of weeks Julie, Rita and Vinny observed Les's flat, taking care that they weren't spotted.

One night they had taken up their usual spot behind the garden wall of a derelict house facing Les's apartment. Although it was August, it had been a dull day, and as the evening drew on there was a chill in the air.

Rita shivered. 'How much longer do we have to stay crouched down here?' she asked.

'Not long now,' Julie replied. 'We can't go rushing off yet; we might miss something.'

'Like what?' grumbled Rita. 'There's not much happened in the last hour. It's worse than watching bleedin' paint dry, and I can't feel my feet they're that bleedin' cold.'

'Sshh,' Julie warned as a car approached the building.

They watched in astonishment as the car pulled up outside Les's apartment building and Jacqueline emerged from the back of it, carrying a package.

'What the fuck is she doing here?' exclaimed Rita, unable to contain herself.

Julie touched her arm to silence her and they waited until Jacqueline had entered the building.

'This is a turn up of events isn't it?' asked Julie.

'I thought she didn't know Les that well,' Vinny commented.

'So did we,' said Rita, '...but it looks as though they had more in common than we realised. I bet they bumped Amanda off between them because they were having an illicit affair,' she continued, letting her thoughts run away with her.

'I doubt it,' Julie replied. 'Why would he be interested in that nasty cow when he's got, I mean *had* Amanda.'

'Search me.'

'Let's wait and see what happens,' said Vinny.

They remained behind the wall for what seemed like hours, but was in fact only a few minutes, before they were rewarded by the sight of Jacqueline exiting the building minus the package.

'Whatever that package was, Les has got it now,' said Vinny.

'Right, can we go now?' moaned Rita.

'Julie intuitively felt that the night wasn't over and that perhaps there was more to see. 'Just give it a couple more minutes.'

'Why, what are you waiting for?'

'I don't know, I just want to see what happens.'

Rita tutted and continued to bang her feet on the ground in an exaggerated manner in order to keep them warm. Eventually a man emerged from the building. He was small and wiry with an unkempt appearance, which seemed incongruous with the middle class surroundings. This made Julie think that he may have emerged from Les's flat.

'He looks a bit of a wimp, doesn't he?' whispered Vinny.

'That's just what I was thinking,' Julie replied. 'I bet he's come from Les's flat and I'd love to know what was going on in there that involved both Jacqueline and that man.'

'Me too,' said Vinny and Rita together.

'There's definitely something amiss going on there and I think the sooner we get to the bottom of it the better,' said Julie.

'I'll second that,' said Rita. 'It beats being stuck out here nearly every bloody night freezing to death.'

Julie and Rita looked at Vinny for his reaction.

'How about this Friday then? Les has been out on a Friday for the last two weeks. There must be a lot of business in the clubs when they're packed.'

The girls consented.

***

Wednesday 20th August 1986

The next morning at work Julie watched for Jacqueline entering the building. Just before nine o'clock, she spotted the unmistakable lines of one of Jacqueline's power suits emerging from behind a group of men from the third floor. Their eyes locked, Jacqueline's full of the usual scorn for Julie but not revealing anything untoward. This time Julie did not look away in shame; she held Jacqueline's gaze. After all, she wasn't the one with anything to be ashamed of, she thought, as her eyes followed Jacqueline heading to the lift. Her intense stare seemed to unnerve Jacqueline, until she broke Julie's gaze with a swift turn of her head before marching towards the elevator.

Julie was tempted to shout something at Jacqueline before she disappeared. She would love to have asked what she was doing at Les's flat, but she bit her tongue. "*Mustn't give the game away,*" she thought. "*If Les finds out we're watching his flat, then we'll never find the evidence we need.*"

Julie knew that Norma had been watching both of them but she didn't confide in her. She remembered Rita's reaction the last time she had confided in Norma and decided that it was best to keep her mouth shut. It wouldn't be long now till everybody found out the full facts surrounding Amanda's death. She just had to be patient for a bit longer.

Chapter 26

Friday 22nd August 1986

It was 11 o'clock on Friday night. Julie and Rita were standing in the narrow, deserted street that ran along the side of the Victorian building in which Les's flat was situated. As they had been watching Les for the last two weeks, they had learnt that his flat was at the rear of the building.

'You watch the back and I'll keep an eye on the front,' ordered Rita.

Julie walked down the side street, and stopped just past the end of the gable wall where she had a good view of Les's bedroom. Her heart was pounding as she thought about Vinny breaking into the flat. She watched the window to see if she could spot any sign of him. A cold shiver ran up her spine and she had the eerie feeling that someone was watching her. She turned around but there was nobody there. She was alone, frightened and vulnerable. The memories of the police cell came flooding back but she tried to stifle them so that she could concentrate on the task in hand.

Suddenly, she saw a shadow fall across the bedroom window. "*Vinny,*" she thought, and she peered around her once more to make sure nobody else had seen him.

As she continued to wait she noticed the tension in her muscles. Although the night was again chilly for August, her hands had become clammy. Her breath escaped in sharp bursts.

"*Come on Vinny, what's taking you so long?*" she thought.

A loud screech sounded in the darkness followed by a clatter of metal. She spun around. Her senses were on full alert as she scanned the back entry where the sound had come from. The sight of two large green eyes glaring at her caused her to gasp in alarm, until she realised that it was just a cat that had crashed into a dustbin.

'Bloody cat!' she cursed.

She noticed Rita heading back towards her. 'Will you be quiet Julie?' she commanded as softly as she could. 'I can hear you half a bleedin' mile off. You'll give the game away!'

'It's OK, it was just a cat,' whispered Julie. 'Vinny's in, go back and cover the front.'

Julie watched as Rita returned to the front of the building. She was just beginning to prepare herself for the ordeal of being alone once more when Rita dashed back towards her.

'Fuck, Les is back!' she announced. 'His car's out the front.'

'Shit, what's he doing back? The clubs don't shut for hours yet.'

'He's with a girl,' Rita replied. 'I don't think they've gone in yet. They were still in the car having a snog.'

'Jesus Rita, we'll have to warn Vinny before Les gets back in the flat!'

'How; we can hardly go and knock on the fuckin' front door, can we?'

'I don't know.'

Julie searched around for something that might help. Instinctively she picked up a stone and launched it at the bedroom window. It missed. She tried again.

Rita joined in, scanning the ground for more stones. A hit. The sound of striking glass. Then another. Rita dashed back up the side street. 'I'll see if Les is still there,' she panted.

Julie spotted Vinny at the window. She waved frantically. A bemused expression ensued. Her hands enacted a series of chaotic gestures. Then, recognition! He was trying to open the window. 'Jesus, hurry up Vinny!' she muttered to herself.

Rita returned. 'They're still in the car!'

Her eyes followed Julie's up to the window. 'Hurry up,' they both mouthed. Eventually Vinny managed to open the window and scoured around for something to clamber onto. He spotted a drainpipe about three feet from the bedroom window.

The girls let out a joint sigh of relief as he began to climb over the window-sill, but then watched with bated breath as he tried to bridge the gap between the far edge of the window and the drainpipe. The drainpipe was old and rickety. It juddered about as Vinny grabbed onto it, trying hard to cling on with his left hand and leg. Suddenly, he took the plunge and let go of the window surround with the rest of his body. He veered towards the pipe.

As his right hand grasped it a bracket broke away from the wall releasing a part of the drainpipe, which swung like a pendulum with Vinny grasping it desperately. Once the swinging had diminished and the pipe had stabilised, Vinny climbed down.

Just at that moment, Julie heard a sound coming from the house that backed onto this one. Her and Rita glanced in the direction of the noise and saw a man at the window.

'What the bloody hell's going on?' he shouted.

'Quick Vinny, we've been spotted!' she warned him and he jumped the last few feet to the ground then appeared on top of the back gate. They ran from the house as fast as they could, and soon heard the sound of police sirens in the distance.

***

Friday 22nd August 1986

Les had persuaded the pretty, young girl to come inside his flat with him. *"This could be my lucky night,"* he thought as he ascended the stairs clutching the girl in a passionate embrace. She was a definite improvement on the other women he had been with since he'd lost Amanda. He knew deep down that there would never be a replacement for his Mandy. The trouble was that he was relying too much on drugs since Amanda had died and in his irrational state he couldn't help trying to recapture what he had with her. This led to disappointment for him, which he would then take out on whichever unwitting girl he happened to be with.

When he drew near to his flat he instinctively knew that something was amiss. This was affirmed when he spotted the front door and noticed that it was slightly ajar. He dashed towards the door and saw that the lock had been forced. In his rage he ran into the flat, examining each room for signs of an intruder.

As Les opened the bedroom door he was shocked to find several bags of white powder strewn about the floor and bed. His first reaction was to stop the girl from seeing them. He met her in the hallway and dragged her into the living room ordering her to stay there and not move.

'What's the matter?' she asked, alarmed.

Ignoring her, Les returned to the bedroom and began to stuff the packages into the wardrobe. He could hear the sound of police sirens becoming closer, and he didn't have time to think of an alternative hiding place.

Once the bags were out of sight, he locked the window, shut the bedroom door and went back to the living room.

'What the hell's going on?' asked the girl. 'You frightened the life out of me.'

Les sidled up to her and adopted his "Mr Charming" persona. 'Sorry love, I didn't mean to scare you but someone's done my flat over and I almost caught them in the act. They escaped through the bedroom window and I didn't want you in there in case you got hurt.'

This seemed to reassure the girl and he began to fawn over her, bestowing her with kisses in preparation for the seduction that was to take place later, all the time aware of the imminent arrival of the police.

By the time the doorbell rang Les was cool and calm, and had formulated his story in his mind.

'Oh hello officer,' he said, as he answered the door.

The two policemen introduced themselves, produced their identity cards, and explained that they had received a call from a neighbour reporting that a man had been seen escaping from an upstairs window.

'Really?' asked Les, the surprise evident on his face as he enacted the role of aggrieved victim. 'I must have just missed the bastard then! I knew someone had been in 'cos of the broken lock, and he left the bedroom window open, but I've had a quick look round and there doesn't seem to be anything missing.'

'Are you sure?' asked one of the policemen.

'Yeah, I reckon I must have disturbed him and the bugger's ran off before he had a chance to take anything. I wish I could have got my hands on the bastard that did this though!' and Les pointed towards the broken door jamb.

'Do you mind if we take a quick look round sir?' asked the police officer.

'There's no need. I told you, there's nothing missing.'

'Nevertheless, we'd like to take a look sir.'

'OK, suit yourself, but would you make it snappy lads 'cos I've got something rather tasty cooking if you know what I mean.'

The policemen nodded in recognition as Les imitated the shape of an hourglass figure with his hands. Then he stood aside to let them enter. Their visit was brief, especially when they spotted the vision of beauty that was sitting on Les's sofa. One of the policemen smiled with envy at Les.

Les accompanied them around the flat and tried to remain calm while they searched the bedroom. The first police officer headed towards the bedroom window to look at the burglar's escape route, while the second officer hovered perilously close to the wardrobe. He glanced around the room and was just about to open the wardrobe door when Les diverted him. 'The bedside cabinet!' he announced. 'I'm sure there's something missing from it.'

Once he was satisfied that the officer had moved away from the wardrobe and towards the bedside cabinet, he continued his charade, holding the officer's attention. 'I can't for the life of me think what it was though.'

After a plausible few seconds spent in deep thought, he added, 'Ah yes, that was it; I had a gold chain on there. I'd not been wearing it 'cos the fastener had broken but don't worry, it's not been taken. I remember now, I took it in to be repaired a few days ago. In fact, that reminds me; I must remember to pick it up.'

The policemen looked at him. For a moment they seemed hesitant. Les decided to steer them into action.

'No officers, there's definitely nothing missing but thanks for your concern. He held the bedroom door ajar, beckoning them towards it. They rewarded his quick thinking by stepping in the direction of the door, taking a last glance around the room as they made their exit.

***

Friday 22nd August 1986

Ten minutes earlier Julie, Rita and Vinny had made the frantic dash from Les's apartment so they could be out of sight by the time the police arrived.

'That was a fuckin' close shave!' yelled Rita as they stopped to catch breath.

'You can say that again,' Julie agreed, clutching her chest. 'Are you all right Vinny?'

'Yeah,' he replied as he examined the grazes on his hands. 'I'm just glad we got away in time.'

'Me too. That was a bit too close for comfort. Did you get a chance to do it?'

'I didn't do the fire, but there's drugs all over the bedroom. There was a box full of them, so I emptied it out everywhere.'

'Oh good,' said Julie. 'Let's hope the police see them when they arrive.'

'Shshsh,' shouted Rita. 'Listen.'

'Shit,' said Vinny. 'They're nearly here. Quick, over there.'

They dashed into a nearby garden, ducking down behind the low surrounding wall. They were now a few streets away from Les's flat and they listened as they heard the police car speeding up the street.

'Jesus, that was another close shave,' said Vinny.

'Let's get home now,' said Rita. 'I've had enough for one night. We've done the job now anyway.'

'We're not going anywhere,' Julie challenged. 'Let's stay put. I want to make sure they arrest the bastard. I wouldn't put it past him to wangle his way out of this one.'

Rita and Vinny reluctantly agreed, and after a few minutes they heard a vehicle coming up the street again.

'Quick,' said Vinny. 'Get your heads down,' but Julie couldn't resist a quick peek over the wall as the vehicle passed.

Once they had heard it round the bend at the end of the street, Julie sat down on the grass and let out a hiss of disappointment. 'It was the police car,' she said.

'So?' asked Rita.

'Les wasn't in it. That bastard's squirmed his way out of it again!'

'He must have heard the sirens and knew they were coming,' said Vinny.

Julie began to hammer her fists against the wall. 'I'm not giving up!' she yelled. 'I'll get that drug-pushing, murdering bastard if it's the last thing I do. If he thinks he can get away with killing Amanda and then taking some tart up to his flat with Amanda only just cold, he's got another think coming!'

***

Early Saturday morning 23rd August 1986

It took Julie a while to calm down after the attempted break-in. Vinny had suggested going back to his place so that they could talk without fear of being watched. Julie had taken some persuading due to her paranoia of being spotted by Clare's school friend, Melanie Butterworth, but they had managed to convince her that it wasn't a problem. It was more important to get out of the present vicinity. If anybody saw them hanging about the streets near to Les's flat, then it was inevitable that they would be linked to the break-in.

The three of them talked inexorably and before they knew it, it was half past two in the morning. Julie surprised both Vinny and Rita by her strength of feeling about Amanda's death, and no matter how much they tried to dissuade her, she was adamant that they should repeat their attempt to prove Les guilty.

Eventually Vinny and Rita had to agree with Julie, because she had stated that if they didn't help her she would risk doing it alone, such was her resolve. However, they would act swiftly, fixing the date for the following weekend because they reasoned that it wouldn't be expected so soon after their previous attempt. They changed the night to a Saturday instead of Friday, because people were bound to be more alert on the same day of the week as the previous break-in.

Julie had also insisted that she would be the one to commit the deed as she couldn't put Vinny through that trauma again. Knowing that she was impossible to dissuade in her present frame of mind, Vinny had grudgingly conceded.

When Julie went to the toilet, Rita had a quick word with Vinny.

'I don't think we're gonna talk her out of this Vinny. She seems dead set on making sure he goes down. I just hope she's up to it.'

'I know, I can't understand it. Why can't she just let the dust settle and find another job? It's not as if she has to live with the guilt of it. We all know that you and Julie didn't kill Amanda.'

'I know, but maybe there's always that doubt in her mind and the only way she can live with what's happened is to shift the blame. Let's hope we do find him guilty, 'cos if we don't I think it'll crack her up altogether. I'd love to know what that Jackie's got to do with it as well. I always thought she was a spiteful bitch. It wouldn't surprise me if her and Les were in it together; two of a kind.'

Vinny shrugged by way of a response so Rita continued.

'There's one thing for sure Vinny, trying to catch him is the only thing that's keeping her going at the moment, and until we do, neither of us is going to find any peace.'

***

Saturday 23rd August 1986

Inspector Bowden had received news of the reported break-in at Leslie Stevens' flat. Recognising that the home of Leslie Stevens was the same property connected with the Amanda Morris case, one of the PC's had been sure to inform him as the Senior Investigating Officer.

The inspector knew that there could be a possible connection but no matter how much he rattled his brains he couldn't think what that connection might be. He went through the facts in his mind, but he had already spent countless hours trying to piece together the evidence and his thoughts were just a jumbled mass, resulting in a throbbing headache. He already had his suspects but couldn't prove anything. Why would they want to break into the flat though? It just didn't add up.

The update told him nothing. A neighbour had reported a man seen climbing out of the bedroom window of Leslie Stevens' apartment, but the description of the man was vague. When Leslie Stevens had returned to the apartment, the intruder had already left, possibly disturbed when Mr Stevens returned early from his night out. Officers had carried out a search of the premises but nothing seemed to be missing. This was verified by the owner, Mr Leslie Stevens.

He sighed and reached for the bottle of paracetamols in his desk drawer, taking two out and washing them down with the remains of his cup of coffee. He was beginning to have his doubts about this case.

Chapter 27

Les had been watching the woman for the last few days. He would like to have watched her for a while longer to get a feel for her movements, but time was against him. He couldn't afford to wait any longer. If she went shooting her mouth off to the police he would be finished. Not having established a regular pattern to her comings and goings, he'd had to wait around the corner for two hours on the off chance of catching her leaving her home. It was fortunate that it was evening so there weren't many people around, otherwise he might have raised suspicion. This wasn't the sort of area where people hung about on street corners.

He'd been on edge since the night when she'd called round to his flat on the pretext of returning an LP that she'd borrowed off Amanda and forgot to bring back. Trust that stupid Ernie to ask for some gear in front of her, the dickhead. Fancy doing it in front of Jacqueline of all people! There was a chance she might not have known what Ernie was talking about. After all, gear could have meant anything and if she wasn't into drugs she might have thought he was talking about something else. But the more he thought about it, he knew that he couldn't afford to take the chance, knowing that at any moment she might realise what had been going on.

It's a good job she fancied him. She was so busy trying to sidle up to him on the couch that she didn't notice him glare at Ernie and quickly change the subject. Ever since Amanda had died she'd been calling round to the flat with some excuse or another – sad bitch! She'd even given him her number; in case he might be feeling down one night and need a sympathetic ear, she'd said. So he rang her and played along just to keep her sweet. The ugly cow made him want to puke but it was the only way to gain her trust and buy some time until he had a chance to do something about her.

When she left her home he began to follow her. He'd done a recce of the surrounding streets a couple of days ago, so he knew where the obscure places were. Unfortunately, these types of houses didn't have back entries, but there was a grass verge surrounded by plenty of bushes on the way to the bus-stop, and a quiet passageway behind a row of shops a couple of streets further on.

He continued to pursue her, hanging back so she wouldn't see him. His heart began to beat erratically. He knew that the moment had arrived. Within the next few minutes he must sort her out otherwise he might not get another chance. Luck was with him as she began to head in the direction of the grass verge.

"Just a couple of minutes more, and she'll be there," he thought. But to his dismay she turned off into a side street before reaching the grass verge. He knew now that any possibility of taking her by surprise and dragging her into the bushes was gone. Although there was a chance she might still pass the row of shops, there was also a chance that she might not.

Fear gripped him. He daren't miss this opportunity! But how else could he carry it off? Then he seized on an idea. He sped towards her till he was within hearing range. As soon as he was near enough he called out her name. She peered over her shoulder, recognition evident in her eyes followed by perplexity at his presence. Before she could voice her concerns, however, he was upon her. Taking advantage of her momentary confusion, he sprang behind her, covering her mouth with his left hand while jabbing the sharp end of a knife into her back with his other.

'Not a fuckin' sound, or you're a gonna!' he ordered.

'Why are you doing this?' she pleaded.

'I said not a fuckin' sound!' he demanded, prodding her viciously with the knife.

He led her through the street, thankful that there was nobody about. His mind began to go into overdrive. What was the quickest way to get her to a secluded spot? They had already walked away from the grass verge. He knew, however, that if he continued to lead her to the end of this street, by turning right at the bottom, they might still reach the row of shops.

They headed in that direction, their progress slow and awkward. He released his hand from her mouth gripping her left arm instead, so that he could walk slightly to the side of her and therefore speed the journey. Before doing so he warned her again not to speak. He kept the knife pointing in her back with his right hand, visible from behind but hidden from anybody ahead of them. Because of their close proximity they would appear just like a courting couple.

As they walked along he hissed a barrage of insults at her, 'Thought you were gonna step into Mandy's shoes did you, you cheeky bitch? She's worth a hundred of you. I don't go in for ugly birds. Mandy was special. Do you hear?'

'Yes,' Jacqueline replied, her voice trembling.

'Shut it, I don't even want to listen to you! You disgust me. You're an ugly, revolting bitch. Now just keep fuckin' moving and keep your trap shut.'

When they reached the end of the road and turned right, Les was relieved to see the row of shops in the distance, highlighted by a billboard and wastepaper bin on the pavement. But his relief soon turned to consternation when he spotted a group of youths gathered outside one of the shops. It was obviously either a chip shop or off licence, which must have been shut when he did his recce, so he hadn't realised the implication. He cursed himself for his stupidity.

'You shout anything to that lot and you're dead meat!' he murmured into Jacqueline's ear. 'If you do as you're told I won't hurt you.'

As they neared the shops his grip tightened, mirroring his unease. He dug the knife deeper into her back, so that it was no longer just a threat but was now beginning to cut through her clothing and was causing her a great deal of discomfort.

Les figured that once they reached the shops he would have to drag her along the side of the buildings and into the back passageway, out of view. He estimated that the gang of youths were about three shops down and he knew that any noise or suspicious movement on approach to the shops would raise the alarm.

They were now about twenty yards from the shops and her co-operation was vital. He marched her nearer still. The youths were now at the point of recognition. Les was sweating profusely with the realisation that, should one of them turn and look in his direction, they would be able to give a good description.

When they reached the shops he was thankful that she didn't put up a struggle. Maybe she had believed his words of assurance that no harm would come to her if she did as she was told. He had lied of course.

His deceit became evident as soon as they reached the passageway at the rear of the shops. He withdrew the knife so that he could turn her round and get a good swing at the front of her torso. There the flesh was softer and the blade would penetrate more easily. Now she did put up a struggle, trying to resist the relentless thrusting of the knife, but it was too late. Jacqueline bled to death in the grimy back entry, surrounded by the detritus of human life.

Once he was satisfied that she wouldn't survive the attack, he covered her body with an old fencing panel and any other rubble he could find. He hoped that by doing so he would prolong discovery of the body for at least a couple of days so that he wouldn't be fresh in anyone's memory. Before he left the back passageway he quickly removed his jacket, turned it inside out and put it back on. That way he would ensure that most of the blood was hidden and in the dark hopefully no-one would notice that he was wearing his jacket inside-out. Now he just needed to make sure that nobody took a detailed look at him while he was making his escape.

As Les walked away from the body he was overcome by a strange feeling of euphoria. He had done it! He had killed in cold blood. He, Les Stevens, had committed the ultimate crime, and he was thrilled by the thought that, should the need arise, he would have no problem in doing it again.

**

Saturday 30th August 1986

Saturday night came quickly; too quickly. Julie was filled with a dread, the power of which she had never experienced before. But she knew that she couldn't back out now; she had to see this thing through!

They met at Vinny's house and set off together. The three of them sat in silence during the journey until Vinny stopped the car a few of blocks from Les's flat as he had done the previous week.

'Right, here goes,' said Rita.

'Are you sure you *still* want to do this?' Vinny asked Julie, but the look of determination in her eyes was enough to persuade him that she was still adamant.

They made their way towards Les's flat, Julie's heart beating wildly. When the building was in view, Julie felt a wave of panic rise through her body and towards her throat, constricting the muscles. She swallowed hard as though trying to quell the panic before it threatened to overwhelm her. They checked to make sure that the lights were out in Les's flat and his car was not parked outside before Julie proceeded further.

Nobody spoke as she went towards the building. She knew that Rita and Vinny had accepted that this was something she had to do. She approached the front door slowly. Extracting a credit card from her bag, she began to slide it into the narrow gap at the side of the door, forcing the lock to shift. She was surprised at the ease with which the door slid open, and she stepped inside and shut it behind her.

She paused for a moment, wiping her sweating palms on her clothing. While gazing around the large hallway she took deep breaths in order to calm herself. She noticed that there were doors to three flats on the ground floor, but she knew that Les's flat was upstairs. Vinny had gone over the details several times with her. She reviewed his instructions in her mind, "*Top of the stairs, full turn at the halfway landing, top of the next flight, turn left as though coming back on yourself, follow the stair railing, and Les's flat is the first door on the right.*"

Julie approached the stairway nervously and began to ascend. First step, OK. Step two, all right. Step three, getting there. Before she had completed her fourth step she heard the sound of a door opening at one of the ground floor flats. In the space of less than a second, she assimilated the facts. "*This person will come out of the door, spot me, unrecognised. They will assume I am a visitor. What would I do if that was the case? Answer: turn around and smile.*"

She enacted the role, smiling fleetingly at the middle-aged man, then continued climbing the stairs. She could feel the man's eyes on her for a moment, then heard his footsteps heading towards the main front door. "*Thank God I shut it,*" she thought, knowing that by leaving the door unlocked, she may have aroused his suspicion. Within a moment he was gone, but Julie's anxiety remained.

Two steps from the landing. One step. Landing. Turn. One more flight to go. She continued warily, her legs trembling. At the top of the second flight she turned left as Vinny had instructed, her clammy hand clutching the rail. She spotted the first door on the right; Les's flat. That was it.

Julie eyed the door. It was solid and the lock was of a type that would require a lot more work than the front door. A new lock must have been fitted since Vinny's break-in, as it didn't fit the description he had given her. She opened her oversized handbag, which she and Vinny had packed with tools. As she searched for a suitable instrument with which to prise the doorjamb, the tools clanked about. Julie shuddered at the rattling sound of metal on metal. She extracted a screwdriver and began to whittle away at the wood surrounding the lock.

The wood was hard and after a couple of minutes of chipping away, she had made little progress. She glanced around her. Julie could vaguely make out the entrance to another flat on the other side of the stair railings. She realised that if someone was to walk out of that flat, she would have great difficulty explaining herself. But her willpower took over.

Julie continued to work at the wood, gradually breaking off tiny pieces. Then, as she became frustrated her movements grew fast and frantic. She hacked away, feeling immense fulfilment as the wood began to fragment until she had worked a gap big enough for the door lock to give way. She gave the door a satisfied push and it swung with ease.

"*So far, so good,*" she thought, stepping inside the flat. The first room she wanted to explore was the bedroom to find out whether Les was still storing drugs there. She recalled Vinny's instructions; "*second door on the right.*"

Unhesitating, Julie set about her business. She pushed the bedroom door open and was horrified by the sight that met her. In the semi-darkness she saw Les sprawled across the bed leering at her. 'Hello Julie,' he sneered. 'I've been expecting you.'

Her first instinct was to run and she spun around. Before she had a chance to get very far, however, Les leapt up and grabbed her from behind. He threw her viciously down onto the bed and jumped on top of her, using his hands to pin her down by her wrists. She saw the madness in his eyes as she lay with her face inches from his.

Julie struggled to free herself but he tightened his grip on her wrists until they felt sore. To her surprise he began to laugh. It was loud, raucous laughter; the laughter of a madman. She guessed that he was as high as a kite on something.

'I've got you where I want you now, haven't I?' he taunted, '... and I can do anything I want with you.' He squeezed her right breast to emphasise his point. 'But before we have a bit of fun', he continued, '... you've got some explaining to do, like for instance, what the fuck are you doing in my flat, and why did you wreck the place last Friday?'

As the realisation of his intentions hit her, Julie stared at him in terror. He had obviously shifted his car and kept the lights off to make it appear that the flat was empty.

'Come on, explain yourself!' he commanded.

She could hear the aggression in his voice, but was still taken by surprise when he struck her forcefully across her face.

'Right, start talking, you dirty slut, or next time it'll be my fuckin' fist!'

She knew that if he found out the real reason for her visit, he would do her some serious damage, so she tried to stall him, hoping that Vinny would come looking for her.

'I wanted some speed,' she improvised. 'I knew I could get it here; you're well known around town, aren't you?'

'Well why not fuckin' buy it down town like everyone else then?'

Julie screamed as she felt another sharp blow across her face, then he grabbed her by the hair as he carried on talking. 'I'm not fuckin' stupid you know! I know why you came here. You're trying to set me up, for a murder that you fuckin' did.'

Despite her terror, the accusation angered Julie and she yelled back at him. 'I didn't kill Amanda, I'm not a murderer!' Smack! She winced with pain as his fist hit her full on the face.

'Don't tell fuckin' lies!' he shouted. He was now becoming terrifying as he continued to bawl at her. 'You and your fuckin' slag of a friend killed Mandy, and now you're going to pay for it!'

He ripped her blouse open, and began laughing again. 'I'll teach you not to try and stitch me up, you cheeky bitch!'

'No!' Julie screamed. 'Leave me alone.'

He covered her mouth with his right hand while he writhed on top of her, pulling her skirt up with his other hand. She put up a tremendous struggle, and he howled in pain as she sank her teeth into his hand. Before he had a chance to recover, she swiftly brought her knee up to his groin. While he gripped his genitals and doubled over in agony, she pushed her way past him and tried to make her escape.

Vinny met her in the hallway and was enraged when he saw the state she was in; her face red and swollen, blood pouring from her nose, her shoes missing and her blouse torn apart.

'Where is the bastard? I'll fuckin' kill him!' he shouted.

Julie watched in despair as Vinny set about Les, raining blows to his head and body.

'That's enough Vinny!' she shouted. 'He's not worth it!'

Vinny carried on and didn't stop until he had spent his last ounce of energy. Then he grabbed Les by the lapels, hoisting him up as he threatened him. 'If I ever catch you near Julie again, I swear I'll be back to finish the job!'

He released Les who slumped back onto the bed with blood pouring from his face.

'Julie, call the police while I keep an eye on him!' Vinny ordered.

'And just what do you think you'll tell them?' Les sniggered. 'How will you explain what you're doing here, especially when I tell them that you've come to buy drugs?'

'You bastard!' shouted Vinny and he went to hit him once more.

'Stop it!' cried Julie. 'He's had enough and this won't get us anywhere.'

'All right, call the police then,' Vinny replied.

'It's no good Vinny; he's got us by the short and curlies. How are we going to prove anything? If they find his drugs, they'll link us to them. I'm already a bloody murder suspect as it is!'

Les gave a satisfied smirk on hearing her words.

'That's right,' he mocked. 'Looks like you'll have to go down for Mandy's murder after all.'

'Oh no!' said Julie. 'This isn't over yet. We know that you killed Amanda and I'm gonna make sure you go down for it if it's the last thing I do! Come on Vinny, let's go,' she sighed.

'Good luck,' Les uttered sarcastically as Julie left the room with Vinny following.

Vinny returned and gave Les one last thrashing. He managed to knock him back down and change his smirk to a grimace before Julie led him away to the sound of Les shouting, 'I haven't finished with you yet, bitch. I'll fuckin' have you!'

***

'Shit!' said Rita. 'What the hell have you two been up to? You look as if you've gone a few rounds.'

'The bastard was there waiting for me,' Julie replied, attempting to wipe the blood from her nose with the back of her hand.

'You're joking!' Then, as Rita noticed Julie's torn clothing, realisation hit her. 'Oh, Julie, he didn't did he?'

'No, fortunately Vinny got there in time but he gave me a few slaps and frightened the bloody life out of me. We're gonna have to get away from here quick. Vinny gave him a good hiding. I think he would have killed him if I hadn't stopped him, and if the neighbours overheard all the racket, the police will be here in a flash.'

'That's what we want, isn't it?'

'No, it's no good Rita. The crafty bastard's got it all sussed. He threatened that if we called the police he'd tell them that we'd come here to buy drugs from him and we'd end up in just as much trouble as him.'

'He wouldn't do that, though,' said Rita. 'He knows he's got too much to lose.'

'Can we afford to take that chance?'

Rita and Vinny remained silent.

'Yeah, but don't worry,' said Julie. 'We'll get him; I'm gonna make sure of it, if it's the last thing I do.'

On hearing these words Rita and Vinny looked at each other with an air of foreboding.

Chapter 28

Sunday 31st August 1986

Julie's parents weren't aware of her injuries until the following morning as she had arrived home late on the Saturday night and disposed of her torn blouse. She made the excuse of tripping over a rug at Vinny's house and banging her face on the edge of the dining table. Despite her mother's comment about bad luck following her around, Julie could tell that her father wasn't convinced. However, they seemed to have accepted her deceit and fortunately didn't pursue the matter. Nevertheless, Betty insisted on fussing and applying Witch Hazel every few hours to ease the swelling.

As the day rolled by Julie tried to find solace by absorbing herself in her familiar family routine. She had spent the day indoors and just finished one of her mother's scrumptious Sunday roasts. It was while she was helping her mother with the washing-up that they heard her father's shouts of astonishment. They dashed in the direction of his yelling and found him in the living room transfixed to the television screen. Their eyes followed his, and they watched and listened as a reporter described the grisly scene where a savage murder had taken place. It was the killing of a young woman just a few streets from her home. She had worked at the Belmont Insurance Company. Her name was Jacqueline Bartlett, and she had been on her way to her grandmother's home when the killer had struck.

Julie felt herself heave and thought she was going to vomit. Her mother led her to the sofa and beckoned her to sit down.

'Is that one of Amanda's friends?' asked Bill, but Betty motioned him to keep quiet.

'I need to get out mam, it's stifling in here!' said Julie.

Before either of her parents could stop her she had her coat and shoes on and was out of the door. She pounded the streets for a good half hour trying to make sense of it all. She experienced a series of emotions: confusion, despair, fear.

Eventually her feet led her instinctively in the direction of Rita's house. She knew as soon as she saw Rita that she too had heard the news; she looked pale and drawn.

'I can't believe it Julie!' Rita kept saying.

'I'm still in shock myself Rita. There's one thing for sure; it was no accident, but what I can't understand is, why? Were Les and Jackie in it together?'

'Maybe Les found out she killed Amanda and it was his way of getting revenge,' Rita suggested.

'Unless she found out too much so he had to get rid of her.'

'I don't know. Maybe in his warped mind he blames us all for Amanda dying. Jesus Julie, he might be after the bloody lot of us, one by one!'

Julie stayed for coffee at Rita's house in the hope that it might calm them both down a little. It didn't. While she was there she rang Vinny who, surprisingly, hadn't heard the news, but once she put him in the picture he was just as shocked as her and Rita.

He suggested that she get a taxi back home just to be on the safe side, which she complied with, realising what a risk she had placed herself under while she had been pounding the streets. Les might even be out there now, watching them and waiting for the chance to dispose of another one of them.

When she arrived home, she wasn't surprised to find Inspector Bowden and Sergeant Drummond there.

'I wondered how long it would take,' she commented cynically.

They didn't take her down to the station; they didn't have much to go on. Instead they interviewed her at home. This time the questioning was brief. Inspector Bowden seemed flummoxed at the fact that she had a good alibi for the night of Jacqueline's murder. Her parents backed her up as she had been watching TV with them on the night of Jacqueline's death. While they were there they also questioned her about the marks on her face but she stuck to her story about tripping over a carpet at Vinny's house knowing that he would back her. She had already discussed it with him and Rita on the previous night in case her parents might raise the subject at some point.

Within less than a half hour the police were gone. Julie could not help but notice that their approach seemed to have changed towards her. It wasn't that they held her in any higher regard; Inspector Bowden still spoke to her as though she was the scum of the earth. The difference was, she concluded, that although he thought her capable of killing Amanda as part of a foolish, irresponsible prank that had gone wrong, he didn't, she felt, find her capable of cold blooded murder.

The person that had done this was sick, a person for whom violence was a way of life. She thought about Les's anger on the night that her and Rita had taken Amanda home, and his maniac behaviour when he had her at his mercy in his flat. She could picture the madness in his eyes and the thought made her tremble. He was fearsome. She could understand why Amanda had always been so compliant towards him. If anything, Julie was more certain now that it was Les who had killed both Amanda and Jacqueline. Despite her fear she remained determined to prove him guilty and see him behind bars.

***

Tuesday 2nd September 1986

It started the following Tuesday. Julie had been back at work for a few weeks and was finding it easier to cope. She had become accustomed to the blank stares and people ignoring her. The scowls and insinuating comments had ceased except for Jacqueline's friends. It was as though the majority of people realised there may be a connection between Amanda and Jacqueline's deaths and that, as Julie had an alibi for the night of Jacqueline's murder, it was possible that she wasn't responsible for Amanda's death either. Some people had begun to say hello to Julie in the mornings. The odd one had even ventured to say a few words to her, although the whole office was still reeling from the shock of the second killing and the vicious way in which it was committed.

'It's nice to see you getting back to normal,' Norma commented. 'I was beginning to think you'd never smile again.'

Then, noticing the wry expression on Julie's face, she checked herself. 'Oh I know you've not had a lot to smile about lately Julie.

It can't have been easy for you, but it is a relief to see that you're starting to get over things. I was getting worried about you.'

Julie chose not to reply. How could she disappoint Norma by confessing that she still thought about Amanda each and every day, still had to fight back the tears sometimes, and still felt determined that she would prove Les Stevens guilty and clear her own name?

Julie had still not ventured to the canteen, and she doubted that she ever would. For her that place symbolised the way she had felt in those first few painful weeks when Amanda's death was fresh in her mind. It was a time when even the mention of Amanda's name could reduce her to tears, and she had been overwhelmed by guilt. She did not need reminding of how she had felt and she didn't need the animosity of Jacqueline's friends to remind everybody what had happened.

She had had a busy morning, even managing to have a laugh with a few of the customers, when she picked up the call. For a moment she couldn't hear anything, then a distorted voice came on the line. Although the caller had disguised his speech, she could hear the next word loud and clear. 'Murderer!' the voice shouted. Then, after waiting a few seconds to gauge her reaction, the caller hung up. Julie yanked off her headset and hurled it across the desk as though it was contaminated.

'What the hell's the matter Julie?' asked Norma.

Julie had to compose herself before replying. 'It was a malicious caller, Norma. Someone's trying to torment me. Why don't they leave me alone?'

'What did they say?'

Julie looked at Norma, her face bearing a pained expression as she uttered the word, 'Murderer.'

'The bloody swines! Who was it? What did they sound like? I bet it was one of Jacqueline's cronies, wasn't it?'

'No Norma. It was an external caller, and I couldn't tell who it was. I think it was a man, but he was using something to disguise his voice.'

'Right, let's ring the police then. I bet it was that Les.'

'I can't do that Norma.'

'Why not, for God's sake?'

'Because I agree with you, I think it was Les. The police won't believe me, and even if they do, they'll find out about us breaking in his flat. We'll end up in more trouble.'

Julie spoke in a flurry hoping to bypass the mention of the break-in, but Norma soon picked up on that. 'You didn't go ahead with it, did you?' she asked, disgusted.

Julie look shamefaced, but knew that she would have to admit to Norma that she had gone against her advice and initiated the break-ins at Les's flat. She hung her head as she related the whole sorry tale to Norma. 'So you see, I can't go to the police,' she added.

Julie had hardly had a chance to recover from this latest ordeal when a package arrived at reception for her. The courier was dressed from head to toe in motorcycle gear, including a helmet. He left the package in such a hurry that it was difficult to notice what he looked like, except that he was tall and well-built.

Julie stared after him in astonishment as she began to open the package. It was similar to a shoe box in shape and size, but it was bright red and the lid was sealed by sticky tape. Julie tore the sticky tape excitedly, half thinking that Vinny had decided to surprise her.

She pulled back the lid and found to her horror that there was a dead rat inside, with a cut down its abdomen and its insides hanging out. Fresh blood from the rat stained the piece of paper that was underneath it. Julie screamed and launched the box across the floor.

Norma didn't speak at first; she got up from her chair and took a look inside the box to see what had alarmed Julie so much. On spotting the dead rat she fled from the building trying to catch up with the courier. A few seconds later she returned out of breath.

'It's too late, the bugger's gone,' she said.

'Get rid of it!' said Julie.

'No, you must keep it; it's evidence.'

'I can't keep it, I can't go to the police; I've told you!'

'Julie, if this carries on, you'll have to go to the police love. You can't let them get away with that.'

Julie decided not to argue any further. Instead she remained quiet for the rest of the day, retreating into herself as she had done once before.

The day dragged by and Julie couldn't wait until it was home time. Finally it reached five o'clock. She set off for the ten-minute walk to the bus stop, but as she rounded the first bend, she had an eerie sensation that someone was following her.

She took a swift glance behind her, but the street was crowded with office workers making their way home and it was difficult to spot if anyone in particular was tailing her. Julie continued to walk purposefully telling herself not to be silly, that no-one would try to harm her on such a busy street, and that she would soon be on the bus home. "*I'm just a bit freaked out by what's happened today,*" she tried to convince herself.

She couldn't shake off the creepy feeling, however, especially as she could hear heavy footsteps in close proximity and they seemed to be gaining ground. As she approached the end of a row of offices, she couldn't resist the urge to take another quick peak as she made an exaggerated turn around the corner while glancing to the side.

It was then that she spotted him. She couldn't have given an accurate description, the glimpse had been so fleeting, but she got the overall impression of a young man, tall, thickset and dark; dark hair, dark eyes, dark clothing. "*Could it have been the courier?*" she thought.

Her thoughts gave rise to panic and she began to quicken her step, trying to increase the gap of seven or eight feet between her and the man. He responded by speeding up as well. She wanted to run, but thought that to do so would let him know that she had seen him. Perhaps if she could try to pretend that she hadn't noticed, maybe she could trick him and make her escape. She was approaching another corner and, as soon as she had rounded it, she sprinted a few yards, then continued walking at a brisk pace when she felt he was in view, hoping that he wouldn't notice the increased distance between them. However, he soon narrowed the gap.

Julie was becoming increasingly frightened. She searched around for a means of escape. She noticed the many people making their way home from work and began to weave in between them trying to hide from view of the man. After a few seconds of dodging, another quick glance backwards told her that she had not succeeded; he was even closer. Her ploy of refusing to acknowledge his pursuit had not worked either.

There was only one thing left to do; she began to sprint, barging into people as she tried to pass them as fast as possible. She could still sense his presence, hear his heavy footsteps, and imagined the feel of his quickened breathing on the back of her neck.

Julie had become so flustered that she could no longer think rationally, and in her haste to be rid of him, she took a turning into an unknown street. It was not one she would normally use, but she was desperate to shake him off.

As soon as she ran into the street she knew she had made a mistake. It was deserted. There was just her and the man, and he was gaining ground. She continued to sprint. Then she found the reason why the street was so empty in the rush hour. It was a dead end.

She carried on running. Hoping for an answer. Searching for a means of escape. But the only doors were those leading out from stores. Fire exits, she thought. The type that lead out of the store, but don't allow anyone to go in. She tried one anyway. She gasped in horror as the door refused to budge, and she felt the man moving in on her. Her sweaty palms began to hammer frenziedly against the glass. Within seconds she had caught the attention of a lady who approached the door from inside the store.

'Help me! Open the door!' Julie cried.

The lady rushed to open the door, her curiosity aroused by Julie's frantic state. It was then that the man stepped into view, and Julie felt him brush against her arm as she fled into the store, leaving them behind. She could hear words being exchanged between him and the lady, and made the most of the few seconds of respite.

Once inside the store Julie began to dash in and out of the displays in order to keep herself out of the man's view. Then she spotted a rail full of evening dresses, standing against the wall of the shop. Julie dashed towards it and hid amongst the garments. The length of the gowns ensured that she was well hidden. She huddled tightly against the wall gasping from exertion and fear.

Julie adjusted the gowns in order to form a peephole. The view from it was limited, but she couldn't risk making it any larger in case she exposed her hiding place. The time spent in her hidey-hole seemed like an age. For a long while there was no sound or movement close to Julie, until she heard the sound of footsteps approaching followed by voices, female voices. Then she noticed them; two middle-aged women fumbling amongst the garments.

'Ooh, this one's lovely Vera,' said one of them as she admired a dress on a nearby rail.

Julie could see part of the woman's back, but the other woman, Vera, was in full view. As Vera approached Julie's hiding place, she stopped and glanced back, admiring the gown. 'Oh yes, Lil. I like that. What about these ones over here?'

She then continued on her mission to examine the rail that Julie was secreted behind.

Before she had a chance to reach the rail, however, Julie noticed a swish of material in her peripheral vision as Lil dragged out the dress she had been admiring. Lil stepped away from the rail and held the dress up against her body, and Julie caught full sight of her.

'What do you think Vera?' she asked.

This action was enough to command Vera's attention, and she approached her friend, cooing in admiration at the vision of the stunning gown against Lil's dark complexion.

'Should I try it on?' asked Lil.

'Ooh yes, it's beautiful.'

To Julie's relief they then made their way towards the changing rooms. She watched until they disappeared from her field of vision, then another shape stepped into the picture. Tall, dark, thickset; it was the man who had pursued her into the shop.

'Oh no!' thought Julie as he faded in and out of view, scanning the aisles. Then he passed in front of her rail and she drew a sharp breath. Within seconds he had gone: it hadn't occurred to him to search behind the rows of clothing. She exhaled in relief.

Julie didn't leave her hiding place straightaway however. She wanted to be sure that he was no longer there, so it was some minutes before she extricated herself from amongst the dresses and began to walk tentatively through the aisles. A faint smile crossed her lips as she saw Vera and Lil standing at the cashier's till chatting; Lil clutching the beautiful garment. Julie couldn't see any sign of the man, so she made her way to the exit at the far side of the store.

She left the store in a hurry and scanned the street for any signs of the man. Julie was now about fifty metres from her bus stop. Once she had reached it, however, she kept going. She was too close to the store for comfort and she figured that if the man had been trailing her before today then he might know which bus she caught for her trip home. Instead, she carried on to the next stop, then the next, walking rapidly and looking back at intervals to see if she could spot her bus, or the man.

When the bus appeared Julie was a good hundred metres from the nearest bus stop, and she had to gather speed to make sure that she caught it. She joined the queue, which now consisted of a couple of remaining passengers. As soon as she stopped running her legs began to buckle and she had to grip the edge of the bus shelter to stop herself falling over.

It was only when she had paid her fare that another thought occurred to her; if he had been observing her and knew which bus she caught, then he might be on the bus already. The colour that had flushed her face after her jog to the bus stop now drained away as she searched amongst the passengers. When she was satisfied that the man wasn't amongst them, she took a seat next to an elderly lady.

The lady turned and smiled at Julie before commenting, 'Make yourself comfortable love. You look as though you could do with a sit down.'

Chapter 29

Tuesday 2nd September 1986

By the time Julie reached home she had composed herself and managed to put on an appearance of normality for the benefit of her family. She didn't wish to confide in her parents about the events of the last day because she didn't want to worry them. "*Haven't I caused enough trouble for them already?*" she asked herself.

She was seeing Vinny that evening so she didn't have to keep up the charade for long. As soon as tea was finished and the dishes washed, Julie was in her room getting changed and made-up. At a little after 6.30pm Julie kissed her parents and Clare goodbye and promised to see them later.

Julie took a taxi to Vinny's house. Although he didn't live far away she didn't want to take any chances after the day that she had experienced. Vinny was already at the door waiting for her.

'I thought I heard a car, and wondered who it was,' he announced. 'What are you doing catching a taxi you lazy sod?' he teased.

The expression on Julie's face told him something wasn't right.

As soon as they were inside the house he challenged her. 'What's wrong Julie?'

'Nothing Vinny,' she replied.

'Come on Julie. I know there's something wrong. Is it something to do with why you got a taxi here?'

'Sort of,' she began. 'It's nothing really. I just didn't want to take any chances, that's all. I've had a bit of a bad day. Someone rang work, and I thought someone was following me home. But it was probably me imagining it. Anyway I'm OK now, so what's the problem?'

Vinny's reaction surprised her. In no time at all he was standing facing her, gripping her arms. 'Don't shut me out Julie. Don't fuckin' shut me out, not again! I want to help you. Can't you see that? But if you're just gonna clam up every time things are bad, then how the fuck can I help?'

'You're hurting me!' she cried.

Vinny released his grip and stared down at the floor, embarrassed. Then, raising his head so that his eyes met Julie's, he said, 'I'm sorry Julie. I didn't mean to hurt you but I need to know what's happening. I don't want it to be like it was before when you wouldn't even see me let alone talk to me!'

'What did you expect Vinny? I was cracking up. It's not surprising after what's happened. And now I've got some fuckin' nutcase after me and I don't know what to do!' As she spoke the words she began to sob, 'I'm scared Vinny. I'm really scared and I don't know how much more of this I can take!'

Vinny began to comfort her and when the tears had subsided, he allowed her to relate the day's events as he listened patiently.

He responded by asking, 'Are you sure it wasn't Les following you.'

'Positive,' Julie replied.

'Then he must have put someone up to it. It's got to be Les. He knows we're onto him after what went on at his flat and he's running scared. Do you think the man who followed you was the same one that delivered the rat?'

'Probably,' said Julie, recoiling at the mention of the rat.

'Right, then we'll have to do something about it. We'll have to report it to the police.'

'Not now Vinny, I'm tired. I just want a nice quiet night when I don't have to think about it.'

'We'll have to do it soon Julie. I think this is all connected with Les. He's already killed Amanda and Jacqueline, and God knows what he might have done to you when he found you in his flat! We can't risk leaving it. What about tomorrow? Can you get the day off?'

'No, not at such short notice. Besides, I've had enough time off recently. We'll have to do it after work. Oh Vinny, I'm so frightened!'

Vinny gently took hold of her shoulders. 'Don't be,' he said. 'We'll make sure there's always someone with you outside work. Don't walk anywhere, get taxis and don't go out alone.

'Chances are he won't do anything to you Julie, not when you've got people with you. Anyway, as long as he's still trying to pin the blame on you and Rita, you're safe.'

'I wish I felt reassured by that Vinny.'

'Don't worry, it'll all be over soon. I'll pick you up from work at five o'clock, and once we tell the police what's been going on, maybe they'll arrest Les. Bring the rat with you! I think Inspector Bowden will need to see that.'

***

Wednesday 3rd September 1986

Julie was feeling nervous when she arrived at work the next day. After greeting Norma she began to search for the box.

'I've already looked; it's gone,' said Norma.

'Gone, gone where?'

'You tell me! Where did you leave it?'

'On the shelf underneath the desk.'

'Maybe the cleaners have shifted it then.'

Julie, however, had other suspicions. It was evidence, and to her it was just too much of a coincidence that the box had disappeared at such a crucial time when her and Vinny were planning to take it to the police station.

'They can't have done,' she said. 'The cleaners never shift anything off the shelves. They just move things that are lying on the floor. They couldn't have taken it Norma. I think somebody else did.'

'What are you saying Julie?'

'That someone else took the box. They must have come in and grabbed it after we went home. What time did you leave last night Norma?'

'Just after you, but I can't see how someone would have got away with walking in the building and rummaging through the desks.'

'Look Norma, that door's always open to the public. Anybody could walk in off the street, and if most of the staff had already gone home then they'd have plenty of time to rummage about.'

'Well, I suppose they could at a pinch.'

'I think it's Les. In fact, me and Vinny are going to the police station tonight after work to tell them what's been happening. I was followed home last night. I think it was the same man that delivered the rat. Les must have put him up to it.'

'You're joking! That must have been awful. Let's hope you have some joy with the police. It's about time this was all over with.'

The rest of the morning passed by uneventfully but Julie received another menacing phone call just after her lunch break. It sounded like the same voice again, taunting her as it said, 'I hope you enjoyed your little present. Pity you haven't kept it, isn't it?'

Before Julie could respond the caller had put down the receiver.

At 5pm she was relieved when Vinny came to meet her and she flung herself towards him seeking reassurance after another trying day.

They arrived at the police station just before five thirty, hoping that Inspector Bowden would still be on duty. Unfortunately for them, he was.

They were led into the same interview room as last time. This time Inspector Bowden had Sergeant Drummond seated beside him and they both appeared to be equally stony-faced. As Julie and Vinny walked into the room, nobody spoke. They weren't offered a seat but they took one anyway. After a few seconds of uncomfortable silence the inspector began talking.

'I hope you've not come to waste my time again,' he stated.

'We haven't been wasting your time. It's not our fault you wouldn't take us seriously!' Julie began, but she was silenced by the touch of Vinny's fingers on her arm.

'We want to report a case of harassment and we think it might be connected to the case,' he said.

'And what case might that be?' asked the inspector, putting them on the spot.

Julie decided to leave the talking to Vinny as her emotions were running high and she knew that she would have difficulty controlling herself.

'The case of Amanda Morris's death and maybe the other girl, Jacqueline, as well,' Vinny replied.

'Would you like to explain how a case of harassment could be connected to the deaths of Amanda Morris and Jacqueline Bartlett?' asked the inspector.

Julie noticed how calm Vinny was trying to remain as he answered each of the inspector's questions.

'Julie is being harassed,' he explained. 'We think it's connected with Les because he knows that we suspect him.'

'How is she being harassed?' the inspector asked.

'I was coming to that. Julie's been getting phone calls at work from a man. She's also had a dead rat delivered to her at work and someone followed her last night.'

'Have you brought the rat?'

Julie watched Vinny's reaction as, unperturbed, he continued. 'The rat went missing, but her colleague Norma saw it as well before it disappeared. She also saw the courier that delivered the rat. We think it's the same man that followed Julie.'

'The word of a work colleague is not evidence enough. I need to see the rat. What about the man? Do you know who he is Miss Quinley?'

Julie flinched as Inspector Bowden addressed her. 'No, I've never seen him before, but he looked similar to the man who delivered the rat, tall and, and … dark.'

'Are you describing Les Stevens?' Sergeant Drummond asked, sounding confused.

'No,' Julie retorted. 'He was much bigger.'

Inspector Bowden re-joined the conversation, his voice beginning to take on a tone of annoyance. 'Then how on earth can you claim that this so called harassment is connected to Leslie Stevens?'

Julie was at a loss for words. She knew that if she described the connection she would have to admit they had broken into Les's flat and that would land them in more trouble. She also knew that Vinny would be aware of her thoughts at this moment, and she heard him jump to her defence as he said, 'We think Les put him up to it. Maybe someone told Les that I spotted him dealing drugs, so he's trying to get at Julie because he knows where she works.'

Regrettably Vinny's reasoning was insufficient to quell Inspector Bowden's wrath.

'Nonsense!' he shouted. 'It's all nonsense. I think you two fabricated this whole story to get yourselves off the hook. Now get out of this station before I have you for wasting police time!'

His voice was still booming in Julie's ears as she marched up the road outside the police station. Vinny was having difficulty trying to keep pace with her as her anger penetrated through to her fast and furious pacing. It took several minutes before he managed to calm her down. Eventually she agreed to let him take her home.

'Why won't they listen to us Vinny?' she asked.

'I don't know Julie. Maybe there's not enough evidence with the rat having gone missing. All they've got is our word for it. For all we know he might be looking into it now. All that might have just been an act for our benefit. After all, if he was going to arrest Les Stevens, he wouldn't tell us about it, would he?'

Vinny's words failed to convince Julie.

***

Wednesday 3rd September 1986

They reached Julie's home a little before seven o'clock. By this time Julie had managed to steady herself and her and Vinny decided to act as though everything was fine, but it was to no avail. She knew by the expressions on her parents' faces when she walked through the door that something was amiss.

'What is it, what's wrong?' asked Julie.

'You'd better sit down Julie, you too Vinny,' said Bill. 'We've been getting some phone calls, not very nice ones.'

'What have they been saying?' Julie asked but, seeing the torment on her father's face, she spared him the anguish of having to give details. 'It's all right. You don't have to repeat them dad. I know all about them. I've been getting them at work as well.'

'Why didn't you tell us?' Bill asked, the hurt evident in his voice.

'I didn't want to trouble you. I've put you through enough lately.'

'Oh Julie love,' said her mother. 'We're your parents. You should confide in us if something's troubling you.'

'I hope you're going to report it to the police,' said Bill. 'They were round here quick enough when they thought they had something on you, weren't they?'

'I already have done dad. That's where we've just been, but they didn't take us seriously. They said we didn't have any evidence. In fact, they said we were just making it up to get me off the hook, and they threatened to arrest us for wasting their time.'

'The cheeky buggers!' said Bill.

Julie couldn't stand the looks of hurt and desperation on her parent's faces. She left the living room and wandered into the kitchen accompanied by Vinny.

'Jesus Vinny, this is awful!' she said. 'I didn't want them to know. I didn't want to put them through it again.'

'I know,' said Vinny, taking her in his arms.

They remained locked together for several minutes, Julie feeling consoled by his silent embrace. It was as though Vinny could home in on her feelings, knowing that she didn't want to hear any more false assurances that things would get better, that her parents would forgive her, or that justice would be done in the end. What use would those utterances be? The only thing that could help her now would be proving Les guilty and at the moment that seemed further away than ever.

She was relieved that Vinny had allowed her those few moments of silence, but when he finally spoke, it wasn't to offer any vain hope through words that held no real meaning. Instead his words were full of meaning and determination as he said. 'I've got an idea. I think it might help.'

Chapter 30

Saturday 20th September 1986

The man was tall and dark with a menacing air about him. He mingled easily in the surroundings of the Blue Macaw, accustomed to the decadence and sleaze that was commonplace in his line of work. He hardly noticed the scantily dressed women with their heavily made-up faces chatting to aggressive looking men covered in tattoos and scars, and blowing endless streams of smoke as they flirted.

To him it was just a way of life; in some ways he could say he enjoyed it. It gave him a chance to lose himself, to explore that other side of him, the sinister side. The man circulated, absorbing his environment but taking care not to appear too obvious. He'd tried to buy drugs in several nightclubs during the last couple of weeks, but it was always the wrong dealer.

The man wanted one person in particular, and he was pleased that tonight he had found that person, Les Stevens. He recognised him from the photographs that he had seen.

After a few minutes he noticed a slightly built man flitting from person to person. He'd also noticed him earlier talking to Les. He reminded him of a whippet. There was always a whippet in these places; the type of man who was nice to all the right people, the people with power, fearful of upsetting them, but at the same time hoping to gain respect because of his connections.

The man knew that he could use the whippet to try to get to Les and it wasn't long before he caught his attention. As their eyes locked he motioned for the whippet to approach his table. He knew the whippet would obey; the man was too imposing to ignore.

'What's your name?' he asked the whippet.

'Ernie,' he replied offering his outstretched hand, anxious to please.

'And yours?' asked Ernie.

'Dan.'

'Dan who?'

'Dan is all you need to know!'

'Oh,' was the only word Ernie could muster.

'You a regular here?' asked Dan.

'Oh yeah.'

'So you know all the movers and shakers then do you?'

'Might do,' said Ernie.

Dan guessed what was troubling Ernie and was quick to point out, 'I'm not a copper, don't worry. I just need to get hold of something and I thought you might know where I can get it.'

'Oh yeah, what is it you want then?'

'Uppers.'

'Yeah, I can get hold of them for you, but it'll cost.'

'How much?'

'Whatever he charges, plus an extra tenner to me for making the introduction.'

'OK, go for it.'

Dan watched, amused, as Ernie shuffled eagerly through the crowds towards Les. Dan knew that a direct approach to Les was out of the question. Les, a hardened drug pusher, would be far too cautious for that.

It wasn't long before Ernie returned and signalled for Dan to follow him.

'This is him,' said Ernie when they reached Les.

'You after some uppers?' asked Les.

'Yeah, that's right.'

'What's wrong with your usual supplier?'

'I've just moved up from London. Things were getting a bit hot down there so I had to get out quick.'

'Oh yeah, how hot? What happened?'

Dan could tell that his obvious Mancunian accent had aroused Les's suspicion.

'Coppers nicked a few dealers. It was getting harder to get hold of anything and a few users were nicked as well. I didn't want to take any chances so I came up here. I'm from Manchester anyway, but a lot of people have moved on since I was last here.'

Les swallowed the tale. 'Right, before we do the deal, no fuckin' hand shakin' or anything, right?'

'Do I look stupid?' asked Dan.

'Right, OK, if anyone asks you're just a mate who knows me from the club. Don't let anyone see the drugs or the money, but if anyone does ask, you were just lending an old mate a few quid right, and the drugs have got nowt to do with me.'

'Sure, I know the score.'

The deal was carried out. 'Cheers mate. I'll know where to find you again,' said Dan.

'Yeah, I'm usually in here or the Hacienda,' Les replied.

As Dan turned to walk away, he noticed Ernie the whippet. He couldn't let such a weak man put one over on him. He had to stamp his authority at the outset if he was going to deal convincingly with these people again.

'And you can fuck off if you think you're gonna screw a tenner out of me, you fuckin' worm!' Then, pointing his finger aggressively at Ernie for Les's benefit, he added. 'I might have just arrived here, but everyone will soon find out who I am, so just fuckin' watch yourself.'

He strode away, nodding at Les while noting his enjoyment at his treatment of Ernie. Les had taken it all in, hook, line and sinker. He just needed to deal with him a few more times now to gain his complete trust, then he could make his final move.

***

Saturday 20th September 1986

It wasn't long after that before Ernie also left the Blue Macaw. Les watched as he disappeared. He had been searching for Ernie for a couple of weeks now, but it seemed that he had been keeping a low profile for whatever reason, probably owed somebody money knowing him. Les wanted to follow straightaway, but he had a few customers awaiting his attention, and he couldn't resist the lure of easy money. Besides, he couldn't afford to turn customers down; he didn't want them to take their business elsewhere.

Unbeknown to Les though, Ernie had been on his way to an important meeting with Leroy Booth, a local gangster and hard man. Ernie had been working for Leroy for several weeks, hence his low profile. Leroy had found that Ernie was a useful pawn due to his meek demeanour. Unlike Leroy and his bully boys, who were forever being pulled by the police, Ernie had the knack of evading suspicion. Leroy had therefore put him to work in a number of areas but advised him to continue his usual activities. Part of Leroy's plans were to find out who his rivals were in the drugs supply chain and Ernie had provided him with some very handy information lately.

As soon as Les had finished with his customers he sped after Ernie. Outside the club he could see him a couple of hundred yards down the road. Les quickly caught up with him.

'Ernie!' he shouted as he drew closer. 'I want a word with you.'

His voice belied the contempt that he felt within.

Ernie swung around, suspecting nothing.

'Hiya Les, what is it?' he asked.

'It's a bit delicate. We'd be better off out of the way so no-one can hear us. Come down here and I'll tell ya.'

Ernie complied with his instruction as Les knew he would, because Ernie was always keen to find new ways of gaining information, respect or both. In his eagerness Ernie unwittingly allowed Les to guide him into a side road followed by a shop doorway, which was deserted at this time of night. Then Les sprung his surprise, taking Ernie's arm and twisting it up his back in an arm-lock.

'You fuckin' dickhead!' he snarled. 'Why don't you learn to keep your big mouth shut?'

He could sense Ernie's pain and confusion as he stammered, 'W-w-what have I done?'

'At the flat, you prat! You mouthed off to that Jacqueline.'

'I don't know what you mean. Who's Jacqueline?' Ernie pleaded.

'You know, that bird that was there last time you came round. Why did you open your fuckin' big trap in front of her?' As he spoke he twisted Ernie's arm tighter up his back.

'Please Les, you're hurting me. I don't know what you're talking about.'

'The drugs dickhead! Why did you have to let her know what we were up to?'

'Shit Les, I didn't realise. I thought she knew. I'm sorry but I thought she was your bird.'

This angered Les more. 'Fuck off! Why would I want an ugly cow like her, you moron.' He released Ernie's arm and shoved him against the shop door.

Ernie stared at him, horrified, on realising his mistake. He had no choice but to wait while Les decided his fate. Ernie didn't have to wait long until Les administered his punishment, kicking and punching savagely.

It was difficult for Les to get at him though; the little wimp had curled into a ball and squeezed into a corner of the shop doorway. When Les grew tired of his exertions, he dragged Ernie to his feet and held a knife to his throat. Now he was really beginning to squirm!

'In future keep your big mouth shut, right!'

Despite his contempt of Ernie, Les had planned to leave it at that. In fact, he was so sure of his hold over Ernie that he hadn't challenged him at the flat straightaway; he was more concerned with how Jacqueline would react if she realised that Ernie was trying to buy drugs from him. And even now, he was confident that Ernie would be so petrified by his threat, that he daren't utter a word to anybody. That was until Ernie made his second mistake; he opened his mouth again.

'What about the girl? What if she says something?'

Les was so hyped up by the thrill of violence that he replied instinctively. 'She won't, not now.'

He cringed as a look of recognition flashed across Ernie's face. Ernie knew what had happened to Jacqueline. Maybe he hadn't seen it on the news with him being NFA or maybe he had and just hadn't realised until now that it was the same girl. Either way, it left Les with no choice; he had to dispose of Ernie as well.

***

Tuesday 7th October 1986

'Julie, you've got to go to the police again. We can't go on like this,' pleaded Betty as she sat beside Julie on their settee while they both digested the contents of this latest threat.

Julie refused to be drawn into another argument. There had been a few over the preceding weeks with each going over the same ground. Julie's parents usually begged her to go to the police, and Julie refused to go through the same ordeal again just to be told that she was wasting police time.

She looked at the piece of paper placed between her and Betty. It was a message made up from letters cut out of newspapers; one of several that had arrived recently. This time, however, the words were even more alarming:-

'Give yourself up or you'll meet the same fate as your friend.'

The word 'friend' was in italics indicating that it was used cynically, and she wondered whether it referred to Amanda or Jacqueline. Julie and Betty didn't discuss the meaning of the letter; they didn't need to. They both recognised the implicit message that it carried.

It had to be from Les. Ever since he had caught her in his flat she had been receiving threats in various forms; letters, phone calls at work and home, and another parcel that had arrived at work just that morning delivered by the same courier as the previous package.

This time Julie was prepared for him though. She abandoned her phone call and chased after him, stopping in time to see him mount his motorbike. She made a mental note of the number plate, and dashed back to the switchboard to jot it down in her diary before announcing to Norma in glee.

'I've got the bastard this time!'

Norma looked surprised. 'What, you mean you got his registration number?'

'That's right!' said Julie before shutting the diary and replacing it in her drawer.

'Good for you!' said Norma. 'Ring the police; maybe they can track him down.'

'They won't believe me. It's not much to go on, is it?'

Norma shrugged noncommittally, failing to reason with her. Perhaps she had reached the conclusion that her reasoning was to no avail.

To be on the safe side Julie also scribbled down the registration number on a small piece of paper and placed it inside her purse. Maybe she was just being paranoid but recent events had had that effect on her and she wasn't taking any chances. She might not be able to use this piece of evidence yet but it might come in useful soon enough.

First she had to see Vinny's plan through and, once it had reached its conclusion, she felt sure that the registration number would prove useful in reigning justice on the sinister motorbike rider, but Les had to be dealt with first.

Norma withdrew her from her pensive mode by asking, 'Don't you want to open it?'

Julie stared at the ominous parcel as she replied, 'Not really, but I suppose I should.'

She began to tear the paper away cautiously before lifting the lid, which was decorated with a cross, representing a coffin. Even though she had tried to mentally prepare herself it still took her by surprise.

Inside the small rectangular box was a picture, which, she guessed, must have been ripped from a horror magazine. It showed a naked woman stretched out on a bed, her body mutilated and bloody. Above her hovered a man with a dagger in his hand, his expression joyful but at the same time chilling.

Julie didn't fail to notice the similarities between the woman and herself; she was also slim with long wavy hair. This picture represented a re-enactment of the time when Les had caught Julie in his flat; a scenario familiar only to those who shared that secret, but in this representation Vinny was absent.

Les had obviously taken into account the fact that few knew about the break-in when he had carried out this sick fantasy. He knew as well as Julie did that it proved nothing in terms of evidence, but its eerie message had a whole wealth of meaning attached to it.

Julie tried to put all thoughts of the picture out of her mind as she made her daily round of the shops during her lunch break, avoiding the hostility of the canteen, as usual.

When she returned to the office, the first thing she did was to reach inside her desk drawer for her diary, but it had vanished, proving her assumption that she had been right in taking down the registration number again.

'My bloody diary's gone,' she said to Norma.

'You're joking!'

'No, I put it in the drawer and it's disappeared.'

They carried out a thorough search of the reception area but the diary was nowhere to be found. While Julie had been on her lunch break Norma had been in the manager's office having her annual appraisal, and one of the office juniors had manned the switchboard.

'It's a good job I wrote the number down again and put it in my purse,' said Julie.

'Yes, it looks as though the mystery courier might have returned and swiped the diary while we were both away.'

That was a troubling thought; someone may have been watching the reception area from the street and waiting for an opportunity. Julie had intended to ask Norma who had manned the switchboard in their absence but they had both become so busy clearing a backlog of calls that it had slipped her mind. Despite her concerns it never re-entered her head, which was a maelstrom of anxieties at the moment. Aside from that, she was too consumed with thoughts of the disturbing threat contained in the parcel.

Chapter 31

Sunday 12th October 1986

Dan woke late. After another night at the Blue Macaw he wasn't in the best frame of mind, especially after what he had been hearing over the last few days. He'd been dealing with Les for a few weeks now and the pressure was starting to get to him. He went to the fridge to grab himself a can of Coke, but as he stared at the empty shelf he remembered guzzling the last one the previous night. A quick scan around the rest of the fridge revealed that he was low on stocks of everything else as well. "*Shit!*" he thought. "*That means I'll have to go to the damn supermarket. As if I didn't have enough on my plate.*"

Before he did anything else though he knew that he had an important call to make. Once he had fixed himself something to eat with the meagre supplies that were available, he reached for the phone.

After the initial greeting the voice at the other end asked, 'How's it going Dan? Have you got close enough to Les yet?'

'A bit too close for fuckin' comfort if you ask me.' Dan replied. 'The guy's a total head case. I've been talking to some of the tarts that he's been with and they say he likes to slap them around. From what they've told me he never treated them with much respect before. What bloke does? But since Amanda died he's gone from bad to worse.'

'Really?'

'Straight up. I tell you, the guy's a fuckin' time bomb waiting to go off. One of the girls said she was almost in fear of her life. She thinks that if she hadn't have done what he asked then he'd have done her some serious damage.'

'Sorry Dan, I didn't know he was that bad!'

'Don't worry about it mate, it comes with the territory but I'm telling you, there's no doubt in my mind that he killed Amanda and the other girl. He's capable of it. There's something else a bit fishy as well. There was this guy called Ernie who introduced me to Les. He was one of the regulars in the Blue Macaw but nobody's seen him since the night I met him. It seems like he's just disappeared off the face of the earth.'

'Jesus! Looks like you'd better act quickly then. He's still sending the nasty letters as well. In fact, they're worse than ever. I'm worried what he might do next.'

'I'll be acting as quick as I can, maybe tonight if the situation's right. I want to see the back of that sick bastard.'

'OK, mind how you go then Dan.'

'I always do.'

***

Thursday 16th October 1986

'For God's sake, I don't believe it! This is turning into a damn serial killer and we're no nearer to finding him now than we've ever been,' Inspector Bowden roared throughout the office for the benefit of everyone in general. He hoped that his shouting would have the effect of shaking up his murder team and would prompt them to come up with something useful. This latest murder had shaken him. Following reports of another body, he and Sergeant Drummond had returned from the crime scene a few days previously and it wasn't a pretty sight.

The body was found on a rubbish tip, buried several feet under the festering, malodorous waste, and it was estimated that the person had been dead for almost a month. Inspector Bowden's guess was that somebody had carried out the killing first and dumped the body later. Whether it had been dumped directly on the tip or via some other means wasn't yet established.

Although nobody had specifically reported Ernie Cummings as a missing person, the police had received an anonymous tip off that Ernie had not been seen around for a while. This was unusual because he used to frequent the Manchester drugs scene. Due to this tip off, the police carried out checks against the information pertaining to Ernie Cummings that they held on their system. This soon led to an identification of the body.

'There must be a connection to the previous two murders. It was the same man for God's sake; he used the same weapon on Jacqueline Bartlett,' he continued.

'Excuse me sir,' Sergeant Drummond interrupted. 'How do we know that the killer was a man?'

'The ferocity of the attacks, of course! I don't think a woman would have the strength to carry out such a brutal attack.'

He then paused to consider the facts before continuing, 'We know the connection between Amanda Morris and Jacqueline Bartlett, but where does this Ernie Cummings fit into it? What do we know about him?' he asked Sergeant Drummond.

'He's a small time crook and drug user sir, no fixed abode and no known connections with either Amanda Morris or Jacqueline Bartlett, but he is known to frequent the Blue Macaw nightclub.'

'The Blue Macaw? Right, well let's get down there and start digging!'

He yanked his coat from the stand and proceeded towards the exit, almost taking the coat stand with him in his haste to get to the Blue Macaw. Sergeant Drummond eyed her half-finished coffee, which she was forced to abandon when Inspector Bowden ordered her to hurry up.

After interviewing several witnesses in the Blue Macaw, Inspector Bowden and Sergeant Drummond found that one name kept cropping up as an associate of Ernie Cummings, but nobody seemed to know his current whereabouts. It was that of Leslie Stevens.

'Well sergeant, we've found our connection,' said Inspector Bowden proudly. 'I suggest we get over to his flat straightaway and see if he's there.'

'OK sir, but one thing's puzzling me.'

'What's that sergeant?'

'Julie Quinley and Rita Steadman; how do they fit into all this?'

Inspector Bowden stared with contempt at Sergeant Drummond. 'Forget them two; that was just a red herring!'

Within minutes they had arrived at Leslie Stevens' flat but found that he wasn't at home. In their desperation to get a result they decided to search the place anyway, and prised open the recently mended front door. As they searched for a clue as to Les's whereabouts, little did they realise that at present he was in another of his favourite haunts; the Hacienda, carrying out his trade.

Another customer of the Hacienda was also planning to carry out his trade there tonight. It was Dan Burroughs and his bit of trade relied on the presence of Leslie Stevens.

***

Thursday 16th October 1986

'Have you seen this Bill?' shouted Betty, and as he approached her she continued. 'It's another one of those letters.'

Stress lines began to cross Bill's face as he digested this latest threat.

'What the bloody hell does it mean?' he asked.

'Oh what does it matter?' snapped Julie. 'It's just one of many. Do we have to talk about it so much? Can't we just forget about it?'

'I've told her to go to the police,' Betty urged, prompting another verbal onslaught by Bill.

'Listen to what your mother's telling you Julie! You're doing yourself no favours by keeping it all bottled up. They should be able to put a stop to it.'

'I've told you both before, it's a waste of time. They don't believe a bloody word I'm saying. I'm a murder suspect don't forget!' Julie retaliated before storming out of the room and heading up to her bedroom.

She didn't realise of course that she was no longer a suspect, and that Inspector Bowden and his cohorts were now searching for Les Stevens, ready to arrest him. In the absence of that knowledge she had already made her own arrangements to deal with Les.

She plonked herself down on her bed where she was seized by an attack of guilt. She knew that her parents didn't need reminding that she was a murder suspect, and it was spiteful of her to bring it up again at a time when they had enough troubles with the threatening letters and phone calls they had been receiving. But she just wished that they would get off her case.

She had enough on her plate herself; there were many things that she hadn't told them, such as the parcel that she had received that day. As soon as her mind began to wander back to it, she put a block on her thoughts and, instead, reached for a tablet to ease the familiar muscle tensions that hounded her. That was another thing that she hadn't told her parents about, her increasing need for something to calm her down, and her fear that she might be returning to the same anxiety state that she had been in not so long ago.

"*Still*," she thought. "*It might all be over soon*," and she tried to comfort herself with the thought that, even at this very moment, her and Vinny's plans might have been carried out, putting an end to this nightmare.

***

Friday 17th October 1986

Dan had visited the Hacienda a lot after finally making contact with Les. The Hacienda and the Blue Macaw were the two clubs that Les frequented the most as they both gave him a steady stream of customers. Dan wanted to gain Les's trust before he could complete his work. So he came here often to deal with Les and to mingle; to see and be seen.

He had made quite a few acquaintances over the last few weeks; some male, some female, and he hadn't gone short of offers. Sometimes he would take up an offer from a girl if he found her attractive enough, but he was careful not to give any secrets away no matter how intimate they might become.

A few of the regulars nodded at Dan as he passed them. He inwardly chuckled to himself thinking about their willing acceptance of him as the character he portrayed. How gullible these people were! His inner pleasure was brought on by the knowledge that tonight was the night. After weeks of planning, scheming and living the life of his alter ego, the time had now arrived for Dan. Quite soon it would all be over and he would be able to heave a sigh of relief as he pocketed the cash and turned his back on the whole sordid affair; at least until the next time someone needed his services.

Dan continued to walk through the nightclub until he reached an area that was near enough for him to achieve his objective. He took a seat at a chipped and stained table and stretched his legs. He was aware that his cool, detached air attracted wary glances from many people, but this added to the thrill. It was reassuring to think that they saw him as the threatening character he purported to be.

A tasty brunette named Paula soon joined him. She leaned tantalisingly across him, revealing an ample cleavage, and asked why he was alone. He ignored her question and sent her to the bar to get him a drink, telling her to keep the change. Her face lit up as he passed her the five-pound note.

On her return from the bar, she decided to sit with him, taking his generosity as a sign of encouragement. "*Shit!*" he thought. "*This could really cock things up.*"

'Do me a favour love, make yourself scarce; I've got some important business I need to carry out if you know what I mean?' he asked.

She pouted sulkily, the hurt evident in her eyes.

'Go on love, go and treat yourself with that change,' he said, winking at her and smacking her bottom as she left the table.

Dan now had Les in his line of vision and he smiled as Les nodded towards him in silent acknowledgement of a known and trusted acquaintance. Les had no reason not to trust him; they had conducted business together a few times, producing a satisfactory outcome for each of them. This had secured Dan a place as one of Les's allies. Dan knew that because of their connection Les wouldn't feel any uneasiness by his proximity, or by the way in which Dan watched him carrying out his business. Les didn't see him as a threat.

Tonight, however, Les was about to discover the true meaning of their relationship. Dan bided his time, waiting for the right moment. He needed a clear path through to Les with no obstacles or people blocking the distance between them. He covertly held the small but heavy mechanism in readiness. After a few minutes he knew that the moment had arrived, and he had to act straightaway.

CLICK. The blinding flash and eruption of noise took Les by surprise. Dan swiftly followed it up with another shot. Les's associates gaped in horror and began shouting and cursing. Some of them searched around for the perpetrator but Dan had vanished long before they had a chance to carry out reprisals.

Chapter 32

Saturday 18th October 1986

Julie and Rita were becoming impatient as they sat in Vinny's front room, and Rita had begun chain smoking to pass the time.

'He's half an hour late now!' Rita complained. 'I bet he's not coming, I bet he's took our money and done a bleedin' runner!'

'Has he 'eck,' Julie tried to assure her.

Rita addressed Vinny, 'Well, what do you think? You're the one that hired him?'

'He'll be here.' Vinny replied. 'He's sound Dan. He's done the job, but he's just got held up on the way here, that's all.

'By the way, he was telling me on the phone that there's been another murder, a guy called Ernie Cummings. Dan knew him and so did Les. He said the police were asking questions in the Blue Macaw. Dan didn't speak to the police though 'cos he was busy in the Hacienda at the time.'

Julie sounded surprised. 'I can't believe it, first Amanda, then Jacqueline and now this Ernie. It's got to be connected to Les, but why?'

Vinny responded by shrugging his shoulders. Rita just wriggled around on the sofa impatiently until they had a chance to digest this latest piece of news, then she resumed complaining. 'How much longer is he gonna be? I'll give him held up!' she said. 'He's cost us enough, the slimy looking get. I wouldn't trust him as far as I could throw him. They're all the same in that line of work.'

'Why, how many have you dealt with before?' Vinny asked sarcastically.

Julie knew that it was unusual for Vinny to resort to sarcasm, and she realised that he must have been growing tired of Rita's grumbling. She rolled her eyes in exasperation and attempted to change the subject. Rita, however, did not react. Julie wondered if perhaps Rita was aware that she was irritating him.

A few seconds later there was a loud, self-assured knock at the door. Without comment Vinny got up to answer it. Julie watched as Dan sauntered in, grinning from ear to ear.

'Evening ladies,' he announced.

They uttered reciprocal greetings and Julie watched him take a seat next to Rita and put down the briefcase containing all the tools of his trade. Before Vinny had a chance to sit Dan addressed him. 'Got any coffee on the go mate?' he asked. 'I'm gasping of thirst. I've had a right job getting here, I can tell you.'

While Vinny disappeared into the kitchen, Dan ingratiated himself with the two girls.

'Sorry to keep you waiting ladies. As I said, I've had a terrible job getting here. I'm sure there's a thousand things two lovely ladies like you would rather be doing with your time. I bet the fellas are queuing up to take you out!'

Julie noticed how quickly Rita responded to his slick charms, despite herself.

'Oh we don't mind, not if you make it worth our while anyway,' she quipped.

'Oh don't worry, it's all signed, sealed and delivered,' replied Dan. 'I never fail to deliver.'

Rita giggled but their flirtation was hindered by Vinny's return to the room.

'Here he is, the main man,' declared Dan. 'Right, before we start getting down to business I thought you might want to take a look at this.'

He passed Vinny a copy of that day's paper and the girls crowded round to read the headlines, "Man Found Stabbed to Death", which were accompanied by a photograph of Ernie Cummings.

'Jesus,' said Rita. 'That's the man that came out of the building where Les lives, that night. Do you remember? It was the same night we saw Jackie coming out of there as well?'

'Oh my God! Yes it is, and now they're both dead,' Julie replied.

Vinny joined in the discussion. 'Like you said Julie, it's got to be connected to Les.'

'Well, just take a butchers at this lot!' Dan interrupted, and Julie watched in awe as he clicked his briefcase open and withdrew its contents. He began by placing several small packages on the coffee table followed by a bound exercise book.

'Drugs,' he confirmed. 'They're all labelled and I've kept details of the types, amounts and dates purchased in this log, all bought from Leslie Stevens of course.'

Vinny nodded, indicating that he should continue. Dan withdrew some envelopes from his case in response and handed them to Vinny.

'This is the icing on the cake,' he said. 'Caught the bastard good and proper, and then took another one just to make sure.'

Vinny studied the photographs. 'These are just what we need,' he said. 'I can't wait until Inspector Bowden sees these. Maybe he'll start to take us seriously at last.'

He passed the pictures to Julie and Rita who looked at them together. Both of the photographs showed Les dealing in drugs with another man. The first shot had captured Les passing a white package to the man with one hand whilst, at the same time, taking money.

'You'd better be quick if you're going to the police with these,' Dan urged. 'That Les will soon be on your tail. You should have seen the commotion when him and his cronies realised I'd photographed him. All hell broke loose. He was shouting at them to grab whoever had taken the shot. This big nasty looking bastard ran towards me, but he couldn't get through the crowds soon enough.'

'Was he dark and thickset?' asked Julie.

'Yeah, that's right.'

'Sounds like the motorbike rider, the one that followed me from work.' she affirmed.

Dan then proceeded to withdraw another document from his briefcase and passed it to Vinny. 'My bill,' he said.

'Bloody hell, you don't mess about do you love?' remarked Rita and Dan rewarded her with a dashing smile.

'Hang on,' interrupted Vinny. 'You've done a brilliant job Dan; I'm impressed, but there's just one last thing I'd like you to do for us.'

This put Dan on his guard. 'Oh yeah, what's that?' he asked.

'I'd like you to come to the police station with us, preferably as soon as possible. I think Inspector Bowden might still need some convincing. We're not exactly flavour of the month right now, and I think it might be better if you were there to back us up.'

'Oh yeah, and I am?' asked Dan.

'So you've met Inspector Bowden before then?' Julie enquired.

'Once or twice, yeah. Poxy old bastard isn't he?'

There was then a few moments silence as Dan mulled over Vinny's proposal.

'We'll pay you once we've been to see the police and cleared this up,' Vinny told him.

Dan sighed. 'Oh go on then, I suppose it would be good to see Bowden grovel for once.'

***

Monday 20th October 1986

The scenario in Inspector Bowden's office had a different air about it this time. This was helped by the fact that Vinny had called the inspector beforehand and explained the evidence that they were going to present. In addition to the drugs and photographs supplied by Dan, Vinny had urged Julie to bring the motorcycle registration number and the latest package she had received along with the threatening letters.

Little did they know that the investigation had now switched emphasis and Julie and Rita were no longer suspects. But Inspector Bowden didn't divulge this information; their evidence could be just what he needed to nail Leslie Stevens. He had already questioned him but didn't yet have enough evidence to charge him.

Amazingly the forensic tests carried out on Jacqueline Bartlett had come up with nothing; no hairs, fibres or prints and they hadn't managed to trace the murder weapon. There was always a chance that tests carried out on Ernie Cummings might show something, but that would mean having to wait. Much better to tie things up now thought the inspector.

At first Inspector Bowden tried a defensive approach. As he read the letters, he asked Julie, 'Why haven't you brought these to my attention before now?'

'Phuh,' sounded Julie, now feeling in control. 'Do you mean to say you would have taken me seriously?'

'Yeah', chipped in Rita, '… just like you did the last time and the time before.'

Inspector Bowden adjusted his tie before replying. 'All cases of harassment are taken seriously no matter what the circumstances,' he stated and, before they had a chance to retaliate further, he cut them short by asking Dan if he could see the remaining evidence.

It was becoming apparent during their time with the inspector that he was impressed by the evidence that they presented before him. However, not wishing to be outdone, he gave Dan a stern lecture about entrapment and said that because of this the drugs would prove useless as evidence. Inspector Bowden then surprised everyone with his next statement.

'These, however …,' he said, as he handled the photographs of Les, '… will prove very useful.'

He marched to the door and shouted at one of his minions to come into the office. Seconds later a young constable stepped inside. The inspector issued a set of instructions and then dismissed the constable and everybody else.

'Hang on a minute!' cried Rita. 'We want to know what you're going to do about it, and an apology wouldn't go amiss either.'

Inspector Bowden glared at Rita.

'Miss Steadman, the evidence is by no means conclusive. We have a lot of work to do before we can prove Mr Stevens' guilt or your innocence for that matter. Now good day!'

He strode from the office leaving them all gasping in bewilderment.

'The cheeky get!' shouted Rita. 'He's in the bleedin' wrong, and he acts as though we're the ones to blame.'

The only reply she received was the sound of Inspector Bowden's voice outside his office addressing Sergeant Drummond. 'Get these people out of my station, and then I want you to come with me. We've got work to do!'

The rest of them remained flabbergasted as Sergeant Drummond led them, retreating, out of the station once more.

Chapter 33

December 1986

The last few weeks had passed slowly but peacefully, to Julie's relief. As Les and his accomplice were being held in custody, Julie was thankful to see an end to the stream of abusive letters and phone calls. It felt strange at first; the daily torment following Amanda's death had become so much a part of her life. She still sometimes found herself tensing as she answered the telephone, half expecting to hear the chilling sound of Les's distorted voice, tormenting her, threatening her and sending a rush of fear coursing through her body. Neither did she have the constant dread of the police arriving on her doorstep at any minute.

For the first couple of weeks after Les and his accomplice had been arrested for the murders of Amanda, Jacqueline and Ernie she still dreaded walking into her home after work in case further threats had been received. Instead of seeing the upset faces of her family, however, she saw happy smiles. Things were almost back to normal, almost but not quite, because Julie knew deep down that nothing would ever erase Amanda's death or the torment that she herself had suffered as a result.

Julie had changed. It was as though she had been forced to grow up, to face life as an adult and take stock. Her relationship with Vinny had also changed; for the better. Instead of seeing Vinny as a stop-gap, Julie now pictured him in a whole new light. He had been the one who had defended her, her knight in shining armour. It had heartened her to think that, despite the accusations, Vinny never lost faith in her and she could always depend on his loyalty. It also shamed her thinking of how she had used him in the past, and she vowed to herself that she would never mistreat him again.

What she now felt for Vinny ran deeper than that though. He had gained her respect and that was an important turning point in their relationship. She no longer viewed him as a dim-witted manual worker; he was strong, determined, and brave. Apart from proving himself by defending her, he was also proving himself in his working life. His decision to work for himself had paid off. Employers trusted a good, reliable worker and because of the many recommendations, he was now receiving more work than he could handle, and he had employed a trainee to help him with the workload.

Julie's work-life was much better too. People now spoke to her instead of ignoring her. Some were even apologetic. One lady had approached her to have a word following Les's arrest, assuring her that she knew deep down that she was all right, and that it was the force of public opinion and the fact that she was arrested that had made her think otherwise.

Things were never quite the same as before though. There were still a few people who didn't bother with her, mainly Jacqueline's old associates, and Julie was reminded of Amanda's death every time she caught sight of one of them. Certain things brought back the dreadful memories too; the space under her desk where the first threatening parcel had sat, and the faint traces of the graffiti on the lavatory wall. Despite the fact that she was no longer under suspicion, Julie could still not face going into the canteen.

Julie didn't go out with her friends as much now, maybe because they had grown out of all those wild nights or perhaps because all of their priorities had changed. Rita spent a great deal of her time in Greece in between doing casual work.

Rita was still planning to buy a bar with Yansis but respected his wishes to invest some of his own money towards it. They had reached a compromise. Rita would put most of her redundancy pay up front, Yansis would contribute as much as he could save for however long they were prepared to wait, and the rest of the money they would obtain by loan. Julie was glad in a way because she was concerned about Rita rushing into things. At least this way it gave Rita a chance to get to know Yansis better before she committed herself.

Despite the recent improvements to the lives of Julie and her family and friends, she still felt that she was living her life in limbo. She was waiting for some great momentous event that could help to erase the pain and sorrow that had surrounded her. That event was the trial of Leslie Stevens for the murders of Amanda Morris and two others, and the start of the trial had now arrived. It was another date that would remain in her memory forever; Monday 8th December 1986.

Julie felt utter trepidation at the thought of the trial. A tiny part of her didn't want the trial to go ahead. Could she face it all again? But she knew that she must. It wasn't only about justice; it was about seeing an end to an arduous chapter of her life and putting it behind her.

Her parents had offered to attend the trial with her but she had declined. She knew what a difficult time it was going to be and she wanted to shield them from any more sorrow. Hadn't she caused them enough grief already? Instead she had agreed for Vinny to accompany her. Despite her concerns about the trial, she felt that Vinny was the best person to help her through it. She was now waiting for him to call and drive her to court. They had arranged to pick up Rita on the way.

Although she had been ready for the last ten minutes, the knock at the door still took her by surprise, shattering her already jangled nerves and making her realise just how worked up she was. Within seconds Vinny had walked into her room.

'Come on then, let's get it over with!' he cajoled with mock optimism.

Julie stepped towards him and took a deep breath as he squeezed her hand in a reassuring gesture. They set off. When they arrived at Rita's house, Julie was invited inside by Rita's mother, a woman in her mid-forties who looked older, her hair streaked with grey, and her complexion jaded and lifeless.

'Come in, I'll give her a shout,' she instructed.

To Julie's dismay Rita wasn't ready.

'You'd better go up, I think she's still tarting herself up,' said Rita's mother.

'Rita, I don't believe you!' Julie cried when she caught sight of her at the bedroom mirror. 'I wanted to be there early today. It's important!'

'Oh give over, we're not that late! Besides, we can make a grand entrance,' Rita replied as she applied another layer of mascara.

'It's a trial Rita, not a bleedin' fancy dress party,' Julie snapped.

'Oh for Christ's sake, lighten up will you? Get back on the bleedin' happy pills or summat.'

That last comment stung Julie to the core. It upset her to realise just how insensitive Rita could be at times. They left Rita's house in silence, a hostile atmosphere surrounding them as they joined Vinny in the car.

'Hiya Vinny, are you all right?' Rita asked.

Julie remained silent as did Vinny. Instead of starting the car immediately, he leaned over and took Julie's hand. 'Don't worry, everything will be all right,' he assured her. 'Why don't you take one of those pills the doctor gave you to calm you down?'

'I don't like to, I thought I was past all that.'

'Just think of it as temporary. It's just to get you through these next couple of days. It's not like you're going to be on them forever, is it?'

'Oh all right then,' Julie agreed, relieved in a way that her use of tranquillisers had been condoned. She had felt the need of something to calm her down for the last two days but had managed to fight the urge, telling herself that she should be able to manage without. Managing without at a time like this, however, was proving very difficult. The previous night, despite a stiff measure of brandy, sleep had evaded her until four o'clock in the morning, making her feel even worse. She reached into her bag and withdrew the small tablet bottle.

Rita must have felt guilty at her own insensitivity, as she said, 'I'm sorry about what I said about the happy pills Julie. You go for it if it makes you feel better. We all handle things in different ways; there's no need to feel bad about it. I wouldn't mind a couple of them myself at the end of the trial topped down with a good measure of Bacardi and Coke to celebrate putting that bastard behind bars.'

Vinny tutted and pounded at the hand break. He then slammed the car into gear and sped up the road. Following her faux pas, Rita remained silent for most of the journey.

When they arrived at the courts five minutes late, they were directed to Court 3. Julie became more agitated on noticing that there was nobody waiting outside the court; they had already gone inside.

'Oh I don't believe it; I knew we were going to be bloody late!' she cried.

'It's all right,' said a court official, 'you're not due to give evidence yet; you've got plenty of time.'

He directed them to a separate waiting area where they were to remain until called to give evidence. Vinny gave Julie a quick kiss goodbye then made his way to the public gallery to watch the trial. As well as Amanda, Les was being tried for the murders of Ernie and Jacqueline.

Although Julie and Rita were being called as witnesses to the night of Amanda's death, Julie felt as though she was being tried herself. She knew that once the defence barrister started questioning her, she would once again feel as though the finger of accusation was being pointed towards her.

They were told that they wouldn't have to wait long but the court officials were unable to specify exactly how long the wait would be. It hadn't occurred to Julie or Rita to bring anything with them to help pass the time; they had other things on their minds. It was doubtful whether they would have been able to concentrate anyway. Instead they spent the time speculating about what was happening in the courtroom, what they could expect and how much longer they would have to wait.

As the minutes turned to hours and the tension mounted, their periods of discussion were interspersed by Rita pacing the room and Julie biting the wicks around her nails.

'You'll have no bleedin' nails left the way you're going on,' declared Rita.

'I'm not biting my nails, I'm biting my wicks,' snapped Julie.

'Your wicks then; look at them, they're going all red.'

'Oh, who gives a shit? They're only bleedin' nails! You're the one that's marching round the room like a demented sergeant major. You're driving me up the wall!'

'Oh, belt up Julie. It's not my fault those bastards are keeping us waiting. They're probably doing it on purpose to wind us up.'

Rita then proceeded to hammer on the door, shouting for attention until Julie yelled at her. 'Will you give over Rita? For God's sake; you're not helping matters! They can't make it go any faster. We've just got to wait until they're ready for us.'

She was on the verge of tears at this point and Rita, shocked by Julie's outburst, stopped what she was doing and took the seat beside Julie. Realising that the tension was getting to them both, Rita took Julie's hand and said, 'I'm sorry Jules, it's just that it's driving me mad in here. I feel like I'm back in that bleedin' cell again.'

Julie didn't respond straightaway, but sat contemplating. After a few moments she spoke:

'I can't do it, I just can't face it!'

'Julie, you've got to face it, you're a key witness,' Rita cajoled. 'Just think of how relieved you'll feel when it's all over.'

But Rita's tender approach was having no effect as Julie was becoming more distressed and refusing to give evidence. After a few minutes and several futile attempts to talk Julie round, Rita was also becoming agitated. As frustration took over she abandoned her persuasive efforts and reverted to type.

'You've got to fuckin' do it!' she shouted.

'You remember what it was like at the police station,' Julie pleaded. 'That bastard defence will make us look guilty, and it'll be just like it was when we were arrested.'

'No it won't! It's just a game to them. Everyone knows what a load of bullshit it is. Besides, we've got a good bloke on our side, and think of the grilling that bastard Les is gonna get when he gets up there. That'll be something to look forward to.'

'I can't do it!'

'You fuckin' can and you will! I don't care how many happy pills it takes Julie; you're gonna do it. Let's get this over with once and for all!' Rita roared with an air of finality that forced Julie to a silent consent. She knew that Rita was right, despite the compelling way in which she voiced her opinion.

***

Monday 8th December 1986

The interior of the courtroom was an unnatural environment for Julie. It reeked of officialdom and, as she walked in, she noticed a number of people in smart suits, gowns and wigs whispering amongst themselves. She caught the eye of Inspector Bowden who stared at her. A feeling of paranoia seized her as she sensed the atmosphere that seemed to descend on the public gallery. Then she spotted him, Les Stevens, standing in the dock. His ferocious glare tore through her, reminding her of the vicious attack that he had subjected her to.

After a few minutes the judge called the court to silence and the multitude of voices faded amidst a rustling of papers. The quietness unnerved Julie and she felt a compulsion to clear her throat repeatedly.

Julie was helped by the fact that Rita had taken the stand prior to her. Just as Julie had surmised, Rita had given a good account. Even as Julie stood trembling in anticipation of her turn in the witness stand, she smiled inwardly at the thought that Rita would have given the defence lawyer a good run for his money.

"*All I have to do is take it calmly, and not let that defence lawyer trip me up,*" she told herself in an attempt at positivity. The looks of encouragement that Vinny and Rita were giving her were also encouraging.

Nevertheless, as she approached the witness stand, she was acutely aware of the ominous silence in the courtroom, the faces that followed her and the evil eyes of Les Stevens, piercing through her, willing her to slip up. She took the Bible in her right hand and swore on oath as instructed, her hand shaking so much that she almost dropped it.

The prosecution barrister began his examination, starting with simple questions although, to Julie, even confirming her name and address in front of an audience of ardent listeners was a struggle.

He seemed a pleasant enough man, late 50s and a little obese, but still with handsome, kindly features and a shock of silver grey hair. He spoke gently, attempting to put her at ease, and within a few minutes his soothing tones had had the desired effect as Julie started to feel the tension drain away from her body, feeling that he was on her side.

By the end of his questioning, he had prompted Julie into giving an account that had the jury almost reaching for their handkerchiefs. The scenario that he had outlined was that Julie, a decent, law-abiding citizen had, in recent months, had to cope with the bereavement of a close friend. As if that wasn't bad enough, she had been labelled guilty of her murder and been persecuted by former friends and colleagues. On top of that, she had also been a victim of Leslie Stevens' callousness as he subjected her to months of harassment because she had threatened to expose him.

She felt relieved when he had finished, knowing that the jury were impressed by his emotive speech. "*So far, so good,*" she thought until the defence barrister stood up. "*Now here comes the difficult bit.*"

The defence barrister was a thin, wiry man with harsh, ferret-like features and an odd twitch to the top right of his lip. His eyes were small and piercing, and his movements hasty and edgy.

He began his cross-examination straightaway, hardly giving Julie a chance to draw breath.

'Now, Miss Quinley, if I can take you back to the night of Friday 20th June once again. You have already admitted to the court that Miss Amanda Morris was extremely drunk when she arrived home that night?'

'Yes,' Julie replied.

'All right, well perhaps we can move back a little to the actual night out itself. Can you estimate how many drinks Miss Morris had consumed prior to returning home?'

'Not really, no. Well, we were all knocking them back really; it's difficult to say.'

'Are you suggesting that you were so drunk yourself that you are unable to say how many drinks Amanda Morris consumed?'

'No, it's just that we were that busy having a good time, that's all.'

'Very well, perhaps you could tell the jury how many drinks you yourself consumed.'

'Objection!' cried the prosecution. 'The witness is here to give evidence regarding Amanda Morris's drunkenness, not her own.'

'I am exploring Miss Quinley's reliability as a witness,' the defence argued.

'Very well, objection overruled,' said the judge.

The defence wasted no time in returning to his question.

'Well, Miss Quinley, can you tell the jury please, how many alcoholic drinks did you consume on the night of 20th June?'

'I don't know, a few…maybe eight or so.'

'Eight drinks or more?' queried the defence emphasising the word eight. 'I think that would hardly place you in a sober frame of mind, would it?'

'I was all right. I can take my drink.'

'Perhaps we can discuss what Miss Morris was drinking that caused her to be so intoxicated.'

"*Oh no!*" thought Julie. "*Here we go.*"

The defence had probably already presented witnesses who claimed to have seen Julie and Rita add something to Amanda's drink, so she knew there was no point denying it.

'We slipped a few shorts in her drink, that's all. We just wanted her to loosen up a bit so we could give her a good night out.'

There were a few disgraced mutterings around the courtroom as the defence said, 'I hardly think your pranks resulted in a good night out, did they Miss Quinley?'

'No,' Julie uttered, feeling her face and neck redden.

'What about when you left the last public house, the Boardrooms, what sort of state was Miss Morris in by this time? Was she coherent? Could she walk unassisted?'

'No, she was rambling on a bit. We had to help her out of the pub, but she did seem to be sobering up a bit while we were waiting for the taxi.'

'And what about when you arrived at her flat; what sort of a state was she in then?'

'Well, she was standing on her own then, and we could understand her a lot better.'

'Would that be when she was singing, "Show me the way to go home", or when she was shouting at the top of her voice?'

There were a few suppressed giggles around the courtroom following this last question. The question was a rhetorical one, designed for dramatic effect and for the benefit of the jury. Julie realised this and did not attempt to answer it, allowing the barrister to move on with his examination.

'What was Mr Leslie Stevens' reaction on seeing the state of Miss Morris?'

'He was livid. He was shouting at her and wouldn't even let us phone a taxi from his flat. He just hurled abuse at us and shut the door in our faces.'

'Wouldn't you say that his annoyance was justified given the state of his girlfriend and the hour that you arrived at his flat?'

'I suppose so.'

'Very well then, let's move on. Can you please tell the court where you were on the night of Saturday the 30th of August?'

This question was the one that disrupted Julie's coping mechanism and she briefly hovered on the brink of hysteria, but managed to recover. Within the space of a few seconds she had held a conversation in her head, debating how to respond:-

"*Shit, I didn't expect this!*"

"*What do I say?*"

"*Deny it?*"

"*No, they'll probably have proof.*"

"*Admit it then?*"

"*Yes, admit it, but justify myself.*"

'I was at Les Stevens' flat,' she said.

She paused for a moment, allowing the spectators time to gasp in amazement. Then, speaking as quickly as possible, she began to describe her motivations for the break-in.

'We knew he was dealing drugs because my boyfriend Vinny had spotted him in a nightclub. We thought his drug dealing had something to do with Amanda's death but we couldn't prove it ...'

'Please keep to the question!' the defence barrister interrupted repeatedly, once he'd spotted that Julie might have been gaining the sympathy of the jury, but Julie carried on, determined to tell her story.

'We'd already been to the police to tell them about our suspicions but they wouldn't take us seriously. They still thought me and Rita had made Amanda overdose. You've no idea what it's like being accused of a serious crime that you didn't do!'

'Isn't it true that you forced your way into Mr Leslie Stevens' property?' the defence barrister interjected, having to raise his voice above Julie's to make himself heard.

'Well, we needed to find evidence to prove him guilty, so we broke into his flat.'

'Causing a great deal of damage in the process I believe,' the defence barrister interrupted once more.

'No,' replied Julie. 'Just a bit to his front door. It was the only way I could get it open,' she replied innocently.

There were a few sniggers in the public gallery following this last comment.

'When you say 'we', do you mean that there were other people involved?' asked the defence.

'Vinny and my friend Rita were waiting for me outside, but it was me who did the break-in on my own. Anyway, I got into the flat and when I went into his bedroom he was there on his bed. I didn't have a chance to find any evidence. He pinned me to the bed and started hitting me. Then he threatened to have his way with me and started pulling my skirt up.'

The noise level rose in the courtroom as people began to whisper amongst themselves.

'It was lucky that Vinny came to find me or I don't know what would have happened.'

The defence barrister had allowed her to relate the last few lines uninterrupted, knowing that the depth of public feeling would not welcome any break in the tale at that point. However, he now seized his chance to switch emphasis.

'Isn't it true that you were also hitting him, and that your boyfriend proceeded to attack Mr Stevens when he entered his premises?'

'I was just trying to defend myself and get away from him, and Vinny was stopping him from hurting me.'

The defence didn't have anything to add regarding that night so he then asked, 'What about Friday 22nd August? A man was reported climbing out of Mr Leslie Stevens' bedroom following a similar break-in. Did you have anything to do with that?'

'Objection!' cried the prosecution, not wanting to give the defence barrister another opportunity to try to blight Julie's character. 'How can this possibly relate to the events of 20th June?'

'Very well, objection sustained,' ruled the judge.

'That is the end of my examination your honour,' said the defence sulkily, to Julie's relief.

As she made her way to the public gallery to take a seat next to Rita and Vinny, she felt her legs almost give way beneath her, and was glad that that particular ordeal was now over.

**

Monday 8th December 1986

'Well, how did it go then?' asked Betty as soon as Julie returned home.

In the background Julie could see her father and sister also awaiting her response.

'Not too bad,' she replied. 'I'm just glad it's out of the way. The jury seemed happy with what I said, and I managed to answer the defence's questions without too much trouble, so let's hope they find him guilty.'

She decided to omit details of the break-in at Les's flat. There was no need to bother them unnecessarily. Inside though she was harbouring other fears. She might no longer be a murder suspect but would she now be prosecuted for the break-in? It would be a lesser crime, but nevertheless, it would still leave her with a police record.

"*Oh I wish this whole bloody nightmare would just end,*" she thought.

Before she went to sleep that night she knelt and prayed for the first time since she had been a small child. 'Please God let justice be done,' she pleaded. It wasn't just a wish, it was a need.

Chapter 34

Friday 12th December 1986

By the Friday Julie was more tired than ever after another restless night. However, it was for her, potentially, the most alleviating day of the trial. She hoped that she would see justice carried out and an end to the tortuous last few months. She took her seat in the public gallery more eagerly than she had done on any other day of the trial. There was still an element of doubt in her mind though as she had no way of knowing how the trial was going to turn out. As a witness she wasn't privy to any information about which way Les intended to plead or what evidence the prosecution had gathered against him.

As Les stood in the witness box a surreal feeling came over her; he really was taking the stand. It wasn't her on trial but him, Les Stevens, the one who had been the true culprit all along. While she waited for the prosecution to commence she looked across at Rita. Julie could see that her friend was captivated by the proceedings; it reminded her of that time when they went to see Flashdance and Rita couldn't take her eyes off the screen.

Once Les had sworn on oath, the prosecution began with the usual questions, verifying Les's name and address before asking him about Amanda's death.

'Can you tell me about the events of the night of Friday 20th June 1986 Mr Stevens? What sort of condition was Miss Morris in when she returned home?'

'She was in a right state, drunk out of her brain thanks to them two.' He nodded his head in Julie and Rita's direction and Julie felt a chill run down her spine as his wild eyes pierced through her. The rest of the courtroom observed her reaction.

'Is it not true to say though, Mr Stevens, that Miss Morris was coherent by this stage?'

'I suppose so but she was still plastered.'

'Can you tell the court what happened once her friends had left?'

'Friends? Huh!'

'Answer the question please Mr Stevens.'

'We had a few words about the state she was in, then I had to help her get to bed.'

'A few words, Mr Stevens? Are you sure that's all you had?'

'Yeah, why?'

The prosecution then made a great drama out of reading a piece of paper that he held in his right hand before continuing. Julie was amazed by the change in his character. He had seemed so affable when questioning her and the following witnesses, but had now become a ruthless zealot.

'I have a statement here Mr Stevens from one of your neighbours claiming to have heard a tremendous amount of shouting and screaming on the night in question.'

'We had a few words, but that was all. They're exaggerating.'

'Similar claims were made by several of your neighbours Mr Stevens. So tell us please, what happened next?'

'What, after I'd got her to bed? I went myself, then that was it till I woke up and saw her the next morning.'

'And?'

'And I couldn't wake her up. I knew there was something not right, so I dialled 999 straightaway.'

'Can you explain why there were amphetamines found in Miss Morris's body?'

'No idea, unless they gave them to her.' Les nodded once more towards Julie and Rita. 'Maybe that's why she was in such a state!' he shouted.

'Do you use drugs Mr Stevens?'

'No.'

'Did Amanda Morris use drugs?'

'No.'

'The search of your flat following the death of Amanda Morris didn't show that there were any drugs present.'

'That's because there weren't!' shouted Les.

'However,' asserted the prosecution. 'A later, more thorough search following your arrest did find traces of amphetamine and other drugs in the carpet. Can you explain the reasons for that Mr Stevens?'

'Dunno, maybe Mandy brought them in with her after she'd been out with them two.'

'Very well Mr Stevens, what about the drugs that you were attempting to sell in these photographs?'

The photographic evidence was passed along the members of jury. As Les noted their reactions, he began to panic.

'I wasn't selling drugs, I was buying them,' he cried.

'Aah, so you do use drugs Mr Stevens?'

'Not often; it's just a bit of fun now and again, that's all.'

'What about Miss Amanda Morris, did she ever use drugs?'

'No.'

'Then why were there drugs found in her body? Come on Mr Stevens, I think that all the evidence is there for the jury to see.'

'Well, maybe once or twice, but I swear I never gave her any that night.'

The prosecutor's voice was taking on a more aggressive tone. 'Then why did police find drugs in the carpet; the same drugs that killed her, Mr Stevens?'

'I don't know, pleaded Les,' becoming desperate. 'We only took drugs a few times. We knew our limits. It was just a bit of fun, that's all.'

The prosecutor's face was a picture of concealed satisfaction as though he knew he had him now; the contradictions were spilling out of him.

Before he had a chance to continue, however, the court became distracted by a disturbance coming from the back of the public gallery.

'Leave him alone!' a pitiful voice whined.

Julie turned round and noticed a scrawny looking woman who was staggering noisily to her feet. She bore the gaunt expression of someone old before her time, with dark shadows beneath her sunken, tired eyes.

'Leave my son alone!'

'Silence!' shouted the judge but the woman refused to be cajoled. As she shouted and slurred inarticulately, Les became agitated.

'Clear off!' he shouted. 'Get her out of here!'

A policeman sped towards her and attempted to remove her from the public gallery. However, she put up a fight, waving her fists and shouting at him, and it took several minutes and the help of another officer before they managed to reach the exit. In the meantime Les was leaning out of the dock, his knuckles turning white as they gripped the rail while he yelled insults at her. 'You fuckin' bitch! You had to come, didn't you? It's all your fault. You ruined my life. Fuck off. Go on. Fuck off!'

'Silence or I'll charge you with contempt of court!' bellowed the judge.

While Les stood trembling with rage the prosecutor continued, capitalising on his emotionally charged state. 'Nice girl Amanda, wasn't she?'

'Yes!'

'A bit different to what you were used to, wasn't she? Isn't it true that you tried to control Amanda Morris and bring her down to your level through the use of drugs?'

Julie could see the lines of fury across Les's face. It was evident that he was having great difficulty controlling himself.

'Well, wasn't that the case?'

'Objection!' shouted the defence.

'Objection sustained.'

Satisfied that his questions were having the desired effect, the prosecutor continued. 'Can you please tell the jury about the night Amanda Morris died? Did you both take drugs that night?'

'No. I've told you, she wasn't a user.'

'A 'user' Mr Stevens; isn't that terminology commonly used amongst the drug dealing community?'

'No. I don't know.'

'Would you even be using that expression if you weren't involved with drugs yourself Mr Stevens.'

'No. I mean, I don't know. I might.'

'So, here she was, full of the party spirit. Didn't she want to continue having some fun? That is, after all, the reason you both took drugs, wasn't it Mr Stevens? To have a bit of fun?'

'No, she asked me for some, but I wouldn't let her have any,' Les replied in despair.

'Aah, so there were drugs in the flat that night?'

Les hung his head in defeat. It was obvious he was in such a state after his mother's performance that he couldn't think straight and thoughts of Amanda were adding to his distress. His voice was low as he conceded and began to describe what had taken place on the night of Amanda's death.

'She wanted drugs, but I wouldn't let her have any. She begged me for them and we ended up having an argument. She was getting hysterical, saying I had no right to keep them from her, 'cos she'd helped to pay for them. I managed to calm her down and we went to bed, but the next morning she wasn't next to me. I went in the living room to find her, and it was a tip. It looked like someone had raided the place.

'Then I saw her on the floor with the empty packet in her hand.'

His voice began to crack as he relived his shocking discovery of the dead body of his beloved Mandy. The prosecutor gave him a moment to compose himself before allowing him to continue.

'She must have found where I'd hidden the drugs. I panicked. I knew I'd get the blame so I cleared the flat out, and then rang 999. It wasn't my fault,' he pleaded, his voice rising in anguish. 'It was 'cos of the state she was in. She'd never have taken that many if she hadn't been so pissed. It's their fault.' He pointed angrily at Julie and Rita. 'They're the ones to blame, they got her pissed!'

The judge urged him to calm down and suggested that the court should adjourn to give the defendant a chance to compose himself.

***

When they returned to the courtroom the prosecutor had switched emphasis and Les was no longer on the stand. The prosecutor produced an exhibit, which he passed along the members of the jury. It was a hunting knife. There were stirrings and mutterings amongst the members of the public as they took in the implications of this revelation. Once the jury had taken sufficient time to examine the exhibit, the prosecutor disclosed that it had been found buried in a woods by a man walking his dog.

The prosecutor then produced photographs of the wounds on both the bodies of Jacqueline and Ernie and these were also passed to the members of the jury. Julie could sense that many people were getting restless as the prosecutor called two expert witnesses to the stand. The first one verified that the wounds on each of the bodies would have come from the same weapon and that the exhibit was almost certain to have been the weapon used for both murders.

The second witness was a fingerprint expert. Julie noted the expression on Les's face when the fingerprint expert confirmed that there were no prints on the handle of the knife and they had most probably been wiped from the handle. However, the expert was able to confirm that a tiny fingerprint had been found on the underside of the bolster. This is the part of the knife that separates the handle from the blade. On a hunting knife it is raised so that when the knife was wiped it is likely that the murderer had missed the print that was on the bolster.

A court official then put some fingerprint images on a display board for the court to view. The prosecutor explained that the two images were of the print found on the knife and a print taken from Leslie Stevens. He then invited the fingerprint expert to highlight the obvious similarities between the two.

While he gave the jury a few seconds to digest this information Rita whispered to Julie, 'They've got the bastard now! Let's see if he can squirm out of this one.'

Although Julie was beginning to feel relieved, she couldn't yet share in Rita's joy; she was finding the whole event too stressful.

Once the prosecutor was satisfied that he had presented sufficient damning evidence, he called Les back to the stand and recommenced his questioning, switching to the night of Jacqueline's murder.

'What can you tell me about Jacqueline Bartlett?' he asked. 'Were you responsible for her death?'

'No,' Les instinctively replied, but his defence was half-hearted, as though he realised that he was now fighting a losing battle.

The prosecution once more drew the attention of the courtroom to a piece of paper he was holding.

'I have a witness statement here stating that Miss Jacqueline Bartlett was seen leaving your premises on the night of Monday 18th August. Can you tell the jury the reason she was at your flat please?'

'I don't know. It was ages ago.'

'Come on Mr Stevens, you must have some idea. Was she a regular visitor or was it just the once?'

'Ah, I remember now. She did come round once, just to bring an LP of Mandy's, but she was only there about five minutes and then she left.'

'Shortly followed by Mr Ernest Cummings, I believe?'

Julie watched the expression on Les's face. His anguish showed and it was discomfiting to see, but she knew that the prosecution barrister had to do this. It was the only way to get at the truth! She then checked herself for almost feeling sorry for Les. It was no more than he deserved. She could tell that Les was losing it and she willed the prosecution to carry on until he broke down altogether and told all. She wasn't expecting him to throw in the towel quite so soon though.

'That prat!' he bawled. 'Why didn't he keep his fuckin' mouth shut? I knew he'd blown it. He should never have mouthed off about the drugs in front of that Jacqueline. I thought she'd blame me but I didn't kill Mandy, I swear!'

His bad language was overlooked in the quest to get at the truth as though even the judge realised that a major revelation was about to occur. The prosecution barrister urged Les to continue.

'She only came to bring an LP, but that prat Ernie tried to buy drugs from me in front of her. I was worried about what she might think. When she went I couldn't stop thinking about it. If she told the police about me dealing drugs then they'd think I killed Mandy. So I had to get rid of her.'

Once he started, he couldn't stop himself, and he went on to describe in detail how he had followed Jacqueline home one night and waited for an opportunity to 'get rid of' her when there weren't many people around.

Julie could feel herself beginning to heave. The rest of the courtroom remained silent, enveloped by an impenetrable tension. Without prompting, Les then described how he had despised Ernie from that night onwards and felt an overwhelming urge to do him some damage. It started off as a vengeance attack, but his rage got the better of him.

As he told the tale he visibly stiffened and the veins on his neck protruded while he relived the scene. His aggression was unabated as he cursed Ernie and continued to plead his innocence in relation to Amanda's death.

The judge again implored him to calm down, but he continued shouting and cursing until he was led from court by two policemen, straining to break free from them and howling pitifully.

It was at this point that Julie left the courtroom. Vinny and Rita followed her out.

'Are you all right?' asked Vinny.

'I just can't watch anymore,' said Julie.

'Don't tell me you feel fuckin' sorry for him?' asked Rita.

'No, it's just the whole thing, I can't stand it anymore. Take us home will you Vinny?'

'I think the bastard got what he deserved anyway,' said Rita, 'and you can piss off if you think I'm gonna go home now and miss the best bit! I'm stickin' around for the verdict, me.'

'Rita, I don't even want to argue about it,' pleaded Julie. 'I just want to go home.'

Julie and Vinny watched Rita disappear into the courtroom.

'Come on then,' said Vinny. 'Let's get you home. It's been a hard few days, and I'm sure Rita will let us know what happens.'

They walked out of the court building for the last time.

Chapter 35

Saturday 13th December 1986

The first thing that impressed Julie about the restaurant was the tantalizing aroma, which hit her even before they had stepped inside. It was a welcoming blend of garlic and baked bread. When she entered she glanced around at the impressive pillars, archways and Romanesque paintings on the walls. The staff were very accommodating and ensured that Julie and Vinny got a good seat in a cosy corner. Julie noticed the waiters' interest in her, but guessed that it was just the Mediterranean male reaction to any woman under 30.

'Well, here we are,' said Vinny. 'You've seen the Bella Vida at last.' His words were a mistake and Julie could sense his discomfort, prompting her to say something to smooth the situation.

'I'm sorry about last time. I was just so worked up by everything that I forgot to ring you.'

'It's all right,' Vinny assured. 'You don't have to keep explaining. You had been arrested when all said and done. You had more important things on your mind. Here have a look at that,' he said, passing her the menu, but she put it to one side while she continued to explain herself.

'It's not all right Vinny; I've been awful to you. Not just since Amanda died but even before that. It's like I was searching for something that I was never going to find, when all the time the man I wanted was right here. I'm so grateful to you for everything you've done for me.'

She took Vinny's hand to reaffirm her words but he responded by diverting his attention to the menu, embarrassed by her emotive speech.

After a couple of minutes studying the dishes on offer, Julie said, 'Wow Vinny, I'm spoilt for choice. It all sounds lovely and this place is really nice.'

'I know,' he said. 'I wanted it to be special. You deserve it after what you've been through.'

She finally made up her mind what she wanted. Although the menu was quite comprehensive, Julie settled for one of her favourites, lasagne, and preceded it with minestrone soup. Vinny opted for a pasta dish in a tomato based sauce (a posh version of Spaghetti Bolognese Julie thought) with breaded mushrooms for starters. As soon as Vinny looked over his shoulder a waiter appeared as though from out of nowhere.

Once they had placed their order, Julie took up the conversation again.

'It's so nice to be able to relax now we haven't got the trial hanging over us.'

'Yeah, pity they didn't do him for Amanda's murder though,' said Vinny.

'Well, at least they got him for Jackie and Ernie's murders, and for drug dealing. He'll serve a good few years for that. I know it won't bring Amanda back but he did deserve punishing. What I can't understand though is why the break-ins were only brought up in court.'

'Maybe because he kept quiet about them at first so the police wouldn't find out about the drugs. Then, when Dan came up with his evidence, Les probably figured that he had nowt to lose so he just went for it. He might have even thought it would help his defence if he made out that he was set up. I still think they should have done him for Amanda's murder anyway,' argued Vinny. 'After all, it was him that got her hooked on drugs in the first place.'

'I know, but I think that, even though he's a total bastard, he loved Amanda in his own strange way. You could tell that in court by the way he kept denying that he'd killed her. Maybe that was what made him crack up on the stand; either that or the fact that his brain was just so addled by the drugs. He's definitely not a full shilling, is he? You know, it freaks me out now Vinny to think that I could have ended up like Jacqueline and Ernie. I dread to think what might have happened in his flat that night if you hadn't have turned up.'

'I know, but I did, so just try to put it behind you now, eh?'

'I wonder why he didn't kill me after the break-in though.'

'He didn't have much chance with us around, did he? You weren't on your own much after that night, especially after that bloke followed you home from work. Besides, he needed you to take the rap. Him and his friend probably tried to put the frighteners on you so that you'd confess to Amanda's murder and get him off the hook.'

'Maybe…Still, I think the whole thing's really sad. Drugs can do strange things to people. I can't believe Amanda was an addict but I suppose it would explain a lot of things. She always seemed to be on such a high when she arrived for work in a morning. Then, as the day wore on, it was as though she was fading away. I just accepted it as the way she was. I never once thought it had anything to do with drugs. Maybe Les might have been a different person without drugs.'

'I doubt it Julie. People like him are rotten through and through. Before you get too carried away Julie, just remember what he's put you through.'

'I know, and it's not over yet. What if they charge me for breaking and entering? I'll still have a criminal record hanging over me.'

'No, they won't do that. You'd have heard from that miserable inspector by now if they were going to press charges. He'll be too busy celebrating his promotion 'cos they've solved two murders. Besides, it's a bit late for that when Les didn't report the break-in at the time, isn't it? Anyway, stop worrying, it's all over now. Let's change the subject. Has Rita fixed the date for Greece yet?'

Yeah, I was just getting round to that. I kept meaning to tell you. She's going next Saturday and the girls are giving her a major night out on Friday to see her off.'

'Oh good. Well, have a good time and no silly buggers, eh?' Julie looked at him. 'Definitely not!'

The food arrived and they both began to drool over it. "*This is a bit different than the last time I was supposed to come here,*" Julie thought to herself. She noticed that Vinny had become pensive too.

'Penny for 'em?' she asked.

Vinny hesitated before replying.

'There's something I've got to tell you. I've kept quiet about it up to now but the time seems right. You see, I've got some unfinished business to tend to …'

Julie's heart sank. Just when she was beginning to think that all her troubles were behind her, Vinny was about to drop a bombshell and he had brought her here to sweeten her up beforehand. She watched him fidget nervously, convincing her even more that he had bad news to impart.

'Well, last time I was here,' he continued, 'there was something that I wanted to do.'

Julie looked at the package that he had withdrawn from his pocket, still only half anticipating what he had to say but nevertheless shocked when she heard the words, 'Julie, will you marry me?'

For a moment she was speechless and Vinny awaited her reply with bated breath. It was what she wanted; she knew now that Vinny was the one, but she just hadn't expected it to happen yet.

'Yes,' she cried. 'Yes of course I'll marry you Vinny,' and she smiled as he put the ring on her finger.

As if from nowhere three waiters appeared and congratulated them effusively, drawing attention to them from nearby tables. When the waiters went back to their work, Julie and Vinny held hands across the table and gazed lovingly at each other for a few minutes before becoming aware of the interest from neighbouring tables. They then withdrew their hands, embarrassed by all the fuss.

'What a way to round off a meal!' said Julie as they returned to their food, giggling like smitten teenagers.

They celebrated by ordering two enormous desserts (Julie's had lashings of vanilla and chocolate ice cream and was covered with a liberal measure of Tia Maria), and a bottle of expensive champagne.

***

Wednesday 17th December 1986

Les sat in his cell alone. His cellmate had disappeared about half an hour ago and Les was making the most of his solitude. He was still becoming accustomed to life behind bars. Despite his nefarious dealings of the last few years, this was the first period that he had spent in prison and it was taking some getting used to.

The lack of home comforts and short supply of drugs was bad enough but the worst part was the constant fear. There were some mean bastards inside and it paid to stay on the right side of the right people. Because he had no previous experience of prison life though, it was difficult knowing who the right people were.

Up to now he had relied on the advice of his cellmate but he was a sly looking bastard and he couldn't trust a word he said. Les knew though that he needed to tread a fine line between showing no signs of weakness to the nobodies and making sure that he didn't upset the people who were somebodies. There was a definite pecking order inside prison and he was starting to find out who was who.

So when one of the prison hard men, Leroy Booth, stepped inside his cell Les instinctively knew that it spelled trouble. His suspicions were reaffirmed when Leroy was followed by four of the meanest looking blokes you could ever expect to meet; all biceps, scars and the smell of stale sweat. They wasted no time in pinning him down while Leroy shut the door and made the brief introduction:

'This is for my man Ernie, you cunt.'

With little time to spare before the prison guards became aware of a problem, Leroy's bully boys began to rain punches and kicks down onto Les while Leroy acted as lookout. Les rolled into a ball trying to protect himself, ironically just as Ernie had done when he had attacked him. His efforts were wasted though; this wasn't about punishment, it was about justice. Nobody killed one of Leroy's men and got away with it, and he had to set an example that everyone would find out about.

While one of the men dragged hold of Les's hair and pulled his head back, enabling another to aim savage kicks at Les's head, yet another reached under Les's body, which had now been levered off the ground.

When the post mortem was carried out it was difficult to tell what had killed Les first; blood loss following repeated thrusts of a sharp implement into his abdomen or damage to his brain.

***

Friday 19th December 1986

As Julie was running late after visiting Vinny, she made a quick call to Rita explaining that she would meet them straight in the club, Saturdays. It was turned ten o'clock when she arrived but she soon found Rita and Debby chatting to a group of men. She pulled Rita to one side.

'I've got some news for you,' she said.

Rita's gaze shot to Julie's left hand which she was resting self-consciously on the strap of her handbag.

'Congratulations!' shouted Rita, 'When did that happen?'

'Last Saturday.'

'You bugger, why didn't you tell me before now?'

'I thought I'd surprise you and I knew you'd be dying to see the ring so I waited until tonight.'

'Ooh, it's gorgeous as well,' cooed Rita. 'Debby come and have a look; Julie's gone and got herself engaged.'

Debby broke off from her male company for a moment to examine the ring. She then returned to the crowd of men, and ensured that one of them passed a drink to Julie.

'It's a pity it's so loud in here; I can't talk to you,' said Julie.

'Sod talking! Let's do some bleedin' drinking and dancing, and having a good time. We've got a lot to celebrate Julie,' shouted Rita before taking Julie by the arm and introducing her to the crowd of men.

When Julie and Rita had tired of the men's small talk, they finished their drinks and Rita dragged Julie off to the dance-floor.

'Come on,' she said. 'The night's only just begun.'

Eventually, when they had danced for about an hour and Julie's legs could take no more, she managed to persuade Rita to go with her for a sit down and a drink in a quieter area of the club.

Julie said to Rita, 'Right, now we've got a moment, it's time I told you my news.'

'I thought you already had?' asked Rita.

'No, not that, my other news.'

Rita raised her eyebrows, displaying her interest in what Julie had to say.

'I had a visitor this morning,' said Julie.

'Oh yeah, come to help you with the wedding list did he?' teased Rita.

'No, not Vinny, you daft cow. It was Inspector Bowden. That's why I was running late. I went to see Vinny to tell him what had happened.'

'Bowden, what did that bastard want?'

'He was the nicest I've seen him actually.'

'Since when was he nice?'

'When he had to come with some shocking news, that's when.'

'What do you mean?'

'Les has been killed in prison.'

'You're joking, that's brilliant news Julie! What happened?'

'Rita, you don't need to sound so overjoyed. It's still a human life even if he was an evil bastard. His family will be grieving.'

'Like as if. The bastard got what he deserved for getting a nice girl like Amanda hooked on drugs in the first place just so he could control her, not to mention the other two people he killed. Anyone who wants to grieve over him needs their head testing. They should be glad to see the back of him.'

Once Rita had finished her rant, Julie continued. 'A rival drugs gang jumped him in his cell. They kicked, punched and knifed him to death … Anyway, the police aren't going to press charges for the break-in at his flat, so that's a relief.'

'I didn't think they would after all the problems they caused us in the first place!'

'You should have heard Bowden, Rita. He apologised for doubting my word and for misjudging us, and he asked me to send you his apologies too. And he said that he might have broken into Les's flat too if he had been in my position.'

'Jesus, I wish I'd have been there to hear him grovel.'

'Oh, don't worry Rita, it wasn't all good. He did suggest that I had put myself in that position by my foolish behaviour, and that girls who go to nightclubs are regarded as being a certain type.'

'The cheeky get!' cried Rita before noticing Julie's eyes looking over her shoulder. She followed her gaze and noticed that it was Vinny who had caught her eye.

'Hiya love,' shouted Julie before standing up, approaching Vinny and embracing him.

'I thought you'd only just bleedin' left him?' asked Rita exasperated, as she grabbed her drink and left the table. 'I'm leaving you two love-birds to it,' she added. 'I'll be on the dance-floor when you're ready Julie. I've got one more thing to celebrate now with that nutcase out of the way. That's made my fuckin' day, that has.'

Rita strutted towards the dance-floor to the sound of "Trapped" by Colonel Abrams, turning to wink at Julie before she disappeared from view.

**

Saturday 20th December 1986

It was the following day. Julie stood by the window with her back to Vinny and Rita. She didn't want them to notice how upset she was. She knew she was being silly but she just couldn't help it. Outside the rain gently ran in tiny rivulets down the pane of glass; a moment's let-up against the heavy downpour, which had lashed down throughout the last twenty-four hours, causing the inside of the windows to steam.

"*Funny how the weather's always grotty when something sad is happening,*" thought Julie.

An aeroplane was cruising along the runway preparing for take-off. She watched as it built up speed until it soared into the air.

'That'll be me soon,' Rita commented, surprising Julie by her proximity. Noting Rita's glee, Julie managed to force an encouraging smile but Rita, as always, could see through her façade.

'Now don't start snivelling Julie Quinley or there'll be no cheap holidays for you!'

'Oh I'm sorry Rita. I am really happy for you; it's just that I'll miss you.'

'I know, I'll miss you too Julie, but I'll ring you as soon as I get there, and I'll keep in touch and let you know how I'm getting on.'

'I know, Rita.'

'Right, well let's tuck into those bloody drinks then. This is a celebration.'

After grabbing her drink she clinked the glass against Julie's and Vinny's and announced, 'To new beginnings.'

She then managed to down her drink in one go. As Julie and Vinny watched, astonished, she commented, 'Well, you didn't think I was gonna fly sober, did you?'

'How long have you got?' Julie asked.

'My flight's at 3.15 so that gives me just over two hours, but I'll have to go through to passport control long before then. That'll be the boring bit, when I'm sat on my own waiting and can't even have a drink. Mind you, I'll be that pissed by then that I won't give a shit.'

'Yeah, I pity the poor bugger that's got to sit next to you for the flight,' said Julie, laughing.

'Whoever it is, his luck's in. Eh, I wonder if there's any good films on. I hope it's not that load of crap they had on last time.'

'Is Yansis meeting you at the airport when you get there?' asked Vinny.

'Course he is. He's a darlin' is Yansis. He wouldn't leave me stranded.'

Julie and Vinny took great care not to mention the fact that none of Rita's family had accompanied her to the airport, and that, if it hadn't been for Vinny's insistence that they gave her a lift, she would have had to rely on taxis at this end. They knew that it was just the way it was with Rita's family and that Rita had long since become accustomed to it all.

It seemed that they had already said all they had to say and Julie didn't want to quell Rita's excitement by discussing anything too mundane. So they confined their conversation to topics that interested Rita; what clothes she had taken, how hot the weather was going to be, what Yansis's apartment was like etc., etc.

As soon as it was time for Rita to go, a last minute panic gripped Julie. This was it; Rita was really leaving! She felt that there was something important she should be doing or saying at such a crucial time, instead of just standing there looking hopeless. Now it seemed to her that their last moments together had passed by in a flash. Before she knew it Rita was in the queue waiting to check her baggage in. She wanted to grab hold of Rita, as though she would never let her go, but Vinny held her back.

'Let Rita do it her way,' he whispered. She watched Rita advancing excitedly up the queue and knew he was right. Rita wouldn't appreciate a heavy emotional scene at such a key time in her life; she wanted to embrace the whole experience, not commiserate it.

As Rita moved to the front of the queue, Julie shouted, 'Have a great time Rita. I hope it all works out!'

'Course it will,' came the reply. 'Come and stay whenever you want. I can't wait to see you both.'

Then she was gone and Vinny was ready with open arms. When Julie had spent a couple of minutes recovering her composure, she finally found her voice.

'Oh Vinny, I'm going to miss her so much; we've been through a hell of a lot together!'

'Don't worry,' he casually remarked. 'She'll be back.'

The End

I hope you enjoyed "Slur". If you want to be the first to find out about forthcoming publications, why not subscribe to my mailing list at: http://eepurl.com/CP6YP? I use my mailing list solely to notify readers about my books and will never share your details with any third parties.

Glossary

A lot of local dialect has been used throughout the book. Although some of these words are used throughout the UK and in other English speaking parts of the world, some of them only usually apply in Manchester and the North of England. The glossary below gives the definitions that apply to the context in which they have been used in the book.

Arsed	Bothered
Bird	An attractive female (now considered an offensive term)
Bloke	Man
Bonk	Sexual intercourse
Boozer	Someone who drinks alcohol a lot /a pub
Bugger	Unpleasant person or just a person generally
Buggered	Ruined/broken
Bugger about	Mess about/waste time
Bugger off	Go away/get lost (usually used in a derogative manner)
A card	An amusing, eccentric person/a character
Chinwag	Chat/talk
Codswallop	Nonsense
To cop/cop off	To meet someone sexually desirable
Cop/copper	Policeman
Cronies	Friends (sometimes used derogatively)
Dead	Very
Dick	Contemptible person/idiot (also a word used for the penis)
Do	Party/event
Dodgy	Suspicious, risky
Dolling yourself up	Dressing up/getting ready (to go out)
Fancy	Feel attracted to/desire

Gabbing	Chatting
Get/git	An unpleasant or contemptible person
Gone to town	Made a big effort (usually used derogatively)
Grotty	Unpleasant/poor quality/not good looking
Having somebody on	Having a joke at their expense
Jacked in	Given up/finished
Lose your marbles	Become crazy
Mither	Fuss/bother/hassle
Mithered	Bothered
Mug/muggins	Someone who is a fool or is gullible
NFA	Of no fixed abode
Nowt	Nothing
Offy	Off Licence (a shop that sells alcohol)
Paralytic	Very drunk
Pissed	Drunk
Plastered	Drunk
Prat	Fool/Idiot
Puddled	Eccentric/insane
Scrubber	A coarse and/or promiscuous woman
Shorts	Measures or spirits such as whisky or vodka
Slag	A woman who is promiscuous or has loose morals
Snog	Kiss and cuddle amorously
Sod	Similar to bugger, or used as a defamatory term especially when used as, 'sod it!'
Sod off!	Go away (usually used in a derogative manner)
Sod you!	An expression of hostility or rejection
Suss	Realise/grasp
Talent	Attractive person(s)
Tart	Promiscuous woman/prostitute
Tarting yourself up	Similar to dolling yourself up but with the suggestion of overdoing it
Tits	Breasts

About the Author

Diane Mannion started her writing career 15 years ago when she began to work as a freelance writer while studying towards her writing diploma. During that time she had many articles published in well-known UK magazines. As part of her studies Diane began work on her debut novel, "Slur", and wrote several short stories. She has since written outlines for a number of other novels.

Despite interest from a couple of literary agents, Diane didn't quite succeed in finding a mainstream publisher for "Slur". Disheartened, she eventually put it to one side while she focused on other areas, but was determined to return to it one day.

Since 2007 Diane has operated Diane Mannion Writing Services, a business offering a range of copywriting, editing and proofreading services to businesses and individuals. One of the areas in which Diane has gained a great depth of expertise over the years is in ghost writing non-fiction books on behalf of clients. Diane therefore took the decision to write her own non-fiction books, which resulted in the publication of "Kids' Clubs and Organizations" in 2012 followed by "Great Places for Kids' Parties (UK)" in 2013.

In the future Diane plans to compile and publish a collection of her short stories, which will be followed by her second novel, "Bad Brother and I". Diane publishes regular updates about her writing on her blog at: www.dianewriting.wordpress.com.

You can also find all her books through her Amazon pages at: http://www.amazon.co.uk/Diane-Mannion/e/B008MX8LD0 (for UK) http://www.amazon.com/Diane-Mannion/e/B008MX8LD0 (for US) or follow her on Facebook at: www.facebook.com/Diane-MannionWritingServices and on Twitter at: @dydywriter.

Also By Diane Mannion

Bad Brother and I

For Adele and Peter Robinson it is by no means an easy childhood. To survive on a tough council estate in the Manchester suburbs of the 1960s and 70s, they have to learn to look after themselves. That struggle for survival is mirrored in their home lives with a slovenly mother and a drunken father who is perpetually angry.

What the children don't realise at first is that their father's violent mood swings don't stem solely from a lack of satisfaction with his load. There is something inherent within him. By the time Adele is old enough to associate her father's behaviour with stories about her mad great grandfather, she is already beginning to notice adverse signs in her brother.

As Peter grows up he engages in a life of escalating crime, which finally culminates in murder, and Adele is disgusted with the person he has become. Meanwhile, Adele is hiding behind a façade of normality and has difficulties in maintaining relationships because of her jealous rages. She is worried that she might also take after her father, and seeks help from a psychologist.

Can Adele manage to overcome her troubled past or will her damaged childhood and fragile mental state have devastating consequences on the rest of her life?

Disclaimer

Proof

Made in the USA
Charleston, SC
20 August 2014